VYING FOR A VISCOUNT

Widows of Mayfair, Book 5

Christine Donovan

ARE YOU SIGNED UP FOR DRAGONBLADE'S BLOG?

You'll get the latest news and information on exclusive giveaways, exclusive excerpts, coming releases, sales, free books, cover reveals and more.

Check out our complete list of authors, too!

No spam, no junk. That's a promise!

Sign Up Here

www.dragonbladepublishing.com

Dearest Reader;

Thank you for your support of a small press. At Dragonblade Publishing, we strive to bring you the highest quality Historical Romance from some of the best authors in the business. Without your support, there is no 'us', so we sincerely hope you adore these stories and find some new favorite authors along the way.

Happy Reading!

CEO, Dragonblade Publishing

Additional Dragonblade books by Author Christine Donovan

Widows of Mayfair Series
Loving an Earl (Book 1)
Pursuing a Duke (Book 2)
Marrying a Marquess (Book 3)
Betting on a Duke (Book 4)
Vying for a Viscount (Book 5)

PROLOGUE

London 1810

MISS LETITIA CAMBRIDGE'S mother meant to achieve what many debutante mothers tirelessly and ruthlessly strived for. She intended to persuade the wealthy, titled, and never-married Graham Fernsby, the Marquess of Rutherford, to marry her daughter without ever participating in a Season.

Thanks to a close friend of Letitia's mother, they'd learned that the marquess, at the age of forty-seven, was finally seeking his first bride to settle down and produce heirs. Realizing the cost of a Season was beyond their current means, they'd invited the marquess to afternoon tea, which, against all odds, he'd accepted. And today was the day he would grace them with his presence.

Letitia had butterflies swarming in her stomach as she sat on the settee beside her mother, waiting for his visit. Beyond his age and title, she knew nothing about him. When she had hoped for a Season, she had studied all the eligible bachelors listed in *Debrett's Peerage*. She had wanted to familiarize herself with them in case she was fortunate enough to find herself dancing with one. Knowing a little about their backgrounds and families would have worked in her favor. She had no doubt the marquess was listed in the book.

Their butler, Mr. Henry, entered the drawing room and announced, "The Marquess of Rutherford."

After the formalities were concluded, Mrs. Cambridge invited the marquess to take a seat. "Knowing this is rather unusual, I thank you for accepting my invitation. Please forgive me if I overstep, but I heard from a close friend that you are seeking a young bride."

Letitia found, to her relief, the marquess to be handsome with dark hair streaked with gray and intelligent amber eyes. He glanced down at his hat in his hands, then looked up, meeting her gaze. He looked at her with kindness and interest. Her breath whooshed from her lungs as his eyes casually roamed up and down her figure. Thank goodness he didn't leer. Her mind had, for some reason, pictured an old man with a hunched back and sinister, leering eyes and a drooling mouth. She could hardly contain her excitement that she'd been wrong. So very wrong.

His eyes flicked to her mother. "You heard correctly." Even his voice sounded pleasant and strong, sending awareness up her spine.

Her mother continued, "What I'm about to say stays between us, and I don't want your pity. I don't know whether you know my family, but I was the daughter of the third Earl of Edgewater. When I chose to marry a gentleman my father deemed unworthy, he cut me off. I took my husband's name and never looked back or regretted my decision. That is, until now. My husband has been gone for over a year, and sadly, I cannot spare the funds to give my daughter the Season she deserves."

"What about your brother, the current Earl of Edgewater?"

Her mother lifted her chin. "I have my pride."

Rutherford's face softened. "I understand completely. I would prefer not to deal with the Marriage Mart mamas, who, no doubt, will swarm me and force their daughters on me. It is degrading for the poor girls and uncomfortable for the gentlemen. So be that as it may, I would like to spend some time getting to know Miss Cambridge and see whether we would suit."

Mother's wide, enthusiastic smile illuminated her blue eyes along with her whole face. One would think Letitia was already engaged to the marquess rather than in the midst of a courtship.

"That is acceptable to my daughter and me."

He turned to Letitia and said, "I would like to hear what Miss Cambridge has to say."

Letitia swallowed her nerves and said not only what her mother expected of her but also what she truly meant. The marquess intrigued her, and so she replied, "I would like to get to know you as well, Lord Rutherford."

"Perfect," he said as he stood. "I will call on you tomorrow for a ride in the park." He bowed. "Good day to you both." Before Letitia's mind caught up with his words, he was gone.

"Well," her mother said. "That went better than I could've hoped. I predict you will marry the Marquess of Rutherford within the month."

Her mother was correct. She did indeed marry the marquess. However, the timeline was two weeks with a special license rather than a month.

AFTER THE WEDDING, Letitia and Graham were happy and kept to themselves for the most part. Although, she felt he spent rather a lot of time at his clubs. But when she gave birth to a healthy boy and heir, he was beyond grateful and proud.

It was unfortunate that all good things must come to an end. On a night of wind-swept, driving rain and violent thunderstorms, five years into their marriage, they quarreled for the first time. Graham was going out for the night and refused to explain what was so important that he would risk going out in such dangerous conditions. He was angry with her and stormed out of the house into the storm without his greatcoat or hat, only to return minutes later, soaked through, rain dripping from him. He marched up the grand staircase and faced her, indecision in his eyes. "I must go. I promise to return by morning."

"I still don't understand why."

"I'm sorry. I must check on my mistress, as she just gave birth."

At hearing his words, her heart tore in two. Why couldn't he have kept the knowledge of his mistress and child to himself? She'd never suspected anything, so why tell her now? Yes, she'd begged to know why he was going out, but why hadn't he lied, as he obviously had in the past? She could have continued living in ignorance.

Tears blurred her vision as she turned her head from side to side. "How could you?"

He leaned down and kissed her cheek, and she fought not to turn away. "Forgive me."

Their eyes met, and she witnessed regret and heartache before he turned and hurried carelessly down the stairs, only to slip halfway down on the wet wood, tumbling over and over until he landed with a sickening thud.

Screams escaped her mouth without her realizing it. She could hardly breathe, and her body shook uncontrollably. Pure instinct had her pulling up her skirts and hastening as quickly as she could down the stairs, careful not to repeat what had happened to her husband. By the time she reached the landing, the butler and housekeeper stood side by side, comforting each other.

Letitia fell to her knees, arched her back, tipped her head up to the ceiling, and screamed at the top of her lungs as her heart was torn from her chest. When no air remained in her lungs, she dropped her head into her hands and sobbed uncontrollably.

Her husband, his eyes open and sightless, lay in an unnatural position. His neck was broken, and he was dead.

The husband she loved.

The husband she provided with an heir.

The husband she thought she knew.

The husband she would never get to apologize to. If she hadn't demanded to know the truth about his quest that night, he would still be alive. She would have had to share him with his mistress, but at least he would be among the living to witness their son grow up to be a fine, upstanding gentleman.

CHAPTER ONE

London 1817

NEWMARKET AND THE thoroughbred racing season were the most exciting things Letitia had ever experienced. She had lived her entire twenty-five years in London. She had never even been to the countryside. Not once. And here she was with her closest friend, Clarice, the Marchioness of Chesterfield, staying at the Red Lion Inn in Newmarket. The inn was a crush. She'd never seen so many people in one place. And the one gentleman she wanted to see more than anything was also staying at the inn. Viscount Greyson. She had first made his acquaintance at the Westport ball at the beginning of the Season, and she hadn't been able to get him out of her mind.

Since Greyson was one of the Duke of Stanton's friends, she knew she would undoubtedly run into him. The Duke of Stanton was courting Clarice, which was why they were in Newmarket. Clarice had her reason; Letitia had hers.

They were having luncheon on the inn's outdoor patio when she saw him. "Oh my," Letitia whispered, "Greyson and his sisters are coming this way. I had hoped . . . but didn't really think . . ."

"Take a deep breath and relax. You don't want to seem nervous or overly excited."

"I know, but it's difficult. The man is so handsome and makes my heart flutter in song."

"Song?" Clarice asked. "He makes your heart flutter in song?"

"You know what I mean. Oh my, he's stopping."

"Lady Rutherford, Lady Chesterfield, what a lovely surprise to find you here," Greyson said as he nodded. "You remember my sisters, Lady Aurora and Lady Anastasia."

"Yes," Clarice and Letitia said in unison.

After a few pleasantries, he asked, "Will we see you lovely ladies tonight at the Ramsbury ball?"

"Yes," Letitia replied, blushing.

"Well, then," he dipped his head and grinned, "until this evening, then."

Letitia leaned forward in her seat and murmured, "I can't believe Greyson's here. I had dreamed of running into him, but now I'm so nervous. It felt as though I had a cloth tucked inside my mouth; it was so dry and hard to speak. I don't remember ever feeling that way before. Indeed, when I met Rutherford, I was young and naïve and overwhelmed with his kindness and generosity. I loved him deeply, and he made my stomach constrict and my heart pound. But Greyson, I cannot explain what he does to me, except to say it's so much more than what I felt with my husband, and I hardly even know him. It makes no sense at all."

"I've never heard of anyone falling in love at first sight, but I believe that is what you did," said Clarice.

Letitia thought back to the first time she'd seen him at the Westport ball. "I never thought it happened in real life, only in novels," Letitia exhaled.

When they finished eating, they went up to their rooms to rest so they would be refreshed for the Ramsbury ball. Letitia rose from her nap rested and began preparing for the ball. She decided on a blue gown, and Penny, the maid who traveled with Clarice, fixed her hair beautifully with cascading curls that bounced as she moved her head. Completely dressed and ready for the ball, she went through the adjoining door to Clarice's room. She was dressed in a lovely green gown that suited her perfectly. They made their way down the hall and exited the inn to find Kirkland standing at their carriage ready to assist them inside. Sitting across from each other to keep from wrinkling their gowns, Clarice tapped on the roof signaling Kirkland that they were ready to go. The carriage wheels creaked as they rolled forward to Ramsbury Ridge Farms.

Thirty minutes later, her insides humming with nerves and excitement, Letitia and Clarice greeted their hosts. Then Letitia found herself entering one of the largest and most beautiful ballrooms she'd ever seen. It was decorated in cream and gold, with chandeliers hanging from the ceiling and hundreds of wax candles casting a soft glow across the room. Delicate floral arrangements were scattered here and there.

"Stanton and Greyson are coming this way," Letitia said as her cheeks heated. "I'm blushing, aren't I?"

"Yes, but so am I," Clarice said.

"Lady Chesterfield, Lady Rutherford," Greyson said as he bowed. "It is a pleasure to see you both again today."

Clarice and Letitia both curtsied. "Wonderful to see you, Greyson," Clarice said.

"Greyson," Letitia said. "I hope you enjoyed your luncheon at the inn?"

His green eyes sparkled as he took her in from head to toe, causing her to blush once again.

"I did, thank you."

The musicians were setting up to play a lively country reel, and Greyson surprised her when he bowed and said, with his gloved hand out, "May I have this dance?" Letitia took his hand, and they made their way to the dance floor to set up for the reel, ladies on one side facing their partners. It wasn't a dance for conversation as they went forward, turned around each other, and then went back. Several times they switched partners but always came back to each other. By the end of the dance, they were laughing, and he surprised her again when he said, "Would you care to stroll through the gardens?"

"Yes," she said, suddenly breathless.

He offered his arm, and she slipped hers through his, and they strolled carefully through the crowded ballroom, out the double doors to a veranda, and beyond to the gardens lit up with torches. When she realized how romantic it was, she almost turned and ran away. It was the first time she'd ever been alone with a gentleman who wasn't Rutherford.

"You seem nervous. Relax. I don't bite."

His comment made her giggle, and her insides eased. "This place is beautiful. The property goes on and on."

Greyson looked at her intently. "The place is, but that isn't what I'm looking at. You are more beautiful than any flower I've ever seen."

Her steps faltered, and her cheeks heated. His words made her unaware of where they were in their stroll until Greyson said, "Here you are" when they came upon Stanton and Clarice sitting on a bench.

Stanton stood and waved to the bench, saying, "Have a seat, Lady Rutherford."

"Thank you, I will."

"I have some bad news to share," Greyson said, a frown marring his handsome face.

"The Jockey Club's betting book doesn't show good odds for Zeus, I'm afraid."

"I'm not surprised, nor does it bother me. I believe Zeus will place. Keep that in mind if you place a bet."

"Place a bet?" Greyson cocked a brow. "Of course I'm placing bets. And to hell—excuse me, ladies—with the odds. I'm betting on my friend."

Stanton held out his hand to Clarice. "Shall we return to the ballroom?"

After Clarice and Stanton left the gardens, so did she and Greyson. To her disappointment, he had been a perfect gentleman during their stroll through the gardens. The closest he came to not being a gentleman was when he brushed his lips against her cheek just before they stepped onto the veranda on their return to the ballroom. "Thank you," he said.

"For what?"

He chuckled. "For spending time with me. I know we've only met a few times, but I feel as though I know you. So I hope you don't think I'm being forward if I ask you to accompany my sisters and me to a luncheon at Lord and Lady Greenville's tomorrow? If you don't already have plans, that is?"

"I would love to."

"Wonderful. We will meet you in the main lobby at one o'clock."

They made their way inside, and it wasn't long before Clarice and Letitia left. The ride back to the inn was quiet as both Clarice and Letitia were lost in thoughts of the men they had fallen for. Letitia had pleasant dreams that night about a green-eyed devil who stole her heart.

The following morning, after taking breakfast in her room, Penny helped Letitia prepare for the luncheon. She wore a lovely sage-green muslin day dress with a matching spencer and bonnet. She'd never socialized with Rutherford during their five years of marriage. Even though it was nearly two years since his death, this would be her first luncheon. Penny assured her she was dressed perfectly, but her stomach still ached from nerves. She couldn't wait until social gatherings didn't leave her petrified. By then, she'd probably be bored with attending such affairs and want to stay home.

She laughed out loud, which made Penny frown. "Is something amiss?"

"No. Nervous laughter."

"Try to relax and enjoy yourself, my lady."

"I will, Penny." Letitia said goodbye to Clarice and left the room right on time. Since her room was on the ground floor, the end of the hall opened into the main lobby, and her breath caught at the sight of Greyson. Dressed in a brown jacket, tan breeches, a cream-and-tan waistcoat, and brown boots, he was without a doubt the most handsome man she'd ever seen.

"Lady Rutherford," he said, bowing as she approached. "How lovely you look today." He offered his arm. "My sisters are already in the carriage. Shall we?"

She had to fight not to giggle like a nervous debutante. "We shall."

He helped her into the carriage, and she took the empty seat facing forward. Anastasia and Aurora occupied the other seat. That meant . . . Greyson would sit beside her. Oh dear, she hadn't brought a fan, and she suddenly felt warm as he sank into the cushion and his booted foot brushed against hers.

"Good day, Lady Rutherford," Lady Anastasia said with a smile.

"Yes, good day," Lady Aurora said.

"Please call me, Letitia."

"We will," replied Aurora.

The ride took about an hour, and Letitia was grateful the twins kept the conversation going whenever it lulled. Greyson was quiet beside her, and she had a feeling he didn't often get to speak around his sisters.

"Greyson told us you have a son," Anastasia said, taking off her gloves and fanning herself with them. "My, it's warm today."

"It is warm, and yes, I have a two-year-old son named Simon."

"Nice name," Greyson said, shocking her that he was paying attention.

"Thank you. It was my father's name."

"I'm sorry. When did he pass?"

"A little over two years ago. Not long before Rutherford."

Aurora sat up straighter, suddenly seeming more interested. "How awful for you. It must have been difficult to lose your husband."

"It was. My mother and Clarice helped me. My mother retired to the country with the Duchess of Blackstone's mother not long ago. They have been friends for years."

"You must miss her." This from Greyson.

"I do, but she's happy, and that's all that matters."

"Our father is unwell," Anastasia added to the conversation, and she could feel the tension filling Greyson's body.

"The doctors think he'll live another six months or so." Again from Greyson.

"I'm sorry," said Letitia.

He shrugged and said, "It is what it is." The carriage came to a stop, and Greyson exhaled. "We've arrived."

The Greenville Estate, a large, four-story limestone home, sat at the end of a long drive lined with white-flowering trees. It resembled a princess's house in a fairy tale.

Greyson exited the carriage first, then assisted his sisters and her. A footman greeted them and escorted them down a stone pathway that wound around to the back of the enormous estate to a terrace crowded with tables, chairs, and guests. Greyson escorted them to their hosts, or at least the ones Letitia believed to be their hosts, since everyone was greeting them.

"Lord and Lady Greenville," Greyson bowed, "thank you for the invitation. May I present Lady Rutherford? And you remember my sisters, Lady Anastasia and Lady Aurora."

"Welcome," Lady Greenville said with a friendly smile. Letitia, along with the twins, curtsied.

"My parents send their regards," Greyson said.

"How are they?" Lord Greenville said. "I was sorry to hear of your father's declining health."

"They both have good days and bad, but thank you for asking."

"Please enjoy yourselves," Lady Greenville said.

All four of them made their way to the terrace and found four empty chairs at a long banquet table.

"How do you know Lord and Lady Greenville?" Letitia asked.

"My father and Lord Greenville have known each other since their Eton days," Greyson replied.

"Do they have children?"

Both Aurora and Anastasia giggled. "Oh yes," Anastasia said "They have a daughter our age and have always hoped Greyson would become their son-in-law."

"Oh," Letitia's heart dropped.

"Their daughter," Aurora added, "Lady Miranda, had other plans. She has recently become betrothed to Lord Centerville."

Aurora fluttered her lashes. "He is most handsome. Look over by the food table. He is the one standing next to Lady Miranda, the young woman dressed in yellow."

Letitia found them but didn't see what was so handsome about Centerville.

Greyson stood. "Letitia, would you care to fix a plate?"

"I believe I would." She took his offered arm, and they strolled to the food table. She was thankful that Lady Miranda and Centerville were walking away. She didn't care to meet the lady Greyson might have married. They fixed their plates with fruit, bread, little sandwiches, and confections, then returned to the table. A footman approached them with a tray of lemonade.

"Come, sister, let's get a plate. Perhaps there are some handsome single gentlemen who will attract our attention. Or rather, we will attract theirs," Aurora said.

"Their exuberance is both refreshing and hard to keep up with," Letitia said with a laugh.

Chuckling, Greyson said, "It can be at times."

"Are you traveling without a chaperone for them?"

"No. You are looking at him."

"Oh. I see." He took her totally by surprise.

"My mother doesn't trust anyone to chaperone them. It's my job for the foreseeable future until they marry. Or at least become engaged."

Between his father's illness and chaperoning his sisters, Greyson certainly didn't have much time for himself. Perhaps her hoping he would want to court her was out of the question. At least until his sisters were engaged.

They played some lawn games after eating, but the twins

were bored and wanted to leave. They thanked their hosts and spent the next hour in the carriage, where everyone fell asleep except Letitia. Her eyes closed every now and then, but sleep eluded her. She was thankful and sad when they returned to the inn.

Greyson escorted her to her room. "Thank you for putting up with my sisters."

"I like them. I believe we shall become good friends if given the chance."

"You may regret saying that." He looked up and down the corridor, making her wonder why, until he bent his head and kissed her. It lasted only a moment, just long enough for her insides to hum.

He stepped back and bowed. "I will see you tomorrow for the race."

Her eyes were riveted to his receding back until he disappeared from sight. She tapped the door, and Penny opened it. "Welcome back, my lady."

"Thank you, Penny."

"Lady Chesterfield said she would see you in the morning. She went out with the Duke of Stanton."

"Would you help me undress and put on a robe? I will be staying in."

"Yes, my lady."

Climbing into bed early, Letitia tried not to get her hopes up about Greyson. It was hard, though, since he had kissed her. It wasn't much of a kiss, but then again, they were standing in the inn's corridor where anyone could come upon them.

Eventually, her eyes fluttered closed, her breathing evened out, and she fell asleep.

As Greyson left Letitia at her door, he wondered what he was doing. He was giving her the wrong idea about them. He could see it in her eyes. With everything going on in his life right now, he didn't have time to court Letitia properly. His father was ill, but so was his mother. Even though he'd hired a nurse to see to their care, he took care of everything pertaining to the earldom and his family's private affairs. Not to mention chaperoning his sisters.

Then there was the one thing he did that took him away on assignments. This past year, he'd been called away with the Black Knights more than he expected. The English people weren't happy with government laws and regulations, and the Knights were trying to help them while keeping the peace. Not an easy feat. He wanted to court Letitia, but his inattention wouldn't be fair to her. But could he risk losing her to some other gentleman? That was his biggest dilemma. His insides ached at the thought of losing her. Somehow, he needed to make it all work.

The first time he saw her across a crowded ballroom at the Westport ball, he couldn't look away. He'd had an advantage over her because he had known her name and a little bit about her. When he looked at her, it was as if she called to him on an elemental level, as if his mind and body recognized her as belonging to him. All his senses, long dormant, were awakened, and he knew right then he had to make her his. He forced himself to remain calm because the last thing he'd wanted was to frighten her away, knowing it was her first foray into society since coming out of mourning. But, bloody hell, he wanted to run across the ballroom, wrap her in his arms, and claim her body and soul. Thank goodness sanity prevailed, and he got his wits about him and remained calm. Remaining calm around Letitia was becoming more difficult the more time he spent with her.

He spent a sleepless night staring at his future, hoping it was brighter than it appeared.

MORNING CAME FAST, and Letitia and Clarice were preparing for the first race of the season, the 2000 Guineas Stakes at Newmarket Racecourse. The Duke of Stanton's horse, Zeus, was racing. That morning, as they took their breakfast in their rooms, Clarice informed her that Greyson and Mr. Hunter would pick them up in an open barouche and take them to Newmarket Racecourse. Knowing she would be spending time with Greyson again today had her heart pounding and her body tingling. Perhaps today he would kiss her again. She could hope.

Letitia was more than thrilled to be in the same carriage as Greyson and his sisters. Clarice was with Hunter, and they were parked side by side right beside the racetrack near the finish line. They were all straining to look for Stanton, who was joining them for the race.

Greyson jumped up, waving his arms and yelling, "Stanton, over here!"

"I thought I'd never find you," Stanton said, acknowledging them and then joining Clarice in her coach. It wasn't long before the race began, and when Zeus came over the rise in the lead, they went wild, yelling and screaming his name. He won!

Greyson turned to her, his eyes bright and his cheeks flushed. "He won!" he said, hugging her and pressing his lips to hers for a brief moment. They were gone almost before she could even register the kiss.

The rest of the day and into the night were a whirlwind of social events. Wherever Letitia went with Clarice and Stanton, she looked for Greyson. She knew he had to be somewhere, but none of the three found him. When they returned to the inn, Letitia, having partaken in too much wine, fell into a dreamless sleep.

In the morning, Clarice and Stanton had to deal with the consequences of her father, the Earl of Portsmouth, showing up in Newmarket. They believed he was spreading rumors about Stanton, trying to ruin him. When Clarice was eighteen, she was supposed to marry Stanton, but her father had forbidden it and then did everything in his power to ruin both of their lives. He was obviously still trying to keep them apart.

Later that day, she traveled with Greyson and Hunter to Ramsbury Ridge Farm to see if they could help in any way. Being there for support was all the help they could give.

The next morning, she found out someone had set fire to Ramsbury Ridge Farms. Thankfully, everyone made it out safely, and even the horses survived the barn fire. It was determined that Lord Portsmouth had paid a young lad to light the fires. Did that man possess a heart?

He quickly fled from England to France, and good riddance to him. Clarice and Stanton could finally build a life together. But first, Stanton's filly, Clover, had to run the 1000 Guineas Stakes. Which she did and won. Letitia was so happy for them, but sad because she needed to leave soon. She had only planned to stay for the first two races. She needed to get home to Simon, whom she missed.

She opted to stay at the inn that night, took a bath, and went to bed early. Her mind battled with all sorts of questions.

Would she see Greyson before she left in two days?

Would Clarice be staying in Newmarket?

Would Greyson call on her when he returned to London?

Was it the end of what she had hoped would be a future with him?

Tears trickled down her cheeks and onto her pillow even as she fell asleep, her heart heavy.

"Wake up, my lady."

"Penny," she said, opening her eyes and squinting at the sun filtering through the curtains. How long had she slept? "What is it?"

"We have work to do." She handed her a note in handwriting she didn't recognize, but quickly realized it belonged to Stanton. "They are getting married today, privately. He is surprising Lady Chesterfield with a wedding breakfast afterward. He already has the private dining room here and the menu. He also took care of inviting people."

Letitia sat up. "What do we have to do? It sounds like he took care of all the details." She glanced at the list. It looked as though they had nothing to do but arrive at noon. She hurried from the bed. "I need to get ready."

CHAPTER TWO

LETITIA'S CLOSEST FRIEND, Clarice, finally married Samuel Radcliff. Watching them leave their wedding breakfast, with love and smiles radiating from their faces, made Letitia's heart feel light and airy for the couple who had gone through the fires of hell to be together. No two finer people deserved a fairytale life than they.

Once upon a time, Letitia thought she had the perfect marriage and life with Graham. Yes, he was nearly thirty years older, but those years melted away over their five years together. They had known each other only a fortnight when they'd recited their vows, yet Letitia had no trepidation or regrets about Graham. At least not at the time they said their vows.

Reflecting on what she now knew, she should have noticed certain things. Things like not attending many social functions despite numerous daily invitations or the fact that they never hosted an event. His excessive time spent at his clubs. Or so he said, and she never once questioned him. Why would she?

Because her mother had married outside her social class, her family had few friends and received very few invitations when she was growing up. Their happy family of three spent most of their time together, and because Letitia had married at eighteen, she didn't know any better. Only after she entered London society with Clarice by her side and spent time with the Duchess of

Blackstone and Lady Langford did she understand that there was a whole other world out there that Graham had kept her from experiencing. She rubbed the pain in her chest. The knowledge that he'd preferred the company of his mistress to hers still wounded her to this day. Letitia still struggled to come to terms with the fact that Graham and his mistress had been together for ten years—as she discovered while going through his papers after his death—before she entered the picture, or rather, the relationship.

The night he died, when he confessed to her about his mistress and their children, was the first indication that he may have kept her secluded from society for a reason. Or at the very least, wanted to spend most of his evenings with his mistress. Or perhaps he was afraid she would hear whispers about him and his longtime mistress. After his passing, she was suddenly overwhelmed by the extent of his deception.

Graham was gone, and there was nothing she could change about their marriage. She had been young and innocent, and up until the night he died, she had been happy and in love. Those memories were what she tried to live by, not the time he spent away from her with his mistress. Not his lies. Deep down inside, she knew Graham had loved her in his own strange way.

Compared with many ladies of society, stuck in loveless marriages, she still believed she was fortunate. She was deeply thankful to have married into the *ton*, even though her grandfather and her uncle were earls. Neither had ever acknowledged her. Her mother had given up her birthright for love. She sighed wistfully at the love her parents had shared, then realized everyone around the long rectangular table was standing and saying their goodbyes. Goodness, how long had she been woolgathering?

"Letitia." At the sound of Greyson's deep voice, her heart pitter-pattered in her chest. He pulled her chair back and held out his large, bare hand, one eyebrow raised inquisitively. "May I escort you to your room?"

Warmth spread to her cheeks as she quickly grabbed her white lacy gloves from the table and slipped her bare hand into his. When she stood, she wondered if he felt the same warmth she did when they touched. He continued holding her hand as they made their way from the large private dining room through several public rooms and down the corridor to the ground floor guest rooms.

"Where did your lovely twin sisters go off to?" she asked as they paused outside the door to her room. She was stalling for time, not wanting her time alone with Greyson to end. Meeting Greyson had left Letitia's world upside down and it still hadn't righted itself. Nor did she want it to.

"Mr. Jacob Hunter is escorting Anastasia for a walk."

Letitia couldn't decipher whether he thought that was a good or a bad thing. Mr. Hunter was one of his closest friends, along with Stanton.

"Do you approve?" she asked as she removed her room key from her reticule.

"Hunter is one of the best gentlemen I know. He's known Anastasia his entire life. It'll take time to get used to seeing them together and courting. Although I think I'm getting ahead of myself. Perhaps it is nothing but friendship."

"Hmmm." She didn't think so, given the way Hunter looked at Anastasia when he thought no one was watching. As for what Anastasia thought, that was a mystery. She was a handful, vivacious and friendly to everyone, making it difficult to tell where her heart lay. Letitia was the opposite of Anastasia, as she'd never learned to school her features from showing every emotion. She would be a terrible card player. That is, if she ever learned to play.

"What about Lady Aurora?"

He coughed into his hand. "Viscount Haddington—excuse me, the Earl of Warren. His father recently passed, and he inherited the title. He is taking her for a stroll through the inn's gardens."

"I met him for the first time today," she said with a smile, trying to put Greyson at ease. "He's very tall. He seems quite taken with Lady Aurora, talking mostly to her throughout the wedding breakfast."

"Yes, he did. I'm still trying to find the connection to either Clarice or Stanton that explains why he was in attendance."

"Does it matter as long as he's a fine gentleman with a good reputation and worthy of her?"

He shook his head. "I suppose not. When are you traveling back to London?"

"Tomorrow." To her utter regret, she knew Greyson would be staying in Newmarket for the time being, as Stanton's horses had more races coming up. Letitia's insides were torn between wanting and needing to see her son, Simon, and craving more of Greyson's company. Her greatest fear was that if too much time passed before they saw each other again, things would change, that the easy, comfortable way of their friendship would somehow be tainted and lost. She was afraid everything they shared was too good and wouldn't sustain the distance of miles and time.

He held out his hand. "Allow me."

Realizing she still held her room key, she placed it in his hand.

Once he unlocked the door and swung it open, he stepped back. He pivoted, took her hand, and brought it to his lips as he dipped his head, his intense dark-green eyes never leaving her face. "Until next time." His warm lips brushed her bare fingers, and she shivered.

He winked as he released her hand, then turned and walked away. She stayed in the open doorway, watching him casually stroll down the corridor while whistling. When she could no longer see or hear him, she closed the door, leaned against it, and sighed deeply. Closing her eyes and picturing his handsome face smiling at her, she whispered, "I believe he still holds my heart."

Her mind wandered to the night they first met at the Westport ball. She was standing with Clarice when her spine tingled with awareness. Her curiosity got the better of her, and her eyes roamed the room once, then twice. Then it happened. Intense green eyes locked with hers, and she couldn't look away. The floor tilted beneath her feet, and her breathing grew labored. All from the powerful glance of a handsome stranger with deep-green eyes.

His mouth quirked into a grin that made her insides warm. The warmth didn't last long when she noticed he had a beautiful young lady on each arm.

All night, she kept an eye out for the handsome stranger who intrigued her, hoping he would ask the Master of Ceremonies to make an introduction. It never happened, and she chastised herself for reading too much into the glance they'd shared. Perhaps he knew she was a widow and was only looking for a dalliance. That was one of her greatest fears—that the gentlemen of the *ton* would like her only for their bed and that she would never experience love or be loved truly and solely. Her fear was being seen as nothing but a widow—the Marquess of Rutherford's used goods. Why would anyone want to marry her and help her raise someone else's heir?

For the rest of the ball, her heart hung heavy in her chest, and she pretended to enjoy herself among her friends, Clarice, Emmeline, and Lilly, even though all she really wanted to do was go home and cry herself to sleep.

Fate had other plans.

As she and Clarice were leaving, she came face-to-face with the green-eyed devil himself, and this time it wasn't just the floor that tilted. Her entire world changed when their eyes met, making her experience things she didn't know existed.

Clarice introduced her to Viscount Greyson, and she somehow managed to go through the proper formalities while they smiled at each other, their eyes never breaking contact. The warmth filling her veins and the fire scorching her cheeks lasted an hour if she remembered correctly.

Then Greyson introduced her to the young ladies with him,

and she felt silly and embarrassed when she learned they were his twin sisters, and later she had trouble sleeping as deep-green eyes intruded on her dreams.

When she went to bed that night, at the Red Lion Inn, she rolled onto her side and hugged herself, knowing those same green eyes would interrupt her dreams that night. And sure enough, she tossed and turned many times, feeling the intensity of those eyes penetrating straight into her soul.

CHAPTER THREE

MONTHS LATER, AFTER a day spent shopping on Bond Street, she returned to Rutherford Manor. She entered the house, greeted the butler, Mr. Henry, and hurried up the staircase, anxious to see her son, Simon, who was two and a half. When she approached the nursery door, she found Simon on the floor, playing with wooden toy soldiers that had once belonged to Graham, and tears pooled in her eyes. He looked very much like his father, with brown hair and amber eyes. He had the same smile, even at this young age. She rubbed the ache in her heart for her son, who would never know his father. Graham had his faults, one big one, but aside from that, he was a kind and generous man. More than generous, in her way of thinking.

When Simon finally looked up, his eyes widened, and he smiled, then yelled, "Mama!"

Letitia dropped to her knees on the carpet and held out her arms for a hug. Simon, a sturdy, rambunctious boy, barreled into her, knocking her onto her back. She wrapped her arms tightly around him, and they giggled.

"My lady," the governess, Mrs. Hartman, hurried to her side. "Let me help you. I keep telling Master Simon to be gentle with you and with all ladies."

Letitia kept hugging Simon. "It's fine, Mrs. Hartman. As long as he doesn't knock anyone else over."

Moments later, she let Simon go and rose to her feet. He went back to his soldiers, some of which were painted red and others blue.

"My goodness, I never expected to be out shopping for so long. How has he been?" she asked Mrs. Hartman, a forty-one-year-old widow with no children of her own, recently hired when Simon no longer needed a nursemaid. Letitia believed it was time for a governess. Someone strict, because Simon was a hellion. A beautiful, happy, and loving hellion, but a hellion nonetheless, and he wasn't even three years old yet.

"He's been a fine boy, and we had a good day today. We read stories, he took a nap, we built a tower with blocks, and you can see he's playing with his soldiers. The poor French don't have a prayer against the English."

Laughing, Letitia ran her hand through her son's hair. "Sounds like you had a full day, Simon. Did you go outside for some fresh air?"

"Oh yes, I forgot," Mrs. Hartman added. "We took a stroll through the gardens, sat on the bench, and went through our letters and numbers. Simon is very bright. He can almost recite the alphabet perfectly. That is, if I can get him to sit still long enough, my lady."

"Thank you, Mrs. Hartman. I don't know what I would do without you. I rely on you so much when it comes to Simon."

Mrs. Hartman's eyes filled with tears, and she curtsied. "I should be thanking you for hiring me when my last charges grew too old to need me anymore."

"Well, we are both grateful for each other." She bent down and kissed the top of Simon's little head. "Be a good boy for Mrs. Hartman."

"Yes, Mama."

After leaving the nursery, Letitia, feeling unsettled, wandered the halls. It had been months since Clarice's wedding. The thoroughbred racing season was over, and most everyone was back in London for the little Season. Everyone except the Duke and Duchess of Stanton, who were on their honeymoon on the Continent. Not a day passed without her missing Clarice, prompting her to think of the Duchess of Blackstone and the Countess of Langford.

Tonight was the Brennan musicale. She had received a note from Emmeline, Duchess of Blackstone, stating that she and Lilly would be attending without their husbands and that they hoped to see her there. She hadn't seen them since the spring, when she'd traveled to Newmarket for the races and they had gone to their country estates for the summer. Receiving Emmeline's note pushed her into accepting the Brennans' invitation. Because truth be told, she was lonely.

When she left for Newmarket, she had no clue how long she'd be gone from home. And to be honest, the two weeks spent there were full of adventure, intrigue, and danger. No danger to herself, but to Clarice and Stanton.

Added to that list of things that happened in Newmarket would be the close friendship she developed with Greyson. Her stomach knotted. At least she believed they had formed a friendship with the understanding of more. Perhaps she had misinterpreted the desire in his eyes and the smooth words he'd whispered to her during their private moments. Had she been wrong about his intentions when he held her hand and stole a few kisses? She blew out her breath. She had heard he'd returned to London in July. Two months had passed, but she hadn't heard from him. Not that she had attended any social functions. The thought of going alone didn't interest her. She was much too shy to venture out alone. However, she thought he would have called upon her by now.

All the more reason to reconnect with Emmeline and Lilly. Yes, they were married, but she didn't think their husbands would mind her going along to a ball, a soirée, or the theater with them.

Heading to her chambers and her desk, she sat down and pulled two sheets of her favorite stationery from the middle drawer. She penned a note to each of them, welcoming them back to London and stating she would see them tonight at the Brennan musicale. She sealed them with hot wax and stamped the Rutherford seal; she rang for her maid. A few moments later, there was a knock on the door, and Jane entered.

"My lady." Jane bobbed a curtsy.

Letitia stood and walked toward her, the muslin skirts of her sage-green walking dress swishing around her. "Please give these to one of the footmen. I would like them delivered immediately."

"Yes, my lady."

Alone once again, Letitia went to the chaise longue on the far side of her large bedchamber and collapsed onto it, stretching out with a pillow beneath her head. She closed her eyes and pictured Greyson's handsome face just before she fell asleep.

⇶⧓⧔

ARCHIBALD FITZROY, THE Viscount Greyson, sat in his family's drawing room, savoring tea with his sisters and their callers. He would refer to the Earl of Warren as Aurora's caller. But when he thought of one of his best friends, Jacob Hunter, calling on Anastasia, he nearly spat out his tepid tea. Hunter's interest in Anastasia was something he never saw coming.

So here he sat in a chair, with Warren and Hunter flanking him in their own chairs, while his twin eighteen-year-old sisters faced them on the settee. Both played perfect hostesses, pouring tea and handing out biscuits, all with smiles and twinkles in their identical green eyes. The same eyes he saw staring back at him in the looking glass every day.

Greyson winced and swallowed a groan at something Hunter said, which made both his sisters giggle. What the devil had gotten into Hunter? He had put on a charming demeanor; even his eyes were soft, dreamy, and full of desire. Soft and dreamy were enough to make him want to gag, but desire tightened his insides. Bloody hell, Hunter was a smooth-talking rakehell. Surely he wouldn't compromise Anastasia?

He reached over and poked his shoulder.

Hunter looked at him as if he had lost his mind.

Well, he just might have. Never in a million years had he imagined Hunter and Anastasia together. He shut his eyes and groaned. No. Not thinking about them that way.

At least when he watched Warren watch Aurora, he saw nothing but innocent smiles and looks. Which made him think, what the hell was wrong with Warren? Didn't he want Aurora? He sighed and slouched in his chair. Hunter was right. He had lost his mind. If only his father weren't so sick and his mother would leave his bedside, even though his nurse was there, to take over the chaperoning duties. A brother should not be chaperoning his beautiful sisters. But he'd promised his mother he would do it. She only trusted him with their safety and reputations. Greyson knew what men thought and wanted regarding a lady. Most of it revolved around getting them naked and in bed. Hell, being naked and using a bed wasn't even necessary when it came to compromising a lady. If he wanted to keep his sisters' reputations pristine, he'd better take his duties more seriously.

After forty-five minutes, Greyson cleared his throat and stood. "I believe, gentlemen, tea is over."

After goodbyes were exchanged, Greyson stopped Hunter from leaving and said, "Can I have a word in private?"

Once again, Hunter looked at him as if he had lost his mind. Greyson made a promise to himself never to have daughters. The strain was giving him indigestion. How did mothers and fathers survive the Season until their daughters wed? He never wanted to find out.

He led Hunter to his father's study, which he had taken over. Not only had he taken over the study, but he was also managing everything pertaining to the earldom and his parents' personal matters. At least when he became the earl, he cringed at the thought because that meant his father would be dead, he would already know all there was to know, and the transition would be easy and fast.

"Sit," he barked, turning to a table behind the desk and pouring brandy into two crystal glasses. He handed one to Hunter, sat in the chair beside him, turned it so he faced Hunter, and downed his drink in one swallow. "What the hell is going on between you and Anastasia?"

Hunter looked at him and smirked, then threw back his drink and set the empty glass on the desk. "I thought it was obvious when I sent her flowers and called on her today."

Greyson glared at him, and he couldn't help but chuckle as Hunter glared right back. "You are an arse. Why didn't you ever tell me you were interested in Anastasia?"

He looked thoughtful. "Because I wasn't really until recently. Not until we spent time together in Newmarket. I've tried to keep my distance for our friendship's sake." He shrugged his shoulders. "Except to stay away isn't really fair to Anastasia or me if there are feelings there to explore."

"What changed?"

Hunter exhaled and ran his fingers through his hair. "I don't know. When we were in Newmarket, I really got to know her." He exhaled. "I've known her since she was a little girl, but when I look at her now, I see the beautiful woman she has become."

Greyson choked on nothing, and Hunter smacked him on the back. "Stop that," Greyson croaked, shoving his arm away.

Hunter narrowed his eyes again. "I thought you were dying."

"You would be happy if I died. Then you could do whatever you wanted with my sister."

Hunter turned serious and looked offended. "You are out of your bloody mind. I would never want you dead. As for Lady Anastasia, you have my promise I will not compromise her." He winked and grinned. "At least not completely until our wedding night."

Greyson jumped up and dove for the brandy decanter, removed the top, and took a swig straight from it. "Christ, give a man a warning before you say something about marrying his sister."

"Sorry." Hunter picked up his empty glass and shook it. "I need more."

"I need more if we're going to discuss marriage." Greyson splashed brandy into both their glasses.

Hunter gazed into the amber liquid. "I'm not ready to offer for her yet. Christ, I haven't even kissed her yet." He took a sip. "She's a hard one to figure out."

Greyson snorted. "Don't I know it."

"I can't tell if she's toying with me, flirting and enjoying my company until someone better comes along—someone with a title and more money than I."

Greyson frowned at the insecurity he heard in his friend's voice. It was something he'd never heard before. Hunter had always been confident around women. He'd never heard Hunter express insecurity about not having a title or enough money. As far as Greyson could tell, Hunter's family was swimming in coin and had prosperous investments. What Hunter must not realize was that many members of the peerage had titles and numerous estates, yet had very little viable coin.

"Anastasia does love to flirt," Greyson agreed with Hunter's earlier statement. "She has an outgoing personality and enjoys being around people, both men and women. But I watched her carefully today, and when she thought you weren't looking, her eyes drank you in. She is more than enamored with you, and I'll eat my hat if I'm wrong."

"Let me get this straight," Hunter said with all seriousness, "not ten minutes ago, you were ready to go for my throat because I was interested in Anastasia. Now you're essentially giving me your approval?"

Greyson crossed an ankle over his knee and chose his words carefully. "She likes you. You like her. The rest is up to you both. I will say one thing. If you can't keep your mouth and hands off her, be smart. I don't want to read about my sister in the scandal sheets. And for the sake of our friendship, swear to me you won't bed her unless you're married."

For the first time since they had entered his father's study, Hunter visibly relaxed. "You have my word."

"Good. I'm thinking of going to Club Knight tonight after the musicale. I just received my membership approval."

"I can't believe you actually went through with the application. Not that I know much about it, except what I heard whispered at Brooks's. I never would've told you about Club Knight if I'd known you would apply to join such a secret club. One that costs a small fortune to join and is so selective, no less." Hunter sat up straighter. "You must tell me everything."

"I'm forbidden from talking about it. Will you call on Anastasia again tomorrow?"

His friend chuckled. "You hate this, don't you?"

"No." He shook his head. "Just getting used to it. Truthfully, having you as a brother-in-law would be wonderful."

"Thanks. When I do propose, she could turn me down."

"She won't," Greyson said, hoping he was telling the truth. "I think I'll get some work done." He raised an eyebrow. "You'll see yourself out?"

"Of course." Hunter paused at the door. "I'll see you at the musicale."

CHAPTER FOUR

As Letitia prepared for the Brennan musicale, she was having second thoughts and wished she had never accepted the invitation. But she would be brave and go. After her maid placed the final pins in her hair, Letitia stood before the mirror, hoping that, if he attended, Greyson would find her irresistible in the blue-and-white evening dress she had chosen. It was one Madam Serena had delivered that morning, and she'd had his tastes in mind when she picked the medium-blue silk. Blue was his favorite color.

Now, if she could get the swarm of bees to settle in her stomach, she might just survive the night. If only she were confident he still cared for her. Her hopes were too high for tonight, and she prayed she wouldn't trip and fall flat on the floor in a heap of silk if she came face-to-face with Greyson.

"You need not wait up for me, Jane."

"Thank you, my lady."

Letitia steadied her legs and managed not to trip, step on her dress, or fall down the stairs. Not that she was prone to clumsiness. However, tonight she felt off-center. Perhaps seeing Greyson's handsome face would make everything right again. She could only hope.

"Have a good evening, my lady," the butler said as he opened the door.

"Thank you, Mr. Henry."

The door to her carriage was open, and the footman standing there held out his hand to help her inside. By the time she sat down and adjusted her skirts, the door was closed, and the footman knocked to signal the driver to drive on.

Nervous excitement coursed through her body. She kept turning her reticule over and over in her lap, giving her hands something to do on the ride to Brennan House. Now that she was on her way, she reconsidered again her decision to attend. Even if Greyson was there, he might not want to see her. If he had wanted to see her, surely he would have called on her by now. Sent a note, flowers . . . anything to show he was still interested in her. She could be making a complete fool of herself by showing up tonight. There was something to be said for the years she had stayed within the safety of her home. Except that, in order to live, you must set aside your fears and enter the unknown. Or in her case, the ever-critical *ton*.

By the time the carriage stopped in front of Brennan House, Letitia was a nervous wreck. She leaned to the side, reaching for the door. It was unusual for her to open it without waiting for a footman, but if she didn't escape from the carriage immediately, she would shout out to the driver to take her home. Her hand was on the door handle when it opened, and she practically fell into Greyson's arms, surprised beyond reason to find he had opened the carriage door.

"My dear," he said, his deep voice and handsome face filled with concern. "You nearly fell."

"I . . . I caught my heel on my dress." She hoped he believed the lie. "Forgive me for giving you a fright. I am perfectly well, as you can see." Her heart pounded so fast she hoped he couldn't hear it.

"I just escorted my sisters inside when I saw your carriage pull up." He paused, then held out his arm. "May I?"

"You may," she said, placing her hand on his solid, warm forearm. She swallowed back a sigh at the thrill of touching him again. Silly to be so excited about such a minor thing, but she couldn't help herself.

"When I saw your carriage, I asked Aurora to save us a seat next to her, if that's acceptable." He paused at the top of the outside stairs landing. "Forgive me. That was presumptuous of me. You're probably meeting someone."

"I am."

His shoulders fell, and she felt a twinge of guilt for giving him the wrong impression. But did he not deserve it for not calling on her for months?

"I'm meeting the Duchess of Blackstone and Lady Langford. Both their husbands are out of town."

"Ahh, then it will be my honor to escort you to them."

"Thank you," she said with regret. She loved her friends, but the thought of sitting next to Greyson made her insides warm.

"How fortunate for me," he said as they entered the large salon and found fifty or so chairs set up in rows, with a narrow aisle between two sections. "My sisters are sitting with your friends, and they left two empty chairs."

"Yes, how fortunate." She believed she kept the excitement from her voice at the thought of sitting next to Greyson for the next hour or so. Even if the daughters of Lord Brennan lacked talent on their instruments, she wouldn't care. Not with Greyson's close proximity.

They stopped in the aisle, exchanged greetings, and then sat. She sat between Greyson and Lilly, Lady Langford, who was expecting her first child. Letitia remembered her time carrying Simon. She hadn't been able to keep much down for the first three months, but in the following six months, she felt wonderful, energetic, and happy.

"You are positively glowing," she whispered to Lilly.

"I feel like I am," she said, resting her hand possessively on her stomach. "Langford didn't want me going out without him, but I told him not to worry. I have three months left. I refuse to be stuck inside now. Winter's coming, and I'll stay inside, curled up in front of the hearth, then."

"Langford's only worried about you." Letitia had that once with Rutherford. Would she ever have a husband again who loved and worried about her? Although she still wondered at times if Rutherford's worry and love were real or all an act.

Her eyes flickered to Greyson, who glanced her way at the same moment and grinned, sending her insides into recurring ocean waves. She couldn't look away as the green of his eyes deepened to emerald. The intensity of his gaze seeped into her soul, causing her cheeks to heat up.

Letitia looked away from Hunter just as Lilly said, "He does."

It was perfect timing when three young ladies, perhaps around fifteen or sixteen, entered the room. Each was dressed in white and looked terrified. One sat at a pianoforte, another picked up a violin, and the last held a flute. Indeed, as they played one piece after another, Letitia didn't think they were half bad. However, she was glad when they stopped, stood, and curtsied to their enthusiastic applause. She wondered how many of the attendees were clapping because they were good and how many because it was finally over.

Letitia was clapping for both. All three young ladies beamed with surprise at the applause. What they would learn in time was that even if they were dreadful, members of the *ton* would act enthusiastic. To do otherwise would be rude, cruel, and scandalous.

Out of the corner of her eye, she saw Greyson, looking dashing in brown and cream, as he stood. As far as she was concerned, he always looked handsome and dashing. He acknowledged a young lady and her mother as they walked by, bowing to them with perfect form. She wasn't the only lady who noticed. Several of the young debutantes had been making calf eyes at him during the performance. Not to mention the Marriage Mart mamas, who, no doubt, couldn't wait to waylay him and practically force their daughters on him.

Oh dear. She panicked. Was he seeking a bride among the

debutantes?

"Lady Rutherford," Greyson's deep voice interrupted her insecure thoughts. "May I escort you to the refreshments table?"

"You two go," Lilly said. "The duchess and I will keep an eye on your sisters, Greyson."

He cleared his throat and gave both his sisters a warning look. "Please do. I expect Hunter will hope for a stroll in the gardens." He looked around the room. "I don't see Lord Warren, but I'm sure he's in attendance and will wish to spend time with Aurora." He bowed to Lilly and Emmeline. "I am indebted to you both."

"Nonsense," Emmeline said with a sigh. "Get Letitia something to drink and eat. She looks flushed. Perhaps she is overly warm and needs fresh air?"

Letitia moved one hand to her cheek. Did she honestly look flushed, or was Emmeline making that up? Their eyes met, and she winked. She had lied to help her with Greyson. It was nice to have friends who understood her.

"Well then, we'll get refreshments and take them onto the veranda." He held out his hand, and she realized she was still seated while everyone else stood. Blushing, she took his hand and rose, finding herself very close to him; she could smell his woodsy cologne and see his eyes darken. He released her hand, stepped back, and waved his arm forward. "Ladies first." Was she mistaken, or did he seem shaken?

Perfect gentleman that he was, he filled a plate with confectioners' treats in one hand and precariously balanced two cups of punch in the other as he followed her out onto the veranda. The fresh night air instantly cooled her cheeks. They stood at the railing, sipping tasteless punch and nibbling delicious biscuits and miniature tea cakes. She'd eaten an early dinner and was surprised she could eat two of the delicious treats. Her eyes met Greyson's, and he smiled as though he knew a secret.

Before she could ask what was so amusing, he said, "You have a little sugar on your cheek." He reached out his hand, never breaking eye contact with her, which had her heart pounding.

"May I?" he asked, his hand hovering over her cheek.

Her suddenly parched mouth refused to work, so she licked her lips and whispered, "Yes."

She was enchanted by the look in his eyes and on his face as he swiped his index finger across her cheek, making her body quiver. He held up his finger. "See? Just a little bit."

She licked her lips again, and all the air vacated her lungs as he licked the sugar from his finger. "No harm done."

Not to you, she wanted to blurt out. How had she forgotten how he affected her during their time in Newmarket? Not that they had spent much time alone together, but when they did, she couldn't breathe or think straight, and her knees weakened. If only she knew how she affected him. Yes, she had seen desire in his eyes tonight, but she knew men could desire someone without it involving their emotions or hearts. If only she could be sure what he felt for her. She had made that mistake once before in Newmarket regarding his feelings. Because, obviously, he hadn't felt the same for her as she did for him if he could go months without reaching out. No note. No visit. Nothing.

"You're awfully quiet, my dear. And the changing expressions on your face have me intrigued as to what's going on in that pretty head of yours." He paused, set their empty cups and the plate on a small table in the corner of the veranda, and returned, making her swallow a groan. He leaned his back against the railing and crossed his arms over his chest, looking thoughtful and serious all of a sudden. "I owe you an apology."

"You do?" she blurted out before she could think better of it. She tried to tell her heart not to get excited or read too much into the apology before she even knew what he was apologizing for, but it was useless.

"Yes. I planned to call on you when I returned to London, but I got caught up in my father's business affairs. Then, before I realized it, two months passed, and I figured you had forgotten me. Can you ever forgive me for neglecting you? I'm not going to lie. My sisters keep my days and nights full with their social calendar. But everywhere we went, I looked for you."

"I imagine they keep you busy, and to be honest, I didn't go out much over the past several months." She honestly could only imagine how busy his sisters' social calendar was, since she'd never had a Season. Instead, she married Rutherford at eighteen without ever attending a ball, the theater, or Almack's, or any other such social event. If she had, and if she had met Greyson, she could well imagine her mother being run ragged to keep her from causing a scandal.

"Would you care to stroll through the gardens? Hunter just disappeared down a path with Anastasia. I should've known she would sneak away from Her Grace and Lady Langford."

Trying to hide her disappointment wasn't easy, and she knew she'd failed when he quickly added, "Forgive me. That sounded as if I only wanted to walk through the gardens to look for my sister and Hunter. I want to keep an eye on them from a distance, but even if I hadn't seen them enter the gardens, I wanted time alone with you there."

He appeared sincere. She exhaled, releasing her disappointment, and said, "I would love to see the gardens."

He visibly relaxed at her answer and held out his arm. She wrapped her arm around his, and they descended the veranda stairs and entered a granite path she knew would weave through the gardens. No doubt the Countess of Brennan had requested stone, making it nearly impossible to hide the crunch of footsteps. The sound of the stone being disturbed would make it easy to locate her daughters when they came of age and snuck off with gentlemen.

After several minutes of walking in companionable silence, Greyson paused by a bench just off the path. "I believe they went that way," he said, pointing to a path on their left. "Do you mind sitting on the bench with me? I don't want to insult one of my best friends by making him think I don't trust him with Anastasia. I'd prefer him to think we came here for privacy."

Removing her arm from his, she tiptoed as quietly as she

could to the black wrought iron bench and sat, adjusting her skirts to keep them from wrinkling. When Greyson didn't move and made a strange face empty of emotion, her stomach tightened. She said, "Aren't you joining me?" How pathetic she sounded.

"Forgive me," he said, shaking his head. "I was listening for footsteps." He strolled toward the bench as softly as possible, his boots crunching on the stone, and he shuddered. "I'm sure they just heard me. But you know what? I trust Hunter with my life. I need to learn to trust him with my sister. I can't think of anyone else I'd rather see her with than him."

"During the times I spent in Hunter's company while traveling in Newmarket, he appeared honest and kind, a true gentleman. He suits Anastasia perfectly. He seems able to rein in her wild nature." Greyson chucked, and the sound eased whatever was left of the tension she'd felt moments before. "It's nice to see you relaxing."

"You're right." He reached over and took one of her hands. "I've been tense. I didn't realize anyone would notice."

As he held her hand, his thumb stroked the underside of her wrist, right across her pulse point. A most sensitive area for her, and she had trouble looking away. Not to mention that her pulse and breathing quickened, making her wonder if he noticed.

"I've missed spending time with you." Greyson's words were soft, and the truth of them melted her heart.

"I have as well."

"May I kiss you?"

Kiss me? Yes. And anything else you want to do. "Yes."

They both pivoted on the bench to face each other. Her knees were tucked between the bench and his. She tipped her chin up, met his gaze, and got lost. Deep, liquid pools of green, tinged with desire. Desire for her. That desire had her insides fluttering. He reached out with both hands, gently cupped her cheeks, and grinned as his gaze dipped to her lips, then back to her eyes. He leaned forward. Her eyes closed, and she held her breath, waiting to feel his lips on hers. When their lips connected, she became lost—lost in the sensations bombarding her from every conceivable direction.

His tongue stroked the inside of her mouth. His thumbs stroked her cheeks, igniting every nerve ending in her body. She fought the urge to climb onto his lap, curl around him, and never let him go. Instead, she kissed him with as much enthusiasm as he kissed her. Little moans and breathy sounds escaped from them both. Her heart pounded right along with his, and she secretly reveled in the fact that she affected him as he affected her.

"Christ," Greyson broke the kiss, touched his forehead to hers, and breathed heavily. "I'd forgotten how good you taste."

"Hmmm," was all she could say, so moved by his kiss and words that she couldn't find her voice.

"I hear footsteps."

All she could hear was her heart pounding and his heavy breathing.

"Well, who do we have here?" She recognized the voice as Hunter's.

"Hunter," Greyson said as he pulled away from her, stood, and adjusted his jacket and cuffs, breaking their intense spell.

Letitia willed strength into her legs and stood, slipping her arm through Greyson's in case her legs failed her. "Mr. Hunter, Lady Anastasia, what a lovely night for a stroll."

Greyson and Hunter laughed at the same time. She didn't miss that Hunter held Anastasia's hand. Nor that her cheeks were pink and her lips swollen, as if she'd been kissed thoroughly. Much like she probably looked right now, too.

"Come," she said, holding out her hand to Anastasia. "Let's walk together and let the men discuss . . . whatever it is they discuss."

Anastasia giggled and, as she wrapped her arm through hers, Anastasia glanced back at Hunter. Letitia couldn't see the look she gave him, but she saw the look in Hunter's eyes and what he felt for her in his expression. He cared for her deeply. And if she wasn't mistaken, Anastasia felt the same. She didn't need to witness the look she gave him to know. Her emotions were all over her face when they first approached.

"How did you like the musicale?" Letitia asked, needing to change the subject. All these emotions swirling between Hunter and Anastasia and Greyson and her were unsettling. Beautiful, sacred, and private, and she was afraid she might break down and cry.

"Come now, Letitia," she whispered. "Ask what you really want to know."

"I really want to know if you enjoyed the musicale." She paused, then inhaled deeply. "Am I that obvious?"

"Yes. I like Hunter. Always have. I just can't believe he cares for me. He's known me forever, and I wasn't always kind or even-tempered. He has seen me throw a temper tantrum and treat Greyson badly." She giggled. "Of course, I was a child then. Thank goodness he sees me as a woman now, not that spoiled girl acting out to get everyone's attention. Being a twin was difficult at times as Aurora and I competed for attention."

"I'm glad he sees you for who you are now. He looks at you as a man looks at a lady he's smitten with."

"You mean how my brother looks at you?"

Letitia's heart leaped. "He does?"

She nudged her shoulder against hers. "Don't be coy with me. He never left your side in Newmarket."

"But he's been back in London since early July, and tonight was the first time I've seen him. I was starting to think he wasn't interested in me anymore. You can hardly blame me for thinking that."

"No, I can't. What a fool my brother is. If he lets you get away, I may have to beat him with his walking stick for being so utterly stupid."

"You wouldn't!"

"No. Never. I love my brother, even if he's annoying and disappears now and then."

"Disappears?" she said, as warning bells rang in her head and her entire body tensed. All she could think about was Rutherford and how he had led her to believe she was his world, when in fact she was only a small part of it. Was Greyson hiding something similar?

"Forgive me," Anastasia whispered, "for upsetting you."

"You haven't."

"You're a terrible liar. I can't explain his disappearances, but I don't believe he has a mistress hidden somewhere. I'm not saying he's a monk, but having a mistress isn't like him. Nor have I noticed him paying attention to any young ladies since he met you."

Frowning, Letitia asked, "Why did you assume I was thinking he had a mistress?"

"Forgive me, but I know about Lord Rutherford's mistress."

Her feet stopped. They stuck to the stone and refused to move. Mortification was the first thing that came to mind. Ever since her husband's death, she understood that most of polite society knew about his mistress and the children he'd sired with her. But she hadn't expected Anastasia to know. Or at least not come right out and mention it. The tension threatening to crack her body into a thousand pieces eased at hearing that Greyson didn't have a mistress, but not entirely. She hated secrets. Could she allow Greyson to court her, if he had secrets? And how could she bring up the subject without raising suspicion? She couldn't. She would just have to stay vigilant. She forced her feet forward, and they began moving as if nothing untoward had happened to stop her in her tracks.

"As his sister, I worry about him, though."

"No doubt. Just as he worries about you." Letitia forced her worries about Greyson from her mind. "He is happy for you and Hunter. Is it as serious as it looks?"

Anastasia exhaled, then laughed. A nervous laugh. "I believe so. If I tell you something, you must promise not to share it with my brother."

"I promise."

"I love him." Her words came out as the softest of exhales.

Letitia held her breath, quickly glanced over her shoulder, then exhaled when Greyson and Hunter appeared deep in conversation. Neither would've heard Anastasia's proclamation of love. "Does he feel the same?" From the looks he gave her, she believed he did.

"Yes. He told me tonight," she said wistfully. "He said he would speak to Greyson soon, since Greyson makes all my father's decisions these days."

"I understand your father has been ill for some time."

"Yes. It's rather sad. His symptoms began slowly; he would get disoriented or confused. Then he started forgetting meetings, people's names, and even us. It's terribly sad on the days he doesn't recognize me. I sometimes avoid his room, afraid he won't know my name or who I am. Then, when I do stop by, and he knows me, I feel guilty for the times I stay away. It's so hard to know what to do. He lies in bed, staring at the ceiling, and my mother barely ever leaves his side. I can't imagine he will last much longer. My mother and the nurse force him to eat and drink. They alone are keeping him alive." Anastasia paused and wiped a tear with her gloved fingers. "Forgive me."

"There's nothing to forgive," she said, tears pooling in her own eyes as she thought of the tragic story.

"My mother's health has declined right along with my father's. She hardly sleeps or eats. She's down to skin and bones."

"I'm so sorry. Greyson has hinted at this, but I didn't realize it was so severe."

"Their health weighs heavily on his shoulders. He feels guilty for staying in Newmarket for so long, but I think he needed the distance to clear his head and enjoy life a little."

Poor Greyson. No wonder he hadn't had time to visit her. All the times she'd thought ill of him for not calling upon her, when the truth of the matter was that he was selflessly taking care of his family. A twinge of guilt, which turned into a thread flowing through her veins, joined another thread of guilt she carried and hadn't made peace with. She was still tortured by the guilt from the night Rutherford died. If it hadn't been for her arguing with him about his mistress and going out on such a stormy night, he might still be alive.

As they approached the stairs to the veranda, Hunter came up beside Anastasia and asked, "May I escort you inside?"

"Yes," she replied with a radiant smile that had Letitia forgetting her woes.

"They look good together," Greyson said matter-of-factly as he stood at her side at the bottom of the steps, his gaze on his friend and sister.

"They do."

"May I?" He offered his arm, and his tentative eyes met hers, making her realize that even after the kiss they had shared not long ago in the gardens, he was still uncertain about her feelings for him. It made her realize he really did regret having ignored her for those long, lonely months right after he returned from Newmarket. At least from her perspective, they were long and lonely. From what his sister said, he had been quite busy and overwhelmed with family affairs.

"You may." She placed her gloved hand on his forearm, and they climbed the stairs to the veranda and into the salon, where he escorted her directly to Emmeline and Lilly.

"Forgive me for monopolizing Lady Rutherford's time," he said as he bowed. "Your Grace, Lady Langford, Lady Rutherford, I bid you goodnight."

Letitia noted that both her friends were watching Greyson saunter away.

"How was your time in the gardens?" Emmeline asked with a sly smile.

"Yes, please tell us," Lilly said, mimicking Emmeline's look.

"Shhh," she said, looking around and relaxing when it seemed no one had heard them. "It was pleasant. We bumped into Hunter and Anastasia."

This time, when Emmeline spoke, she lowered her voice. "We tried to watch her, but Anastasia's a slippery one. We knew she was with Hunter and would be safe . . . well, relatively safe, anyway. I know you were upset with Greyson and his neglect of you, but I recognize the look of interest in a man's eyes. Perhaps he has a very good reason for his neglect."

"He did explain, and so did Anastasia." Tears threatened to appear, and she fought them off. "A note would've been nice. But he made no promises to me in Newmarket. Just a passing comment about calling on me, which I took too seriously. It was hardly a declaration of undying love and commitment." By the widening of her friends' eyes, she knew she'd said too much. What was going on with her tonight? One moment she was almost paralyzed with guilt, and the next she was ready to cry her eyes out. Oh, dear, her hand covered her stomach. She must be close to getting her courses.

Lilly sighed and took her hand. "He hurt you—more than I realized. You care more deeply for him than I thought. For that, forgive me for not being there to support you."

"Don't be silly." Now she felt bad for Lilly feeling bad. "You and Emmeline were at your country estates until recently. If I recall correctly, I made only one small comment about it in my letters to you both. Hardly a cry for help. I'm a grown woman, a widow, and a mother. I can handle the disappointments that come up in life."

Emmeline took her free hand in hers. "We know how strong and resilient you are. We wish you hadn't pined away for Greyson alone."

"Thank you. Both of you. If you don't mind, I think I'll go home now."

"We will walk out with you," Lilly said. "My little unborn baby and I are ready for bed."

Emmeline and Lilly saw her to her carriage and left after exchanging hugs and promises that things would improve. As she sat inside her carriage, listening to the clip-clop of the horses' hooves and the creaking of the wheels, she began to believe them.

When the carriage stopped, Letitia startled awake. "I must be more tired than I thought," she said to herself just as her footman opened the door, lowered the steps and assisted her in alighting from the carriage.

Mr. Henry greeted her at the door. "Welcome home, my lady. Miss Jane is waiting for you."

"Thank you, Mr. Henry. You may retire for the night."

He bowed. "Thank you, my lady."

Feeling weary from all the stimulation of being around so many people, she trudged up the stairs on tired legs, her hand gripping the banister tightly with every step. After spending time in Newmarket for the races, she thought she would be used to crowds by now. But somehow tonight was taxing on her, making her wonder if she would ever get used to the London social scene. Crowds didn't bother her; she just needed to get acclimated to them, and she never really had the chance while married to Graham. She supposed that, since she hoped to spend more and more time with the *ton*, she had better get used to the social whirl. Perhaps tonight's fatigue had more to do with being in private with Greyson and the kiss they shared? It was as though no time at all had passed since they were together in Newmarket.

When she entered her chambers, she said, "Did you forget I told you not to wait up?"

"My lady." Jane curtsied. "I didn't forget. I wanted to wait for you in case you did have need of my services."

"Thank you. Please loosen my dress and stays. I can take care of the rest myself."

"Yes, my lady," Jane said as she did as asked.

Jane closed the door quietly when she left. Letitia stripped down, poured water from a pitcher into the basin, wet a cloth, scrubbed her skin, and dried off. She used tooth powder on a cloth to clean her teeth. She went behind the screen in the far corner of her room to take care of personal needs. Then she put on her night rail that Jane had left on her bed and draped her evening clothes over a chair to keep them from wrinkling.

She climbed into bed, turned onto her side, and snuggled beneath the coverlet, sighing heavily. Being in bed beneath the covers felt decadent rather than a nightly occurrence. Her mind drifted to the kiss she had shared with Greyson. It felt so natural to her, like coming home after an extended visit away. Did he feel it too? Or was she alone with her feelings? Sometimes it was hard to read Greyson. One moment, his emotions were plain as day, like an open book, and the next, the book snapped shut. When his guard was down, his gorgeous green eyes were a window to his soul. When he protected himself, they were a dark abyss, swirling green and black, lacking any emotion whatsoever. Those glimpses made her skin prickle. Seeing him devoid of emotion didn't sit well with her. He was meant to be joyful and unguarded, not shut off from the world and his surroundings.

Tonight wasn't the first time she'd caught a glimpse of this side of him. A time or two in Newmarket, she had witnessed it, which made her wonder why. He should always be joyful, open, and approachable.

She rolled onto her back, stared up at the ceiling, wondering what Greyson was doing. Was he home and in bed, thinking of her as she was of him? Had he visited one of his clubs for a nightcap? Did he do that every night? There were many things she didn't know about him. Little things she wanted to know. Big things she hoped to know one day. For the first time, she let herself acknowledge that they were, in some ways, strangers and, in others, well acquainted.

What she learned from Anastasia that night was that he was an intensely private person when it came to his family and their troubles. As she thought back to their time in Newmarket, to the horse races and the nightly balls and soirees they attended, she never sensed that he felt guilty about being away from his parents. Yet according to Anastasia, he did. Not only was he private, but she was also beginning to think he hid his feelings deep inside.

CHAPTER FIVE

AFTER LEAVING THE Brennan musicale, Greyson rode to Club Knight. It was a large three-story townhouse, much like any other home on this street that bordered on fashionable London. Greyson had been here many times before, but never inside the club rooms. He usually entered from the back and went down the stairs to a private, windowless room with two secret entrances. A room where gentlemen loyal to the Crown met and planned. A group of spies that didn't report to the Home Office. The Home Office didn't know about them. At least, not yet they didn't. It was getting harder and harder to stay in the shadows and keep their existence secret. They reported directly to the Prince Regent and had been formed at the conclusion of the last war with Napoleon.

But the organization wasn't what brought him here tonight. Tonight, he was a club member for the first time, and he would see the inside of these walls in a different light. Greyson hesitated on the stoop, his heart pounding. He stood to the side as several members came and went. He chose to attend tonight because it was a regular night with gambling, billiards, and socializing. No dancing or masquerade to contend with.

Perhaps his heart was pounding because he felt guilty. Guilt for witnessing the disappointment on Letitia's face, for never calling on her for two months. What a complete idiot he was.

Yes, he'd been busy and had gone out of town several times on assignment, but he could have sent a note. Why hadn't he? His stomach tightened. He didn't deserve her. That was partly why he stayed away. Working for Prinny as a Black Knight—yes, that was what they called themselves—was dangerous. He didn't know if he could court Letitia seriously or even marry her while endangering his life as a Black Knight. Not to mention keeping watch over his mother and father and chaperoning his sisters. It wouldn't be fair to Letitia. He wouldn't be able to give all of himself to her, which was what he always said he wanted when it came to marriage.

Tonight, he was going to indulge in cards. Relax in an atmosphere where one could be oneself without worrying about ending up in the gossip rags. Not that his name appeared in them often. In fact, not in quite some time, thankfully. Not since he had nearly found himself with the parson's noose around his neck for stealing a kiss from Miss Emma Honeysuckle when he was all of twenty years old. How could he not kiss her with a name like Honeysuckle? His idiot friends, Stanton and Hunter, had dared him to kiss her. He had almost not escaped that one. But those days of being a rake and stealing hearts were over for him. Debutantes didn't interest him anymore. There was too much to lose if one wasn't careful. He would prefer to marry for love, not because a pistol was being held to his head. Even so, the lady marrying him would have to understand his past, value his present, and accept his future.

He worked hard to keep his private affairs secret, even from his two closest friends. There were times when it was difficult. Right after Letitia left Newmarket for London, he went on assignment for a sennight. It hadn't been easy to make Stanton, Hunter, and his sisters understand why he had to leave. Thankfully, Clarice, now the Duchess of Stanton, had chaperoned Anastasia and Aurora during his absence. The harsh words exchanged with Stanton and Hunter weren't easy to swallow. Goodness knew what they thought at the time. Not to mention the fact that it wasn't the first time he'd bailed on them. Every time he left in a hurry, he witnessed the disappointment in their eyes. His body, his mind, and his soul were tired, and he needed an escape.

All of this led him to Club Knight, a place where you could have a tryst between two willing partners, and the knowledge would never leave the club. Perhaps if he hadn't met Letitia, he might have visited those rooms on the upper floor. However, his days of rendezvous were over, even if he couldn't have her. His escape that night would have to be in the form of card play.

After opening and closing the door several times, the doorman finally said, "Are you coming in?"

Greyson stared at the card in his hand, embossed with the word Knight. Nothing like hiding in plain sight. He handed it to the doorman, who flipped it over, no doubt to inspect it and make sure it was authentic.

"Welcome. The usual rules apply tonight."

He took the card back and put it in his jacket pocket, then stepped into the foyer. His eyes widened as he took in the dimly lit interior.

"Mr. Knight is in attendance this evening," the doorman said. "Would you like him to give you a tour?"

"If it's allowed, I'll wander around myself."

"Stay off the third floor unless you know what it's for and what you want," he warned.

"I believe it was explained when my acceptance notice arrived, but thank you for the reminder. I'm really here for the cards."

"All the tables are set up in the ballroom. Go up the stairs and turn right."

He hurried up the stairs and whistled when he entered the ballroom and saw all the tables, most of them full, not just with gentlemen but with ladies as well. He was used to attending men-only gambling hells, though ladies of dubious reputations were present, not to partake in card play but to serve and entertain the gentlemen. The sight of ladies sitting at tables and playing cards with men was intriguing, to say the least. He walked the perimeter of the room, recognizing many members of the *ton*.

"Welcome to Club Knight, Greyson."

The gentleman who approached him wore a mask that covered most of his face. A face Greyson knew was burned and scarred in the war. He was dressed entirely in black, except for his fine white linen shirt. He had recently married a young widow by the name of Charlotte Beauchamp, making her his duchess.

"Tremont, or do you go by Knight here?"

"I prefer Knight while inside the club. It adds to the mystique. I was surprised to find your application cross my desk."

"Why?"

"Mayhap there were rumors from Newmarket during the spring about you and Lady Rutherford."

His stomach clenched up tight, causing stabbing pain. "How in the hell?"

"So tell me why you are here."

"Perhaps I'm here for the gambling." He had been admitted to the club, so why was Knight hammering him?

His Grace . . . Knight chuckled. "I admit some members come for the gambling and nothing else."

"Perhaps I came to gamble, play billiards, and relax without having to be perfect all the time."

"Oh, come now, Greyson. You can do that at any of the other gambling clubs around London. There must be another reason."

"Christ, Knight. Give a man a break. The truth is, I do want to gamble, wear my shirt unbuttoned if I so desire, and not have to explain myself to anyone. Chaperoning my sisters during the Season, the racing circuit, and now the start of the Little Season, not to mention my father's declining health and my mother's right along with his, has me wanting peace."

"You will get that here and more. I also understand that demons are fighting to take over, but you would be wise to fight them back."

"Perhaps I just want to satisfy some desires with a willing partner." Why the bloody hell did he say that?

"I'm disappointed in you. Perhaps you have a willing partner in Lady Rutherford. Perhaps you should visit her and devote your energy to solidifying your future with her. Or better yet, bring her here."

"I don't think that would be wise. I also can't imagine what business this is of yours."

"It's not. Although I do have a vested interest in my Black Knights."

"Are we finished here?" He'd been tense since arriving thirty minutes earlier. The last thing he expected was an interrogation by Knight. Knight was someone he knew well since he headed up the Black Knights. Most of the time, he was in an odd mood; tonight, he was even odder than usual. Greyson would have thought it was because he'd applied for membership, but as he looked around the room, he noticed a few Black Knights in attendance, so that couldn't be the reason.

"Yes, but please keep in mind what I said before you do something you regret."

Without replying, Greyson moved to the first available chair and sat down. "Deal me in." He removed several bills from his billfold. To his misfortune, he found himself at a vingt-et-un table. Glancing around the round table, he tried to hide his annoyance at the other three players. Miss Constance Sherman, her cousin and cousin's husband, the Earl and Countess of Haversham. Greyson had courted Miss Sherman briefly a year ago. Their personalities were too different. It didn't take him long to learn they would never suit.

"Miss Sherman, Earl, Countess," he said as he picked up the one card the dealer had dealt him.

"Greyson," Miss Sherman said with a smile. "I haven't seen you in ages."

"I've been quite busy these days," Greyson replied to Miss Sherman. "I hope all is well with you?" He picked up another card and smiled inwardly as he held two tens. The object of the game was to get as close to twenty-one as possible without going over.

"I am very well, thank you for asking," she replied, eyeing him like candy. Quite unsettling, to say the least. When he'd courted her, the typical roles had been reversed. He'd had to fend off her amorous advances. He knew if he had bedded her, she would have expected a marriage proposal, which he had no intention of making. He'd ended the courtship, to her disappointment.

"Another card, Greyson?" the dealer asked.

"No."

"Then place your cards down, face up."

He won the hand and received a nasty look from Miss Sherman, who held a jack and an eight.

Oh well. One shouldn't gamble or play cards if one can't lose graciously. After playing several more hands of vingt-et-un, which he lost, Greyson stood and bowed. "Ladies, gentlemen, since this is my first night at the club, I'd like to look around." He would stay clear of the third floor, where ladies and men went looking for company. As much as his body needed relief, since it'd been months since he'd bedded a woman, he just couldn't do it. The only woman he wanted in his arms and in his bed was Letitia, even if he wouldn't. It wouldn't be fair to her. He couldn't commit to a relationship just now because of the Black Knights.

Ever since the war with Napoleon ended, the people of England had been suffering and starving. People were out of work as machines replaced them. The new Corn Laws, since they were passed in 1815, limited the amount of grain that could be imported, which kept grain prices and profits high. This benefited landowners and farmers, but the working classes were struggling to feed their families as food costs continued to rise.

The laws had been widely protested since they were passed—it wasn't hard to see why—but ever since the Pentrich Rebellion in June, Greyson had been particularly busy. The uprising, led by Jeremiah Brandreth, had ended badly. He had believed he would lead his group of farmers, knitters, and out-of-work industrial workers, armed with crude weapons, to Nottingham, where they would meet fifty thousand other men and then march on the Tower to demand government reform by force. Unfortunately, they had been deceived by a man—an informant and agitator—who approached Brandreth and encouraged the march. Light Dragoons stopped them long before they made it to London, and Brandreth and several other men were now awaiting execution. Greyson was still cleaning up that mess in his work as a Black Knight, as the repercussions from that rebellion weren't over yet.

More and more rebellions were occurring in smaller groups. The Black Knights were tasked with keeping the peace and dispersing the protesters without bloodshed. They hoped to reach them before the local militias, Light Dragoons, yeomanry, or infantry soldiers arrived, drew their weapons, and made arrests. Most often, they arrived too late. Sometimes Greyson felt as though the Black Knights weren't doing enough or making any difference. While Prinny still feared a copy of the French Revolution happening in Britain.

Greyson poked his head into a few doors, finding a billiards room, a library, and several salons. Having seen enough for one night, he made his way to the door and retrieved his coat, hat, and gloves from the doorman.

"Leaving so soon, Greyson?" Knight said from a dark corner of the entry hall. The man could make himself invisible in broad daylight.

"Yes, I feel the sudden urge to be alone."

"I totally understand." He paused, then stepped farther into the entry. "Remember what I said—bring Lady Rutherford next time. I would love a formal introduction."

"I will take it under advisement." Greyson walked to his carriage and told his driver, "Home, Hughes."

When he finally arrived home, he dismissed his valet for the night and prepared for bed. Lying in bed on his back, he willed his exhausted mind and body to sleep. It wasn't easy. It took over an hour of reliving the time in the garden with Letitia and then his visit to Club Knight before he finally fell asleep, a particular blue-eyed, beautiful lady smiling up at him in his thoughts.

CHAPTER SIX

THE FOLLOWING MORNING, after she was dressed in a pretty pink linen day dress, she visited Simon in the nursery to find him having breakfast. She sat with him for a time, then made her way to the morning room to break her fast. After descending the stairs to the entry hall, she saw a lovely vase of hothouse roses in a variety of colors on the entry hall table. Her heart flipped with excitement as she plucked the card tucked among the roses. There was one word scribbled on the card. "Greyson." She flipped it over and over, hoping for more words, but alas, there were none. She fought her disappointment. So he was a man of few words. She could live with that. The important thing was that he sent her flowers. Roses in a rainbow of colors. Perhaps he would call upon her today?

As a footman approached, she said, "Please have these flowers brought into the family drawing room."

The footman bowed. "Yes, my lady."

Letitia continued into the morning room, where filtered sunlight streamed through the large windows. It was one of her favorite rooms in the house. On a sunny day, she could enjoy her morning meal, the warmth of the sun invigorating her and giving her the energy to start her day. Not that she ever had much to do during the day, but she loved knowing she could accomplish anything that came along.

A footman entered the room with her plate and hot chocolate. She never had the cook bother with hot plates on the sideboard, filled with all kinds of food. She was one person and preferred the same breakfast every day. Two buttered eggs, sausage, and toast with cream and jam. If she ever wanted something different, she had Jane pass it along to Mrs. Woods, the cook.

After she ate, she made her way to the family drawing room. When she entered the room, decorated in shades of blue and cream, and saw the roses from Greyson on the table beside the settee she always sat on, she smiled. She picked up the embroidery she had been working on from a basket on the other side of the settee and sat down. Even though she hadn't known if she would see Greyson again, she had started a set of four handkerchiefs with the initials ARF for Archibald Robert Fitzroy. She was using thread in black, gray, and red. She was on the second one and had no idea if she would ever give them to him. Still, it gave her something to do. She'd made enough pillows and pillowcases over the years; she had a small cedar chest filled with them.

Someday, if she ever had another child and it were a girl, she could make pinafores embroidered with all sorts of pretty, colorful flowers to wear over her dresses. If only, she sighed.

The day dragged on, as many did. She took luncheon in the nursery with Simon. Then she curled up on the chaise longue in her room and read a book of poetry for a spell. Just in case Greyson came for afternoon tea, she dressed in a lovely blue day dress and made her way to the green drawing room, where she greeted visitors.

She'd just about given up hope when a footman entered the room and announced, "Viscount Greyson."

All the air whooshed from her lungs at the sight of him in brown-and-tan riding clothes. He removed his hat and gloves, placing them, along with his riding crop, on one of the two chairs facing the settee, then turned to her and bowed, appearing a little out of breath. "Lady Rutherford. Forgive me for arriving late for tea, but it couldn't be helped."

"No need to apologize. Please sit."

"Thank you," he said, sitting in the comfortable upholstered chair facing her.

"Would you care for tea?"

He chuckled, and it was nice to see his guard down, his humor radiating from his eyes. "Thank you, but I must decline." He leaned forward, his elbows on his knees. "You see, I've just had tea at my house with Hunter and the Earl of Warren. I've drunk enough tea for a week. But thank you, anyway."

"So that is why you are past teatime?"

"Once again, forgive me. I nearly had to throw Hunter and Warren out. I mounted my horse and rode like the devil to get here."

"You never have to stick to proper visiting hours with me. You may drop by anytime. And," she said, motioning with her arm toward the vase of roses, "the roses are beautiful. Thank you for thinking of me." She'd had Jane move them again from the family drawing room to the public one.

"Whether you wish to believe me or not, I think of you often."

Heat suffused her cheeks. "As I do you."

"Forgive me if I hurt you in any way."

Just her heart and her pride. Which, of course, she would never admit. Instead, she redirected the conversation to something Anastasia had said that had been puzzling her. "May I ask a personal question?"

"You may ask, but I may defer answering."

"I suppose I have two questions. Before I ask the second question, I want to know if you plan to court me. Sending flowers and calling on me would lead me to believe you do. However, with you, I can never be sure what you are thinking or planning." There. She asked the first question. A perfectly logical one, as far as she was concerned.

"I would like to court you, but you need to understand that I have other obligations. I wouldn't want to make you feel neglected, as you did in the past few months. Can you accept my life as it is now? I won't be as attentive as some suitors."

"I understand better now than before, which leads to my second question. Anastasia recently said something in passing—please don't be angry at her for mentioning it—that you disappear occasionally, sometimes for days or even a sennight at a time." For one brief moment, he looked angry, then it was gone. "I only ask because Rutherford kept things from me. He led me to believe he spent his days at his club and even some nights, but it was all a lie." She paused and inhaled, gathering the courage to continue. "If you disappear because you are hiding a mistress, then I will not be courted by you."

His expression softened. "I can promise you I have no mistress or bastards, nor do I plan to." He cleared his throat. "Honestly, when would I find the time? As for my leaving from time to time, it's so I can escape and have time alone to keep my sanity or to take care of estate business."

She now felt terrible for asking. "Thank you for being honest with me."

"Can I ask you a question?"

"Yes. And I'll answer if I can."

Chuckling, he said, "Fair enough. I understand you married Rutherford before you came out."

"Yes," she said.

"Did you love him?"

Oh dear, that was a complicated question that made her insides ache. "Yes. I loved him as a naïve eighteen-year-old would, and I continued to love him until he died. After he died, when I saw other couples in love, I realized my marriage wasn't anything like theirs. And when I watch Emmeline and Lilly with their husbands, I realize what Rutherford and I shared was a comfortable, almost companionable love, not the passionate love I witness among my friends." She had asked for honesty from him; she could give him no less.

"I see."

"Have you ever been in love, Greyson?"

She could see she'd shocked him with her question because he wasn't quick enough to school his emotions.

"No." He cleared his throat. "Enough questions. I would like to invite you somewhere tonight." He paused, studying her face.

"Go on."

"It is not your typical place. It is an exclusive club for those who have . . . Let's just say there is an extensive application process, and membership comes at a steep price."

"You have piqued my interest." She leaned in, her heart beating a tad faster than it was. "Is this a secret club of some sort?"

He grinned. "Actually, you would be correct. It is a secret club only because members can be themselves. Both men and women are welcome. There's gambling and billiards, and twice a month, there's a masquerade ball where nobody needs to reveal themselves."

"If it is so secret, how can you take me there?"

"I'm close with the owner, and he suggested I bring you."

"Hmmm, why would he do that?" Did that mean Greyson had talked about her? Warmth spread through her chest.

"It doesn't matter; what matters is that he did. I do not believe he offers guest passes often. I myself just became a member."

"I see."

"There's more. I don't want you to be shocked to learn that rooms are available for private use. That's not why I'm inviting you." He combed his fingers through his hair and groaned.

His composure was falling apart, and she was surprised by it. It was most unusual.

"You're quiet. Did you understand what I said?"

"Yes. Forgive me. My mind wandered. Yes, I believe I get the gist of it."

"Will you accompany me tonight? Before you answer, the club doesn't open until midnight."

"Midnight?"

"Yes, I suggest you rest up. I'll pick you up at half eleven."

Funny, she didn't remember agreeing to go. But after he described the club, nothing could keep her away. She'd led such a sheltered life, first with her parents and then with Rutherford. It was high time she left the house and started living. "I'll go if you promise not to leave my side."

"I won't leave you alone." He stood, gathered his things, turned to her, and bowed. "Until tonight."

"Yes," she murmured. "Until tonight."

After dinner, she forced herself to take a nap, telling Jane to wake her at ten so she would have time to prepare for her foray into the world of secret clubs. She had never known such clubs existed, and she planned to enjoy herself.

➤➤➤◄◄◄

FOR THE REST of the day and into the evening, Greyson spent most of his time in his father's study. He'd invited Letitia to Club Knight that night because his sisters had no social engagements on their calendars for that evening, which he was very thankful for. It gave him a reprieve from his chaperoning duties. He knew he complained about escorting his twin sisters, but the truth was, he enjoyed spending time with them. Once they wed, he didn't know how often he would get to see them as they started their new lives.

For what felt like the hundredth time, he glanced at the clock. Was it broken? Surely it was later than ten. At this rate, he'd be an old man before the clock struck eleven. When it did, he poured himself a generous measure of brandy and downed it in one gulp, savoring the warmth as it spread down his throat and into his stomach. He needed something to fortify himself, for he risked much by taking Letitia to the club. What if she was horrified? What if she looked at him differently, as if he were depraved for wanting to belong to such a place?

At ten past eleven, he made his way to the front hall, knowing the carriage was waiting for him.

"My lord," the butler, Henderson, said, assisting him into his overcoat and handing him his gloves and hat. "The carriage has been brought around."

"Thank you, Henderson. No need to wait up. I expect to be very late, or early."

"Yes, my lord."

"Please mention it to Dalton. I may have forgotten to tell him the same."

"Yes, my lord."

Greyson exited his family's townhouse and, before entering the carriage, told his driver, Reed, "Rutherford Manor. Then on to Club Knight." Once he was settled, he knocked on the roof, and the wheels began to move, sure and steady. With most members of polite society still attending one event or another, the ride to Rutherford Manor and then on to Club Knight should be unencumbered by traffic. Greyson rubbed the constant ache in his chest, the one he'd had ever since he invited Letitia to accompany him tonight.

Was he doing the right thing? Would she take one look around the club and demand that he take her home? Would that be the end of their courtship? Did Knight know something about Letitia that he didn't? Perhaps they were acquainted, although Greyson didn't see how. Did Knight's wife know Letitia? That would make much more sense if she did, since they were both widows and of a similar age. That must be it. That must be the reason Knight suggested bringing her as his guest.

When the carriage slowed to a stop, Greyson exhaled. "It's now or never," he mumbled to himself from inside the plain black carriage he used for assignments. He deemed it wise to use it for club visits as well. Nor did his driver or his groom, standing on the back of the carriage, wear his father's livery. Greyson always found it valuable to travel with his groom rather than a footman, in case the horses needed immediate attention or came up lame. When the young groom, Stevenson, opened the door, he climbed out and found himself face-to-face with Letitia. It took him a moment to compose himself. How had she managed to break through the barriers he had trained so hard to conceal?

"Lady Rutherford." He stepped back, creating space between them so he could bow. "Forgive me. I didn't see you there."

"Apologies. I didn't mean to startle you. It's such a glorious night that I thought I'd wait outside for you to arrive. Breathe in the crisp night air and watch for any shooting stars."

"Did you see any?"

"No," she replied, placing her small, delicate, gloved hand in the one he offered to help her into the coach. "But the stars were vibrant and twinkling. Positively mesmerizing."

Greyson followed her into the coach and sat on the bench beside her, since the carriage was small and had only one bench. He tapped the roof, and the wheels engaged. "Are you comfortable? This is not my usual carriage."

"Yes, I noticed that. Did you break a wheel?"

"No. Nothing of the sort. I prefer to arrive at Club Knight without my family's crest on the door. No need to draw attention to myself and set the gossiping tongues wagging." Her breath caught, and he quickly added, "No one will recognize you with the hood of your cloak covering your lovely hair and face."

Her breath caught again. "But what about once I'm inside? What then?"

What an idiot. He should have prepared her better. He reached over and covered her hands, which gripped a small velvet pouch, on her lap. "Forgive me, Letitia. I neglected to prepare you better for the club. Every member and guest signs a confidentiality agreement. They may never speak of who attends the club or what goes on inside. I will take you directly to the owner, as you need to sign such a document."

"But how do we know no one will talk?"

"We need to have faith in the establishment and in the owner's ability to protect us."

"Do you?"

"Yes. Or I wouldn't be bringing you here tonight. Try to relax and enjoy the night. And don't be surprised to see people you know."

She turned one of her hands palm up beneath his and curled it around his gloved hand. "I trust you. I know you wouldn't bring me here if it weren't safe or if my reputation would be at risk."

Damn, his heart was pounding right out of his chest. "I stake my life on it." His life and anything else he had to give.

The carriage came to a stop, and Greyson opened the door. His driver and groom, whenever they took this unmarked coach, except for arriving at Rutherford Manor, had strict instructions never to leave their posts in case they needed a quick getaway. He didn't expect such a thing when visiting Club Knight, but one never knew, especially since the secret Black Knight meetings were held here.

He climbed out, leaned back inside with his hand out, and, with a smile he hoped would ease Letitia's nerves, said, "Shall we?"

Her eyes flickered from his hand to his face and back, making him wonder if she was having second thoughts. Then she smiled shyly, placed her hand in his, and stepped out of the coach. "We shall."

His chest swelled as he took a deep breath, having held it while waiting for her to take his hand. When he exhaled, it came out shaky with relief. She dropped his hand and quickly slipped her arm through his, moving close so they touched from shoulder to hip. "I can feel you trembling. We don't have to go in." Her entire body vibrated against his side, making him question once again his decision to bring her here.

"That is kind of you to say. But I think we both know I do. If we are to begin a courtship, I want no secrets between us."

Bloody hell! There would be one huge secret hanging between them. One day, he would speak to Knight about it.

Greyson often wondered whether the wives of the other Black Knights knew of their husbands' secret work. Of course, he was getting ahead of himself, thinking about being married to Letitia. As he thought the words, his insides warmed, and so did his heart. Perhaps he wasn't getting ahead of himself. Only time would tell. By now, they had reached the top of the outside stairs, and they faced a large man checking memberships.

"Card," he said in a soft voice, nearly a whisper.

Greyson handed over what looked like a calling card, but it bore a single word embossed in black ink. *Knight.*

The guard, Samuel Cutter, handed the card back and opened the door. They were greeted by another club employee. He didn't know this man's name. It was only the second time he had seen him. He knew Samuel Cutter because he was a Black Knight.

"Welcome, Lord Greyson. The usual rules apply. Mr. Knight expects you in his study."

"Thank you . . ."

"Mr. Savage," the man supplied.

"Thank you, Mr. Savage."

During all this time, Letitia hadn't let go of his arm or moved an inch away from his body. Her trembling had only gotten worse, and he feared she would run out the door screaming. Except he knew she wouldn't. She was the type who followed through on her decisions once made. Much like him, if you discounted the time he said he would call on her and didn't. Something he would forever regret. Otherwise, his word was sound.

He moved his arm forward, indicating a corridor straight ahead from the entry. "Shall we?"

"Excuse me, Lord Greyson," Mr. Savage said. "May I take your things?"

Greyson chuckled, stepped away from Letitia, helped her remove her cloak, and handed it to Savage. He then removed his greatcoat, hat, and gloves and handed them to Savage as well.

He lowered his voice and said, "Letitia, would you care to take off your gloves? No one bothers with them here."

Her eyes widened, and she nodded. "I suppose so." Once she removed them and handed them to him, he added them to the pile Savage was holding in his arms.

"Thank you, Mr. Savage. We will go see Knight now."

Letitia quickly slipped her arm through his again and walked with him out of the modest entry and down a corridor lit by wall sconces. They passed several doors, some open, some closed. The billiards room was full of players and spectators. She never took her eyes off the end of the corridor, and he felt like an arse for putting her through this trying visit. He could only hope she would relax at some point. And if she didn't, at least she knew this one secret about him, since she had a rightful aversion to being lied to.

"The door ahead on the right."

Greyson knocked softly on the wood trim, and when he heard Knight say, "Enter," he opened it, unwrapped her arm from his, and waved Letitia in ahead of him. Please let him be doing the right thing by bringing her here.

CHAPTER SEVEN

FOR THE ENTIRE ride in the unmarked carriage, Letitia thought she would cast up her accounts at any moment. Her mouth was as dry as a desert, and her body wouldn't stop shaking, no matter what she did. At least ten times, she almost told Greyson to turn around and take her home. The only thing stopping her was that he was sharing this secret part of himself with her. It couldn't be easy for him, and she wouldn't and couldn't take it lightly. If she asked to go home, she truly believed their courtship, if this was what they had, would end, something she didn't wish to happen. When he told her he wouldn't leave her side and would keep her safe, she believed him. He was an honorable man. Better than most. He showed his goodness every day, from worrying about his parents and hiring a nurse to see to their health and comfort, to chaperoning his sisters. Greyson cared deeply about his family. No wonder he took off for several days at a time to relax and refresh or visit his family's country estate.

Her parents had instilled in her the importance of family because only the three of them remained after her mother's family disowned her. Unfortunately, her father had been raised by an elderly aunt after his parents died in a carriage accident—all the more reason to cherish one's family.

When they arrived at the club, she wasn't sure her legs would support her weight. She had never been weak-kneed, but at that moment, she thought she might be. She wrapped her arm tightly around Greyson's and clung to him as they ascended the stairs. The blood rushed so fast through her veins and pounded in her ears that she could hardly hear the behemoth of a man speaking softly to Greyson. When he opened the door, she felt as though Greyson dragged her up the single step so they could enter the townhouse. A townhouse, she might add, that looked like any other residence on the street. No one would ever know it was a private club.

In the owner of Club Knight's study, she stood trembling and lightheaded, her vision blurry. Greyson, as if sensing her discomfort, moved beside her and took her hand in his large, warm one. The skin-to-skin contact anchored her, and she cleared her vision after blinking several times. When her eyes focused on the man behind the desk, she gasped, then mumbled, "Forgive me, Your Grace. I thought we were meeting a Mr. Knight." She blinked a few more times, in case her eyes were playing tricks on her. But no. The gentleman behind the desk was none other than the Duke of Tremont. Unless someone was pretending to be him. She'd never been introduced to him, but she had seen him and his duchess on Bond Street a time or two, which caused those around her to whisper about the disfigured duke who had bravely fought the French. Also, no one else she knew of wore a black mask that covered most of one side of his face, ending just shy of his mouth. He had sustained burns while serving as a naval captain. That was the extent of what she knew about him. That, and people called him an enigma.

"Have we met?" he said in the deepest voice she'd ever heard.

"Forgive me," she said, curtsying. "Not formally, but I have seen you on Bond Street."

He chuckled. "Yes, I suppose I'm hard to miss. People do like to gossip about me and hurry to cross the street, hoping to keep their distance. I promise you my injury is not contagious and I do not bite."

"Oh dear," she said, placing her free hand on her chest. "I

meant no disrespect . . ."

"Relax, Lady Rutherford," he interrupted. "You have not insulted or displeased me in any way. I've come to terms with my disfigurement." He waved toward the beautiful lady, close in age to her, standing beside his desk. "And so has my wife. Lady Rutherford, have you met my wife?"

"No, I haven't." She faced the duchess and curtsied again. "It's an honor to make your acquaintance, Your Grace."

"Please take a seat, both of you," Tremont said.

She nearly dove to the nearest chair, leaving the one farthest from the door for Greyson. She refused to meet Greyson's gaze. He must think she'd lost her mind.

"Now, we can get down to club business. Inside the club, please refer to me as Mr. Knight or Knight. We don't use titles here. At Club Knight, we are all equals. You may address my wife as Charlotte. May we call you Letitia?"

"Yes." No titles? Everyone was equal? The Duke of Tremont was Mr. Knight? What strange world had she entered?

"Greyson," he snickered, "refuses to be called by his given name, and he is not the only one. Though it has nothing to do with standing and everything to do with hating one's given name. Anyway, I presume he explained the club's secrecy and its members, and that I need you to read and sign a confidentiality agreement to visit this evening." He paused, and his eyes shifted from her to Greyson and back. "It is highly irregular for me to allow a visitor inside these walls. However, I have known Greyson for some time, and I asked him to invite you."

She was having a hard time not staring at his masked face. She was mortified that she couldn't look away until Greyson cleared his throat. "Letitia, are you unwell?"

"No, I'm sorry. Yes. Greyson explained everything. I'm ready to sign the document."

"Good." His Gra . . . Mr. Knight slid the paper across his desk toward her. She reached forward and picked it up. Her eyes scanned the words. Short and to the point. She took the pen Mr.

Knight held out to her and scribbled her name.

"Thank you," Knight said, putting the paper in the middle drawer of the desk. "Now for some refreshments. I think you could use a little sherry to calm your nerves." He looked at his wife. "My dear, would you pour sherry for Letitia and yourself, and brandy for Greyson and me?"

Charlotte handed out the drinks, and Letitia took a sizable sip, hoping to settle her nerves.

After Charlotte took a sip, she said, "We have never met, but I am friendly with Clarice and have heard her mention you. I'm so happy for her and Stanton. I only wish Nathaniel and I had been able to attend the wedding. I received a letter from her the other day saying how much they are enjoying Venice."

"I received one as well and look forward to their return next month."

"As do I. If you both are wondering why my husband mentioned inviting Letitia to Club Knight for a visit, it was because of me. Call it women's intuition, but I thought you would fit in. I also believed we could become friends."

"Thank you. I believe we can become friends, too."

"We will not monopolize any more of your time," said Knight. "Please enjoy your time at the club. Please close the door on your way out, Greyson."

Letitia placed her empty sherry glass on Knight's desk, stood, and walked out of Knight's study, holding Greyson's hand. She felt two sets of eyes follow her into the corridor. Once Greyson shut the door, she said in a low voice, "I'm shocked to find that a duke owns this club. Do you know his reason for opening it?"

Greyson paused, then pulled her into an empty room. "Yes. He wanted a place for people like him to go without everyone staring and whispering about him. He also wanted to employ men who fought in the war alongside him and now have physical deformities, making it nearly impossible to find employment. Another reason was to give members of the *ton*, who were willing to pay his exorbitant membership fee, a place to go when they wanted to be free from all the propriety and formal rules governing other establishments. Don't get me wrong, Club Knight has its rules. But come, you can see for yourself."

"I have a question before we go. Knight hinted that you dislike your given name. Is that true?"

"After everything you were just told by Knight and me, that's what you want to ask?" he chuckled. "Yes. While growing up, my parents called me everything from my real name—Archibald—to Archie, Arch, or Baldy. Then one day, when I was ten, I stomped my foot and yelled, 'My name is Greyson.' And that solved that."

"Oh, I see. But really, Archibald is a fine name," she said with a smile.

He grinned back. "Then perhaps one day I'll let you use it. Meanwhile, let's go look around and enjoy ourselves."

They made their way back to the entry, where the main staircase was, and climbed up to enter what looked like a ballroom transformed into a gaming room. Round tables filled much of the center of the room, while comfortable settees and chairs were tucked into the corners for relaxing and socializing.

Considering how many people were in the room, she wasn't bombarded by overly loud voices. Servants moved about with trays of drinks, and she spied a banquet table overflowing with food. Chandeliers hung from the ceiling, all lit, casting a warm glow throughout the room. Wall sconces added to the lighting. Even so, the large room appeared serene.

"Would you care to try your hand at a game of cards?" Greyson asked, his hand squeezing hers lightly.

"I don't know how to play," she replied.

"If you will allow me, perhaps I can teach you. But not tonight. This is not the place to learn."

"I would like that very much. I've wanted to learn." Glancing around the room again, she said, "Do you mind if we sit on one of the settees?"

"Not at all," he said, leading her toward the far corner of the room, near the glass double doors that opened onto a veranda, where a vacant settee stood. "Would you like a glass of wine?"

"Yes, please."

Greyson waved a nearby servant over. "Two glasses of wine, please."

"Yes, sir."

He handed Greyson two glasses of red wine, and he, in turn, gave her one. She took a sip. Her jumbled-up nerves were beginning to settle now that she was on the outskirts of the gaming tables, where she could observe from the shadows. As best she could count, there were eight round tables surrounded by chairs, occupied by both ladies and gentlemen. She knew that ladies gambled, but they usually did so at private card parties attended only by women. Seeing ladies mixed with gentlemen was strange. She, of course, never attended a ladies' game night, but she knew of them.

"Do you recognize anyone you know?" Greyson asked, pulling her out of her thoughts.

Because she spent so little time socializing, she recognized only a few people by sight. Those she recognized were people she had met in Newmarket. Most likely, if Greyson told her the names and titles of some of the other patrons, she would recognize their names even though they'd never met. "A few people from my time in Newmarket."

"Are you feeling less anxious?"

"I am." Even though butterflies still swarmed in her stomach. More from curiosity than nerves. As she watched people at the card tables, others strolled around the room, and still others congregated on chairs and settees. She wondered what everyone's names were and what brought them here. Her eyes fell on a couple nearby. They embraced and kissed most scandalously. Her eyes widened, and she couldn't look away. The only time she'd ever come close to being kissed like that was by Greyson during their time at Newmarket and the other night in the gardens. Not that Graham hadn't kissed her, just not in such a way, not all-consuming, like what she was witnessing. In the open.

"That is Lord and Lady Hammond. They are good friends with Knight and a couple deeply in love. Don't be fooled by them, though. They help Knight keep an eye on the patrons in exchange for free membership, but don't repeat that."

She turned her head away from the couple and looked at Greyson. "How do you know this? I can't imagine it working well if all the members know."

He chuckled, put his arm across the back of the settee, and said, "Lean back and relax. I won't ravish you in public, but I would like to hold you."

She shimmied back until she was up against the back of the settee. Greyson immediately rested his arm on her shoulders, and she sighed, leaning toward him.

"See? That didn't hurt. And it feels nice," he said with a touch of amusement. "As for other Club Knight members knowing about Lord and Lady Hammond, there are very few who do."

"You didn't answer my question about how you know."

"Hmmm. I may have recently joined, but I've been friends with Knight for some time. Before he opened these doors, he sought advice from several of his closest confidants."

"I see." She didn't really understand, since this was the first time Greyson had mentioned a friendship with Knight, or rather, the Duke of Tremont. How did they know one another? Had Greyson served in the Navy, as Knight had? She didn't believe so.

Her eyes traveled the room. Almost everyone was focused on their cards. Yes, perhaps the ladies and gentlemen were dressed more casually than usual for a night out in London, but overall, she wasn't as shocked and scandalized as she thought she would be.

"Do you have any thoughts or questions?"

Greyson's query drew her gaze back to him. "Why all the secrecy?" she asked.

Instead of answering, his hand caressed her bare shoulder as her short sleeve slid down, exposing her skin with a little help from him. Now that was something that would never happen in a proper London ballroom. The warmth of his fingertip swirling in circles on her skin sent heat pooling between her thighs. Goosebumps rose on her arms, and she rested her head on his shoulder. The action felt natural, even though others were around, and it would be considered scandalous anywhere else. It would make headlines in the gossip rags.

"Does this feel good?" he murmured, resting his head against the top of hers.

"Yes," she said, exhaling.

"Most of what happens during card playing is mild. The masquerade ball is another matter. People dress most scandalously, more so than at any other masquerade ball I've attended. Of course, this is all hearsay, as I've yet to attend one here. And have you forgotten about the third floor?"

The heat consuming her cheeks intensified. She had forgotten. Greyson explained there were rooms for couples seeking privacy. Did that mean . . .?

"From what I've been told, couples can go up together for a private engagement. Single men and women can wait outside a vacant room, hoping someone will join them. One does not go up there unless they are prepared for a very intimate encounter."

"Oh my," she whispered, closing her eyes and picturing herself and Greyson in one of those rooms as he ravished her. She fought the urge to rub her thighs together to ease her discomfort.

"Have I shocked you?" His voice was soft and seductive as his fingertips traced her collarbone, making her swallow back a moan.

"N-n-not at all." Oh dear, what a conundrum. A battle was forming between her body and her mind. She wanted nothing more than to go to the third floor and have Greyson's hands all over her, and hers all over him. Did she dare? "Can you take me up there?" Had those breathy words really come out of her?

"Letitia, I promised you and myself that we wouldn't go there tonight."

"When is the next masquerade ball?"

"Next Tuesday."

"Will Knight allow me to attend?"

"If you wish, you can apply for a membership. I will cover the cost."

"I would like that. When you were here before, did you go up there?" Her stomach sank with dread as she waited for his answer.

"I've yet to visit the third floor." Her body eased, knowing he spoke the truth.

Greyson, to her regret, righted her sleeve. He removed his arm from around her and stood, holding out her hand. "Shall we go?"

She really didn't want to leave, but she supposed it was for the best. How embarrassing. She had practically asked him to bed her. No. Not practically. She *had* asked him. "Yes." She took his hand, stood, and they strolled out of the ballroom. They collected their things from the doorman and went out into the cool night air, which did wonders in extinguishing the fire burning inside her.

They rode in silence to Rutherford Manor, and she wondered what he was thinking. Was he shocked that she had asked to go to the third floor? She was a widow and well-versed in the carnal acts between couples. She and Graham enjoyed their time in the bedroom. Since his death, she missed the connection she had felt when wrapped in his arms, the feeling of being cherished and made love to until her body reached the pleasure of release.

"You're quiet," Greyson's soft voice echoed inside the small coach.

"I was thinking you must be shocked by my suggestion that we visit the third floor," she said, exasperated and mortified, fighting the urge to cover her face with her hands and hide. "I can hardly believe it myself. Forgive me if I made you uncomfortable."

Just then, she noticed the carriage had stopped, and she wondered how long they had sat in front of her home.

"Will you permit me to see you inside?"

She shouldn't, but because of the hopeful way he asked, she replied, "Yes," a little breathlessly.

Mr. Henry greeted them at the door and took their coat and cloak. "You may retire for the night, Mr. Henry."

"Thank you, my lady." Mr. Henry bowed and headed toward the kitchens.

"Come with me," Letitia said, leading the way up the stairs and into the drawing room, where she'd had afternoon tea with him just that afternoon. It seemed like days ago to her now.

Sitting on the settee, she invited him to join her. They faced each other, their knees touching. She took a deep breath and said, "I'll understand if you don't want to see me again."

He reached out immediately, taking her hands in his, and looked at her with one eyebrow raised. "Why on earth would you say that?" He moved one hand to cup her cheek and looked at her questioningly.

She stayed frozen in place, fighting the urge to lean into the warmth of his hand. "Because you must think me a wanton."

"My darling Letitia, you are no such thing. As far as I know, you have been with only one man, your deceased husband. And even if you have been with others, it wouldn't matter to me. You intrigue me. You make my heart pound and my breath seize in my chest. I desire you as I've never desired another. I was flattered that you had the courage to speak your mind and consider taking me into your bed . . . into your body."

"I . . . I . . ." Words escaped her, and the knot in her chest eased at his words.

"I must be totally honest with you about forming a courtship." He looked at her, his eyes intense and touched with sadness, and she knew she wouldn't like whatever he had to say next. "I feel it would be unfair to you at this time if we formed a courtship. That is not to say we can't see each other and attend society functions. But my life is not my own, and I have many responsibilities, more than you know. When I do court you seriously, and I do plan on it, I want to give you all my attention. Can you find it in your heart to be patient with me and not give up on us?"

Tears pooled in her eyes, and she blinked them away, mad at herself for almost crying. She would be truthful with herself because seeing each other and going to functions together sounded an awful lot like courting. If he couldn't commit to her now, she would take what he could give. There was no other gentleman she'd met who intrigued her or made her heart flutter like he did.

She smiled, even though it was tinged with sadness, cupped his cheek, and said, "I trust you." She leaned forward and kissed him.

It was a kiss that turned sensual quickly, and before she understood what was happening, she was swept into Grayson's strong arms and gently lowered across his lap. She wrapped her arms around his neck and sighed into his mouth. It took only seconds for him to devour her. His tongue swirled inside her mouth, tasting her. When she joined her tongue with his, she felt the rumble of his groan from deep in his chest vibrate against hers. That wasn't all she felt. His manhood, hard and straining against his breeches, pressed against her bottom, and she swiveled her hips, intensifying the friction and making him groan again. He eased his lips from hers and placed light, barely there kisses down her neck, across her collarbone, and back up her neck, beneath the sensitive spot below her ear. Her entire body quivered with desire for this man.

"Greyson . . ." she purred as his hand reached beneath her skirts.

"Easy, my dear. Stop me if this isn't what you want."

His hand continued caressing up her calf, over her knee, and along the inside of her thigh. A stampede of wild horses couldn't make her say stop. Oh dear, what did that say about her? She wanted this man and what he was making her feel. She sometimes wore pantaloons, but not tonight. There was nothing between his hand and her womanhood. His fingers finally brushed her curls, and she sighed deeply.

"Letitia," Greyson exhaled as his fingers parted her folds and his thumb circled her nub. "So wet." He kept circling. "So warm." More circling. "Come for me." He inserted one long finger, then removed it and pushed it back inside repeatedly.

She clutched the lapels of his jacket and buried her face there as her stomach fluttered low, her legs began to tremble, and her body shattered into a million tiny pieces of intense pleasure. Greyson didn't speak as her body exploded. One hand stayed beneath her skirts, drawing out her pleasure, while the other splayed against her back, holding her tightly. Her body felt languid and weak, and she was thankful he held her; otherwise, she would likely slither to the floor in a lifeless heap.

After perhaps a moment, Greyson righted her skirts and said, "Letitia, look at me."

Did she have to? She inhaled, then raised her head, seeing desire in his eyes and a soft smile. "That was beautiful. Thank you for giving yourself to me. For trusting me."

Oh dear, she blinked back tears at his words. With no words of her own, she brought her mouth to his and kissed him gently, not to arouse their desires but to let him know how much she appreciated and cared for him. She did care for him. In fact, she'd fallen in love with him during their time in Newmarket. However, she would keep those words to herself until the time was right.

When she broke the kiss, he eased her off his lap, and she stood on wobbling legs. Greyson rose, straightened his jacket and cuffs, then raised her hand to his mouth, and brushed his lips across her fingers. Their eyes met, and his smoldered. "Goodnight, my dear. Weather permitting, would you join me for a ride in the park tomorrow?"

"I would like that very much," she answered, and then he was gone. Poor Greyson must be uncomfortable in his breeches. Her thoughts darkened. Would he visit a brothel to ease himself? Go back to Club Knight and visit the third floor? If only she'd never known about Graham's mistress. It made her question Greyson, and it wasn't fair to him. He wasn't Graham, with his secrets. Not to mention that he'd told her he didn't have a mistress.

Jane met her as she entered her chambers. She helped her undress, then slipped a clean night rail over her head. She removed all the pins from her hair, combed it, and braided it. "That will be all for tonight, Jane."

"Yes, my lady."

After her maid left, she performed her nightly toilette and slid beneath the counterpane. Her body was still warm from the lingering effects of what Greyson had done to her, she didn't want to feel embarrassed, but she was. Sleep eluded her for quite some time.

CHAPTER EIGHT

W HEN LETITIA SUGGESTED going up to the third floor at Club Knight, Greyson almost relented. But he believed she would regret it afterward and that it would put an unnecessary strain on their friendship. He would never have regretted it, but he feared she would have. The tension on the carriage ride to her townhouse tightened his chest. Perhaps he should never have introduced her to the club. It wasn't for everyone. Even though she appeared agreeable, he wasn't convinced.

When they arrived at Rutherford Manor, he escorted her inside, determined to convince himself she was fine and then take his leave. He hadn't planned to pull her onto his lap and kiss her, a kiss he would remember always. Next thing he knew, his hand was wandering of its own accord, and his mind had to hurry to catch up. To his utter surprise and delight, Letitia melted under his exploring hand, a hand that brought her up and over the edge to oblivion and beyond. He'd always suspected she was a sensual woman. Tonight confirmed his suspicions.

As he returned to Club Knight for a secret meeting of the Black Knights, his chest ached at the memory of her words. "I can't abide secrets." Rutherford's secret life had caused her irreparable harm. How could he maintain his secret life without causing her the same harm?

"Bloody hell, I can't let her go. I've never felt this way about anyone. I owe it to both of us to see this relationship to fruition," he mumbled to himself.

His driver stopped the carriage one street over, and Greyson hopped out without a word to either his driver or his groom. No words were needed. Reed knew to stay close by. He pulled the collar of his coat up and his hat low, shielding his face from onlookers. He softly tapped the secret code on the backdoor of Club Knight, and it opened, letting him into a dark back corridor. They changed the code each sennight for security. One could never be too cautious when dealing in business involving secrets, investigations, and spying.

The man who opened the door closed it behind him and locked it without a word. He need not speak, as Greyson knew where to go. The less one said, the better. He opened the well-oiled door on the left, closed it silently behind him, and walked down the stairs without a creak. Knight prepared well for their secret meetings.

As did Greyson. As he'd prepared for his role within the Black Knights. Greyson had worked hard to hide his emotions when he needed to. It was essential and a lifesaver while on assignment. He practiced in front of a mirror, learning to school his features. It wasn't as easy as one might think. Keeping his expression neutral came easily to him. The hard part was his eyes. They tended to be overly expressive without his knowing it. He had worked extremely hard to make them look bored or emotionless. It was a necessary skill if he wanted to stay alive. However, it often interfered with personal affairs. He had to remind himself to relax around his family and friends lest they begin to think he didn't care about them, which was the farthest thing from the truth. When it came to Letitia, he appeared to gush his feelings openly. Not that he could see, but he felt his guard drop and could read her emotions. Another thing he was trained to do. Words were one thing, but the expression on someone's face said it all.

As he descended the last step, the room came into view, lit by numerous wall sconces. It wasn't large, perhaps twelve feet square. The dirt floor was covered with a rug. Eight wooden chairs stood in a circle, with a low table in the middle, laid with bread, cheese, a decanter of brandy, and eight glasses already poured. Greyson nodded to those seated in the chairs. Knight, Lord Hammond, Lord Cain, Baron Cooke, retired Captain Sweeney, Mr. Thomas Tobias, and Mr. Samuel Cutter.

"Now that we're all here," Knight said, picking up his glass of brandy. "Let us get down to business. I had an interesting meeting with Prinny earlier today, and he's most worried about further uprisings due to the Corn Laws and job and wage cuts by industry and mine owners. There's been more unrest in Derbyshire because the leaders of the Pentrich Rebellion are still imprisoned and awaiting execution. Also, word is that other towns are planning marches demanding the repeal of the Corn Laws."

Greyson spoke up. "What is the plan going forward?"

"Everyone in this room understands the plight of the English people. They have been suffering since the conclusion of the war with France. Citizens continue to voice their dissatisfaction with the government, and quite frankly, who can blame them? Our job is to end these rallies or rebellions amicably so no harm comes to the good people of England. We need to find peaceful ways for them to be heard without it turning to violence. That is our job at Black Knights, and we must do everything we can to accomplish it.

"We'll travel in pairs to the rumored rally sites and do what we can to quell any unrest and keep the peace. We must use our false names. Which, of course, is why I'm staying here." He paused, then added, "You were all hand-picked by me because you support the causes of the protests but you don't want the citizens of England to suffer. Our job is to keep the peace. We are caught in a conundrum because our other job is to keep the royal family safe. We shall strive to do both without bloodshed.

"Cain, Sweeney and Hammond, you will travel together to Derbyshire, where the Pentrich Uprising originated Greyson and

Cooke, you'll go to Bristol. The miners and their owners are not happy with the price of coal. See if you can come up with a solution. Tobias and Cutter, you will pair up and travel to Nottingham.

"Our intelligence is still working to pinpoint the details. You leave for the assignment on Wednesday. That should be sufficient time to wrap up your affairs and come up with plausible excuses for your upcoming absences. All of these uprisings are in the infant stages and not expected to become organized for several weeks. Before that happens, I have faith in your abilities to help those involved and come up with a way they can be heard without violence."

Knight poured himself another brandy and downed it. "That will be all for now."

Greyson thought about staying behind to have a word with Knight, but decided against it. The man looked ready to snap in two, no doubt from the strain of his earlier meeting with Prinny. Instead, he left with the rest of the Black Knights.

Riding home in his unmarked carriage, Greyson's thoughts turned to Letitia and to how this assignment was coming at the worst possible time. What could he tell her to explain such a lengthy absence? And what about his sisters? He'd never asked his married cousin, Lady Charity Colbourn, to chaperone them, but he would send a note asking. Thankfully, she often offered her services.

Letitia looked in the mirror over her dressing table, satisfied with her appearance for the carriage ride in Hyde Park with Greyson. She was dressed in a cream muslin day dress, a blue pelisse trimmed in cream, and a matching hat and brown leather half boots. There was a breeze today, so she grabbed a lap blanket and warm gloves as she left her room. At four in the afternoon, the time to see and be seen riding in the park, it could be chilly, as the sun was low on the horizon this time of year.

As she descended the stairs, Greyson's deep voice reached her ears, and her cheeks heated at the memory of what had happened last evening in the drawing room when they returned from Club Knight. How could she ever look him in the eye today without blushing? As she reached the last few steps, Greyson watched her with intensity, adding more heat to her cheeks. When her feet met the entry hall floor, he bowed, straightened, and said, "Lady Rutherford, you look lovely today. Are you ready for our ride?"

"Yes," she answered, taking his offered arm as Mr. Henry opened the door for them. Greyson helped her up and into the mid-rise phaeton while a stableboy held the horses' reins, keeping them steady. Greyson joined her on the seat, took the reins from the stableboy, and off they went at a slow clip toward Hyde Park. "This reminds me of our time in Newmarket in the spring."

He looked at her and grinned. "Yes, it does me, too. I look forward to the next racing season."

"It was my first time attending a thoroughbred race, and it was an eye-opening and fun experience. All the excitement that came from horses running on a flat course."

He chuckled. "It doesn't take much to entertain people."

"Do you miss Stanton?"

"Yes. I imagine you miss Clarice. Stanton sent word, and they should return to London in early November."

"That's what Clarice wrote in her last letter." As he expertly handled the phaeton and horses, Letitia remembered the time they spent in Newmarket. She attended two races with Greyson, the 2000 and 1000 Guineas Stakes. Both races were won by the Duke of Stanton's horses. While visiting Newmarket, she and Greyson had very little time alone, but it was enough for them to share several kisses. Still, nothing compared to last evening. She moved one hand to her lips, and her gloved fingers hovered over them.

"What are you thinking about, other than when the duke and

duchess will return?"

Greyson's voice pulled her from her thoughts. "Nothing, really."

He chuckled and turned to meet her gaze. His eyes were full of heat and something like amusement. What a strange combination. "You lie."

She coughed. "Guilty. I lie. At first, I was thinking of Newmarket."

"Yes. And then?" he prodded.

Did she dare admit what she'd been thinking? "About our kiss last night and how it was nothing like the few kisses we stole in Newmarket."

He snorted, then coughed to cover it. "Christ. Are you trying to torture me with memories of last night?"

"Greyson, please. You're making me embarrassed."

"I wish I could hold your hand and reassure you that there's nothing to be embarrassed about. But the entrance to Hyde Park is coming up, and I need both hands on the reins. Anyway, I would've kissed you in Newmarket as intimately as last night if I'd thought you were ready. I didn't want to frighten you away with my desire for you."

She nudged his shoulder with hers. "And that's supposed to make me feel less mortified?"

"Oh, my dear Letitia," he said, his voice softening to a low murmur. "Never be mortified when it comes to me. Finally, a lull in the traffic so that we can enter the park. It appears the entire *beau monde* is out and about this afternoon."

"Which makes me think," she said, her pulse calming somewhat after their discussion of kisses. "Are you not derelict in your duties to Aurora and Anastasia by taking me for a ride?"

"Not at all. I expect we will see Hunter, Anastasia, Lord Warren, and Aurora, since the four of them went for a ride together." He paused and chuckled. "So I'm not derelict in my obligations at all."

She smiled, happy for his sisters. "I'm glad to hear that. When do you think Hunter will ask for Anastasia's hand?"

"Soon. I expect Warren to wait a bit before he asks for Aurora's. He seems to take things at a snail's pace. I wonder how he ever gets anything done regarding his estates. Aurora doesn't seem bothered by this trait. It would drive Anastasia crazy, which is why she is with Hunter and Warren is with Aurora."

"Hmmm. It is all so exciting. What does your mother think?" His entire body visibly tensed, and she regretted her words. "Forgive me."

"For what?" he asked, keeping his eyes on Rotton Row, his horses, and the carriage directly in front of theirs.

"For mentioning your mother, I know how much you worry."

"It is I who should be apologizing to you. You've done nothing wrong in inquiring. Mother is thrilled for them—two fewer worries for her if they make good matches. Before you ask about my father, he has appeared to rally and has his wits about him, but not the strength to leave his bed. I fear it is short-lived. I can hardly believe he has lasted this long since taking ill. Mother's health has improved right along with his. I pray hers will last. I want my mother to live long enough to see her twin daughters happily wed and perhaps to become a grandmother."

"What about you? She must want you to marry." She covered her mouth with her hand and groaned. What had gotten into her to say such a thing? "Once again, I must beg your forgiveness for asking what is no concern of mine."

He placed both reins in one hand and set the other on the hand covering her mouth, brought it down to her lap, and squeezed it gently. "If I have any say in the matter, it will be of great concern to you."

He took his hand away and once again held the reins properly. She missed the connection, even though they both had gloves on, which kept them from touching skin to skin as they had last night. She made a strange sound, as no words would form in response to his comment. It wasn't the first time he had hinted at something more than a courtship between them.

Could she allow herself to hope?

Risk her heart without a guarantee?

Believe in his honesty?

"I do believe I see the Duke and Duchess of Tremont," stated Greyson. "He's usually not one for riding in the park at this hour. He prefers to ride early in the morning. The duchess must have convinced him otherwise on this glorious day."

Even though they touched from shoulder to knee on the small seat, she leaned her head closer. "I'm still shocked he owns the club," she whispered.

"It's more than that. He owns the residence next door, and many of his men who served with him on his ship live there with their families and work for him at the club. It's his way of supporting them because he feels responsible for the attack on his ship, which took many lives and injured scores of others, including himself, when he tried to save his wife's first husband who was also his best friend."

"Oh, I had heard rumors that her husband was killed in the war, but I had no idea that Tremont and he knew one another. How fortunate they were to meet and marry."

"Indeed, how fortunate."

"On a different topic, did you write your letter requesting membership in Club Knight? If so, I can pick it up when we return and deliver it to Knight tonight."

She shivered at the thought of belonging to such a place. The interesting question was whether it was nerves or excitement. "Yes, I have. But what if I change my mind?"

"When your membership is approved, you are under no obligation to visit the establishment if you do not choose to do so."

"But what about the fee?"

"You let me worry about that."

"You never said how much it cost, except that it was an exorbitant amount. I feel guilty for having you pay."

He pulled the carriage off the path onto a patch of vacant grass. He held the reins in one hand and reached for her hand with his free one. "I suggested this. I invited you there in the first place. If you want to join, I will pay the fee. If you choose not to join, no harm done. The fee is not due until you are accepted into the club. We still have time."

She looked at their joined hands, sighed, and smiled to herself. "I'm being silly. Of course I want to join. I want to spend time with you and get to know you better in a private setting, other than my home." The home she had shared with Rutherford.

"My thoughts exactly," he said, letting go of her hand and bringing his up to caress her cheek. "You are amazing. Do you know that?"

She broke into a wide smile, her cheeks flushed, and her heart raced. All because of his hand and his words. How strange that it took so little on his part to make her feel cherished.

"Did you hear what I said?"

She shook her head. "Thank you for the compliment, but I'm rather dull and unexciting. Not amazing at all."

He caressed her cheek again, and the look he gave her spread warmth through her body. "You think too little of yourself. You are raising a young boy who will one day inherit an earldom. You run a household by yourself, and as far as I know, you never seek help from anyone. I would say that makes you amazing in my eyes."

Unexpected tears pooled in her eyes, and before she could wipe them away, he wiped them with his hand. Her tears darkened his brown gloves. "I didn't mean to make you cry."

"They are not sad tears, but happy ones. What you said touched my heart. But to be honest, my life is hardly a hardship. I adore my son, and I have a governess who takes great care of him and loves him as well. My servants are proficient in their work. My housekeeper, Mrs. Peterson, runs a smooth household with the help of the butler. I choose the daily menu. I hardly find enough to do in any given day. My life is easy, and I sometimes feel guilty for it."

"Don't feel guilty. You are doing exactly what you are supposed to do. You are managing a household and raising your son. We should move back onto Rotten Row before some carriage driver gets annoyed with us for stopping on the grass." Greyson merged the horses and carriage back onto the path, and they rode on in companionable silence back to Rutherford Manor.

"Thank you for a lovely ride," she said as he helped her down from the phaeton.

"You are most welcome, and thank you for allowing me the pleasure of your company." He bowed, took her hand, and pressed his warm lips to the underside of her wrist, where the glove ended. The contact left her quivering inside. When he released her hand and stood straight again, he winked at her. "Do you have an engagement this evening?"

It took her a moment to focus her mind on something other than the handsome devil standing in front of her. "As a matter of fact, I do not."

"Would you care to dine with my family and me?"

"I would love to."

"I will send my carriage for you at half seven."

He jumped onto the perch and left, glancing back once before turning the corner and disappearing from view. Then she panicked when she realized it was probably after five and she had much to do in the next two hours.

She hurried past Mr. Henry when he opened the door and made haste up the stairs and to her chambers, calling out to Jane as she entered her dressing room, going through her dresses.

"My lady," Jane said as she entered the dressing room.

"Oh, Jane. Thank goodness. I'm going to dinner at Danbury Hall, and the viscount is sending his carriage at half seven. How will I ever be ready in time?"

"My lady," Jane said in a soothing voice. "Come and sit by the fire, and I will bring you some evening dresses to choose from. If I recall, you mentioned the viscount's favorite color is blue. Perhaps a blue dress?"

"No. I always wear blue. Perhaps the burgundy one. The more I think on it, the more perfect the burgundy one seems. I don't believe he's seen me wear that color yet."

"The burgundy dress it is, my lady."

Jane entered the dressing room and returned with the burgundy dress, matching shawl, and reticule. After dressing her, Letitia sat at the dressing table while Jane worked her magic on her hair. Using the curling rod, she curled her entire head of hair, then pinned it up, leaving some curls to cascade down the back of her neck, where they bounced as she moved her head. Letitia thought she looked beautiful, if she did say so herself.

"My hair looks amazing, Jane."

"Thank you, my lady. It's easy with your thick hair and light coloring. Your paleness, set off by the rich color of the gown, is striking. Burgundy was the perfect color choice. All you need is a little color on your cheeks and lips. I made some this morning, hoping you would like to try it. May I?"

"Please."

Jane brushed a light touch of beetroot rouge onto her cheeks and carmine beeswax onto her lips, then wiped some off with a piece of linen. "Perfect. Very soft, but it enhances your cheekbones and full lips."

"I hardly recognize myself. Thank you, Jane." Letitia stood and stepped back from the mirror, then turned around, admiring herself. "You outdid yourself. I shouldn't be late."

"Have a wonderful time, my lady," Jane said as she curtsied, then left, leaving the door to her chambers open, knowing Letitia was right behind her.

CHAPTER NINE

GREYSON RETURNED HOME and went directly to his study, where he wrote to his cousin, requesting her assistance during his upcoming assignment-related absence. He had just finished when a footman entered and announced Hunter.

"Would you like a drink?" Greyson asked, turning the letter over so Hunter could not see what he had written.

"No."

"Letitia and I didn't see you in Hyde Park. Were you there?"

"Yes, we saw you, but we were several carriages ahead of you. The ladies wanted the roof up because the wind was chilly."

"Hmmm."

"What, hmmmm?" Hunter inquired.

"Nothing. You seem nervous. Did something happen?"

"I'm here to request your permission to marry Lady Anastasia and to negotiate the marriage contract."

Greyson tried to hide his smile as he opened the desk drawer and took out Anastasia's marriage contract. Before his father took ill, he had drafted both his sisters' contracts. He slid the document across his desk. "This is the contract my father already prepared for an event like this. He went so far as to incorporate the pin money and how you will provide for her and any children in the event of your death. Let me know if you are agreeable to it." He should be. Both his sisters came with ten thousand pounds to be placed in a trust in their names. Their husbands would control the interest it accrued, which was the standard for marriage agreements.

Hunter's eyes moved across the document and down. "Everything looks acceptable to me. No need to have my solicitor look at it."

Greyson handed him a quill dipped in ink, and Hunter scribbled his name and date on the contract with a shaky hand. Greyson was surprised by Hunter's nervousness, since he was an easygoing fellow, and it took a lot to make him jumpy.

"Phew," he said, relaxing back in the chair. "I didn't expect to be so nervous." He ran his hand through his hair. "In fact, I'll have that drink now, if you don't mind."

"Not at all. I need one too after seeing my friend look like he was going to vomit on my desktop." He stood, moved to the sideboard, poured two glasses of brandy, and handed one to his friend. "So, when do you plan to ask Anastasia?"

"Tonight, if you'll allow me to come to dinner."

"I'm sure Cook can whip up something special. I already invited Letitia, and I could send a note to Lord Warren. We'll make a night of it." He drained his drink, wondering whether, if and when he planned to propose, he'd be as nervous as Hunter. Most likely. "So when will the big day take place?"

Hunter choked on his drink. "Christ! Give a man a warning before you blurt out something like that!"

"Sorry," he grinned. "Having never gone through it myself, I'm enjoying your discomfort."

"Funny. If she says yes, which I believe she will, I hope you'll have the banns posted this Sunday. After three Sundays, we can wed. That is, unless Anastasia wants a large, fancy wedding, which I pray she doesn't. Waiting months will not be easy for either of us."

A strange sound came from Greyson. "Please, I don't want to think of the two of you together like that."

Hunter snickered. "Why? It never bothered you when I spoke

of other ladies."

"Have a care. This is my sister, not one of your other ladies."

"I know. I'm just teasing you for remarking that I looked like I was about to vomit."

Greyson inhaled and let it out slowly. "I'm so happy for you both. She will say yes, and, with any luck, you will be married in a month."

"Yes. I hope."

Greyson leaned forward, his elbows on his desk and his fingers steepled. His demeanor grew serious. "I have a favor to ask."

"Anything," Hunter replied.

"On Wednesday, I need to leave on business for perhaps a fortnight. There's an issue at our country estate that needs attention. Since my father can't go, the matter falls to me. Could you and Anastasia pay Letitia a call or two while I'm gone? Now that I'm practically courting her, I hate the idea of her staying home alone without visitors while I'm away."

"Of course we will. But you do realize she has friends. Close lady friends she visits, and they visit her. You, Greyson, are not her only friend."

"I know that. What do you take me for?" He held up his hand. "Don't answer that. Yes, she is friends with the Duchess of Blackstone and the Countess of Langford, but their husbands keep them very busy."

"We will visit."

"Thank you. I'm asking my cousin, Lady Charity Colbourn, to come and stay while I'm away. Lord Colbourn is so busy with his clubs and political aspirations that he will hardly notice she's gone. I want you to understand that I trust you with Anastasia, but I need Lady Charity to keep a close watch on Aurora. And if the nurse or my parents need anything, she will be here to help. Having her here puts me at ease when I can't be."

"I do understand," Hunter said. "I've known you since before Eton, and I know how you are. How you pretend all is well while your insides are being tossed around, worrying over too much responsibility."

He leaned back in his chair and sighed. "I hope I'm not that obvious."

"Not to others. To me and, most likely, to Stanton. Once Anastasia and I wed, you will have one less sister to worry about. I love her and will take good care of her. You will see us all the time, since my townhouse is only five doors down from yours."

He groaned. "Don't remind me. Seriously, though, thank you. I know I won't have to worry about Anastasia, as she will be in good hands with you, my kind and loyal friend."

Hunter stood. "I must go if I'm to be back for dinner. What time did you say?"

"Half seven and not a minute sooner."

As Hunter left his study, his laughter faded with his departure.

Greyson knew Anastasia would have a good, loving, and fulfilling life with Hunter, so why did his heart ache? Because he wanted what they would soon have with Letitia. With his work with the Black Knights, was it possible? Some of the members were married, so he knew it could work. It was just that Letitia was wary of deceit, and he didn't know how to avoid it.

On Wednesday, he had a long ride ahead of him, one that would take several days. That would give him plenty of time to figure out how to make a future with Letitia work. Meanwhile, he'd better send an invitation to dinner to Warren, or Aurora would be cross with him. Once the note was finished, he folded it, sealed it with wax, and affixed his seal. Someday soon, he would become the Earl of Danbury. He would no longer be Greyson. It was an odd feeling to contemplate.

He hurried out of the study, rushed to the front door, and handed the note to Henderson. "Please have a footman deliver this straight away and wait for a reply."

"Yes, my lord."

He was halfway up the staircase, turned around, and hurried back down. "Henderson, please inform Mrs. Shepherd that we will have three guests for dinner and to prepare something special. Oh, and one more thing. Please send the carriage to pick up Lady Rutherford for half seven."

"Yes, my lord. Is there anything else?"

"No, Henderson, that is all."

He went back up the staircase. Before he made his way to his chambers, he stopped by his parents' room to see how his father was faring. When he knocked and entered, he found the room stiflingly hot, a large blaze burning in the hearth, and all the curtains closed. "Mother," he said as he opened the curtains, "it is hot as Hades in here."

"Please don't open a window. Your father was chilled earlier and is finally sleeping after struggling to rest most of the day."

He closed the curtains on the windows he'd just opened. "I'm sorry. I should've checked on you both earlier today."

"Nonsense," his mother said from her place in the big bed. She was sitting up, propped by a bevy of pillows. "You have your sisters to chaperone, Lady Rutherford to court, and the earldom to run. You can't possibly do everything. You stop by at least twice a day, and your father and I appreciate it. We couldn't have asked for a better or more caring son. Also, Mrs. Clark is wonderfully adept at her job as a nurse. You needn't worry about us."

His throat tightened. To him, it sounded as if his mother were saying goodbye. He pushed it aside, blinked to clear his eyes, and said, "Hunter has asked permission to marry Anastasia."

Both of his mother's hands covered her heart. "Oh my. I'm going to cry. This is wonderful news. I couldn't be happier, and your father will be too when he finds out. When is Hunter proposing?"

"Tonight. He's coming for dinner. Actually, Lady Rutherford and Lord Warren are as well. Are you up for dining with us?"

His mother sighed. "It's so last-minute, and there isn't time to make myself presentable. Perhaps next time."

He moved to his mother's side, bent down, and kissed her

cheek. "Next time, then. Besides, you and Anastasia have a wedding to plan."

Her eyes brightened, and she smiled. "We do. Now, be off with you. You must look your best for Lady Rutherford."

"Yes, Mama." Greyson strolled down the hall, past the staircase, and down the corridor that housed his chambers and those of his sisters. Most single gentlemen of means and of age rented bachelor's quarters. Greyson had once lived in such quarters, but when his father took ill, he moved back home. Bachelor's quarters could be rowdy, making peace and quiet hard to find. It wasn't a hardship for him to move home. In fact, he was glad to be home.

After Dalton stopped fussing over him as they prepared for that evening, he went downstairs and into the drawing room, where he found both his sisters looking magnificent in their evening dresses. He bowed. "Ladies, how lovely you look."

Both Anastasia and Aurora giggled. "We have gentlemen to impress," Anastasia said, twirling around.

"Thank you for inviting Warren, brother. I would've felt like the fifth wheel on a carriage, awkward and unwanted."

"Christ," he said as he combed his hair, messing up the job Dalton had done with a comb. "I never heard back from him."

Aurora smiled. "I intercepted the note when it arrived. He is coming."

"Good. Six for dinner is the perfect number."

"Did you send the carriage for Lady Rutherford?" Aurora asked. "It is the proper thing for a gentleman to do when he invites a lady friend to dine."

"My, aren't you a wealth of knowledge tonight?" He paused and grinned. "Yes, I did. In fact, all our guests should be arriving any moment."

Just then, Henderson entered the room, with Hunter and Warren on his heels, and announced, "The Earl of Warren and Mr. Hunter." He then left, no doubt to await Letitia's arrival.

"Would you gentlemen care for a glass of sherry?" Greyson

asked as they each moved to stand beside the sisters they were courting and exchanged greetings. He'd noticed two glasses of sherry on the table in front of the settee when he asked. His sisters had already helped themselves. He didn't blame them. It was a nice way to start the evening, taking the edge off one's nerves.

"Yes, please," Warren said.

"Please," Hunter said, whispering to Anastasia, then joining Greyson at the sideboard against the wall. "I'm going to propose tonight after dinner in the gardens," he said quietly. Greyson handed Hunter his glass of sherry, and he downed it in one gulp. "Another pour, please."

"Sherry is supposed to be sipped, not downed in one swallow. If you don't take it slow, you'll be too inebriated to propose."

"I'll sip this one. I need to relax. I'm tied up in knots, and I don't want her to suspect anything."

"Once you ask her and she says yes, the knots will surely untie themselves, and you can breathe easily again."

"How did you know I can't breathe?"

"I didn't. Just a guess. Is something else wrong with you? You seem unlike yourself."

He glanced back at Anastasia. "Ever since I left your study today, I've been questioning her feelings for me. What if I misread her and I'm nothing but a diversion until someone better comes along?"

"We have gone over this before. So what if you don't possess a title? Anastasia can keep her courtesy title, only when you marry will it be 'Lady Anastasia Hunter.' Also, you have more money than many young men our age, and you and Anastasia are a perfect fit for each other."

"I think I believe that . . ."

"No thinking. It is so." Greyson picked up two sherry glasses. "Come, before Anastasia wonders what we are whispering about."

After he'd handed Warren his sherry, Henderson entered the

drawing room, this time with Letitia following him. "Lady Rutherford," he said, bowed, and left the room. Greyson walked to Letitia's side. It took effort not to run to her. She looked beautiful in a deep-burgundy evening dress. He hoped the gardens wouldn't be too crowded after dinner, since he intended to find a private spot in which to ravish Letitia. Well, not ravish exactly. More like kiss and hold close. But he hoped he would get the chance to ravish her soon.

His eyes roamed over her and settled on her face, on her eyes, which were full of mirth. "You look gorgeous, my dear."

"Thank you," she said, and a delicate red flush tinted her cheeks.

He held out his hand. "Come. Let's get you a sherry." They made their way across the room, and he poured her a glass of sherry then handed it to her.

"Thank you," she said just before she took a sip.

He couldn't take his eyes off her lips, wishing he were the glass and that her luscious lips were on him. He cleared his throat to hide the moan that almost escaped.

"I'm surprised to find Warren and Hunter here. You didn't mention they were coming to dinner."

"It was an even more last-minute invitation. I hope you aren't bothered by their attendance."

"Why would I be?" she said with a smile. "I enjoy their company, and I'm sure Anastasia and Aurora are happy with the turn of events."

"I'm sure they are. Ahh, the dinner bell." He held out his hand again. "Shall we?"

She placed her hand in his. "We shall."

Since Greyson didn't feel comfortable at the head of the table while his father was still alive, he and Letitia sat on one side of the table, side by side. Warren, Aurora, Hunter, and Anastasia sat across from them. In his opinion, it was a nice, cozy, and intimate dinner party. The perfect prelude to Hunter's marriage proposal to his sister. And perhaps he could steal those kisses he daydreamed about from Letitia.

The first course was served. It was a squash soup with just the right amount of nutmeg, cinnamon, and cream. Roasted chicken, mashed potatoes, and carrots followed. Then came fruit, nuts, and dishes of blood pudding.

Greyson didn't think he could move by the time all the dishes were removed. He didn't believe he had overindulged, but his stomach felt as if he had. "Shall we retire to the drawing room? I had the pianoforte brought in. Perhaps Aurora would grace us with some music?" He could have predicted Aurora's groan at his request. She was quite good at playing, but she preferred to play for herself when no one was around to hear her.

"Must I, brother?" Aurora said, and he heard the frustration in her voice.

"Oh, Lady Aurora," Warren said, looking at her with a wide smile, "I would love to hear you play. Perhaps we could play a duet."

Her face softened, and she smiled at Warren. "I didn't know you played."

"Yes, quite proficiently, I might add." How strange. When some gentlemen said such a thing, they would come across as boasting, but not Warren.

"Well, then, I would love to play a duet with you."

"It's settled then," Greyson said as he stood, slid Letitia's chair back, and held out his hand. She took it as she stood. "We shall go to the drawing room and be entertained by Aurora and Lord Warren."

Everyone stood and made their way back into the room they had occupied earlier, and Greyson was thrilled to see the pianoforte already in place.

CHAPTER TEN

DURING THE CARRIAGE ride to Danbury Hall, Letitia fidgeted with her gloves, repeatedly taking them off and putting them back on. For some reason, she was most anxious to see Greyson again, even though she'd ridden with him in Hyde Park only hours earlier. When she arrived, the butler escorted her into a lovely navy-and-cream drawing room, where she was pleasantly surprised to find Lord Warren, and Mr. Hunter in attendance as well. Her anxiety from the ride over subsided immediately, and the pain in her stomach eased.

The thought of having dinner with Greyson excited her when he'd asked. As she prepared for the evening, panic had settled in, but now she was elated to find she wasn't the only non-family member at the table. The conversation was easy, the food abundant, and the idea of Aurora and Warren entertaining them at the pianoforte was perfect. She loved to play, but she would not share that knowledge tonight. Being a spectator and enjoying the music was something she hadn't had when married to Rutherford. Whenever he was home for dinner, she played for him.

She found herself seated on a navy velvet settee beside Greyson. Warren and Anastasia sat on an identical settee, facing them, with a low round table between them, while Warren and Aurora played a lovely sonata by Ignaz Pleyel.

"Having Aurora play was a wonderful idea," she whispered between songs.

"Thank you. And Warren asking to play was like a fireworks display."

"Yes. He is quite good. They both are." She sighed and let herself rest against the back of the settee. Her eyes closed, and she hummed along to another arrangement, which she knew well. It was one of her favorite arrangements by Handel.

The settee dipped as Greyson moved closer to her and murmured into her ear. "You seem to know this song well. Do you play an instrument?"

Her body tensed, but she forced it to relax. "I play the pianoforte, but don't ask me to play tonight. It is Aurora's and Warren's night to shine. They are perfect for each other and sound lovely. I hope he proposes soon. If he does, you can have a double wedding for the twins."

He chuckled softly. "Indeed. Wouldn't that be the wedding of the Season?"

For the following arrangements by several different composers, they listened in silence, holding hands, much as Anastasia and Hunter were doing.

When Aurora expressed her exhaustion from playing, Hunter and Anastasia rose. Hunter said, "With your permission, Greyson, I would like to take a stroll in the gardens with Anastasia."

"You may," Greyson replied.

Once they left, Warren and Aurora sat on the settee they had just vacated.

"You both play beautifully," Letitia said, smiling and at ease.

"Thank you," Aurora said. "I can't believe Warren plays. And can play as well as I can—even better, actually. I've never had so much enjoyment playing in front of people before."

"It was my pleasure to play with you, Lady Aurora," Warren said with a lovesick smile and puppy-dog eyes meant for Aurora and Aurora only.

"I second what you said. It's good to play with an equally talented musician," Aurora said, smiling.

Greyson cleared his throat and said, "Do you mind if Letitia and I walk through the gardens? I will call your maid down to chaperone if you deem it necessary."

"Brother," Aurora scoffed, "Warren and I will stay right here and do nothing but hold hands. You can trust us."

"Yes, well," he cleared his throat again and looked directly at Warren. "Do I have your word, Warren, that you will do nothing but hold my sister's hand while I'm gone?"

It was so sweet to see Warren blush. "Yes, Greyson. Hold hands. Nothing else. You have my word."

"Good," he said as he stood and held out his hand to her. Letitia placed her hand in his and stood. She pulled her wrap more snugly around her shoulders, knowing it would be crisp outside since darkness had settled.

As they exited the double doors onto the veranda and descended the stairs to the gardens, she said, "Poor Warren. You embarrassed him."

"I did no such thing," Greyson said.

She removed her hand from his and slipped her arm around his elbow, so they were very close, their bodies bumping against each other as they walked. "You did. He blushed. It was so sweet. He cares a great deal for Aurora."

"Yes, I noticed that. Not the blush, but the caring for her. Honestly, a double wedding would be perfect."

"I hear an exception coming."

"Except Warren is a patient man who does things on his own time. Which, I might add, is at a snail's pace."

"Perhaps, when it comes to marrying Aurora, he will surprise even you. Mayhap when he learns that Hunter is proposing this very night, he will realize it is time for him to propose to Aurora. I predict he will come knocking tomorrow to discuss the marriage contract."

"You are a romantic at heart, Letitia. And I . . . like that about you."

If her hearing didn't deceive her, she believed Greyson had almost said *love*. If her heart could soar, it would soar into the sky and circle all the stars and planets with utter joy. She had fallen completely in love with him during their time in Newmarket, and that love had intensified since then. Perhaps he felt something close to love? She could hope. "Thank you. You know, my parents married for love. So it was all I'd known growing up. It wasn't until I married Rutherford that I found out very few couples in the *ton* marry for love. Some do, and they are the lucky few."

"I know you said you came to love Rutherford after you married, but did you love him when you married him?"

Hearing the trepidation in Greyson's voice shocked her. After all, Rutherford was dead and posed no threat to him. "Not when I married him. I hardly knew anything about him, but, as you know, over time I came to love him.

"I see."

She hadn't noticed, but he led her to a private alcove with a bench, surrounded by evergreens and shrubs. "Does it bother you?"

"Please sit." Letita sat on the cool wrought iron bench, and Greyson joined her. "Yes and no." He combed his fingers through his hair several times, then sighed. "He was your husband. I have no right to be jealous of what you two shared. And the fact that he is dead makes me feel like a terrible person."

"Nonsense," she said, patting his thigh. "Perhaps I'd feel the same if the positions were reversed. What I will say is that Rutherford is gone. You are here with me. I choose to be with you."

She turned on the bench so their knees brushed, and she cupped his cheeks with her bare hands, having left her gloves in the dining room. "Let's not waste this precious time alone tonight, talking and thinking about my deceased husband. We are together. We are alive. Will you kiss me already?"

His deep laughter filled her heart. "When you say it like that, I'd better comply."

And so he did. He took her wrists and put them around his neck. His arms encompassed her waist, and his warm, wonderful lips landed on hers, and she was entirely lost. She twirled her fingers through his thick, soft brown hair, which brushed the top of his jacket collar. It only took a moment for her to realize their tongues were twirling around and around at the same pace as her fingers in his hair, which had him groaning into her mouth.

He took the kiss to new heights. His tongue no longer twirled and danced with hers. It devoured every crevice of her mouth. His lips pressed against hers, almost painfully, but she knew it was because he was lost in her, out of control with his need to kiss and taste her essence. When she thought she might die without air, she tore her mouth away, buried her head beneath his chin, and breathed deeply, her chest heaving to take in much-needed air. His heart thumped against her, and his chest rose and fell with his deep intakes of air.

"Letitia," he said in a shaky voice, so unlike him. "Forgive me if I caused any undue pain to your lips."

"There is nothing to forgive." She brushed her fingers across her swollen lips. "They are tender, but it's a good feeling. Caused by something we shared and enjoyed together."

"Thank you for saying that, but I should've been more gentle."

"No." She lifted her head and met his dark-gray eyes. "I want you to be yourself with me. Don't try to be someone you're not. There is time for gentleness and time for what we just experienced. Never apologize for being true to your instincts and affections."

He gently squeezed his arms that were wrapped around her waist. "How'd I get so lucky to find you?"

"I don't know," she flirted. "You were at the Westport ball, a beautiful lady on each arm, and I felt bad for you."

He chuckled. "You took pity on me?" he teased. "I believe it was the other way around. I saw this beautiful woman and felt empathy for her as all her married friends surrounded her."

"Funny, but a total lie."

"I have something I need to tell you." The moment he began to speak, his body language changed. Gone was the relaxed, carefree Greyson, replaced by the tense version she'd met a time or two. "On Wednesday, I leave for Danbury Estate. There are things I need to take care of. I must meet with the estate manager. Correspondence can only convey the information he wants to share with me. I feel I owe it to my father to visit at least once a year to check on the tenants, the servants, and the manager, to ensure he is doing his job adequately. I refuse to let the estate be run to the ground by the manager, as has happened many times when the title holder prefers London and neglects his other properties. People suffer, buildings fall into disrepair, and animals suffer, to name a few."

Letitia pulled away from his arms and looked at him. "You would never neglect your duties, so you don't have to convince me otherwise. Go. Take care of whatever needs tending. I will be waiting when you return."

He brought both her hands to his lips, kissing one, then the other, before returning them to her lap. "Thank you for understanding."

"Did you think I wouldn't understand?" Everything he said rang true and was what the lords of estates did. They often visited their country estates. Why did he think she wouldn't understand?

"I knew you would. It's just that we've finally begun courting, and I have to leave."

"Are you afraid some other gentleman will come into my life, sweep me off my feet, steal me away to their castle, and ravish me?" She was only half teasing. Part of her believed he thought that way. Which was silly, since she hadn't seen him for months after Newmarket, and no gentleman had come calling on her. Not even once, and he knew this.

"Yes and no," he exhaled. "At least I hope not. And if some

other man calls on you, I'd hope you'd send him away with his self-esteem bruised and a shattered heart." He kissed her gently. "Because you are mine." He kissed her again, and she tried not to fall off the bench in shock at hearing him say those words.

He jumped up, his hand out. "Come, my princess. I need to make sure Warren hasn't ruined my sister. If he has, that double wedding will happen quite quickly."

Letitia was glad to hear his voice; his expression and demeanor were back to normal. She took his hand, and they strolled back through the gardens, swinging their joined arms back and forth like children. "Do you think Hunter proposed yet?"

"Bloody hell, I forgot about them. You make me lose myself in your lips. And to answer your question, yes. It was probably the first thing he did when he got her alone. I hope they're either back inside the drawing room or will be soon. I'd hate to have to go looking for them."

"Yes. That could get awkward."

"Please, don't remind me."

"Greyson, I'm shocked," she huffed. "You can pull a lady into your arms and kiss her senseless, but you can't accept Hunter doing the same with Anastasia?"

"I know. I know. It sounds ridiculous, but she's my sister."

"With one of your best friends, about to be married to him."

"Once again, I know. I wouldn't want her married to anyone else. It's still . . ." He paused.

"Hard to think about and witness," she said.

"Exactly."

"I don't understand men. Oh, look," she said softly with a smile, and her insides warmed with joy.

"What?"

"Shh. Look who's on the veranda."

"They look happy together," he murmured, tightening his grip on her hand.

"They do," she sighed.

They ascended the stairs, and only when they stood on the

veranda did Hunter and Anastasia notice they were no longer alone.

"Jacob proposed," Anastasia said with exuberance.

Letitia kissed Anastasia's cheek. "Congratulations to both of you."

"Yes," Greyson said, kissing his sister's cheek and shaking Hunter's hand. "Congratulations."

Anastasia looked positively glowing in the lantern light. "Can we marry as soon as the banns are posted?" She reached for Hunter's hand and intertwined their fingers. "We don't want to wait or have a large wedding. Only close family and friends."

"That sounds perfect," Greyson said with a wide grin. "Let's go inside, open a bottle of champagne, and toast the newly engaged couple."

The four of them entered through the double glass doors and straight into the elegant navy drawing room, laughing and chatting. Warren and Aurora were sitting on the settee, their heads together as they shared some intimate words, if Letitia had any guess, by the blush staining Aurora's cheeks.

"Hunter proposed," Anastasia said to Aurora, who hurried off the settee and over to her sister, hugging her.

"How exciting," she exclaimed. "I'm so happy for you. Can I help you plan?"

Letitia watched Warren closely. He looked slightly uncomfortable, but otherwise like his usual affable self. She really hoped he would propose to Aurora soon. She wouldn't want any jealousy to come between the two twin sisters, who at times seemed like two halves of one soul. If Letitia were in Aurora's place, she would be ecstatically thrilled and happy for her twin, yet wish it were herself instead.

She found herself sitting beside Warren while Greyson and Hunter popped open the champagne bottle at the sideboard. "How wonderful for Lady Anastasia and Mr. Hunter," she said, hoping to gauge what Warren was thinking.

"It is," he said, leaning close and lowering his voice. "May I confide in you, Lady Rutherford?"

"Why, yes. I'm a wonderful keeper of secrets."

"I'm surprised Hunter beat me to it. I was going to call on Lord Greyson to ask his permission to marry Aurora." He paused and exhaled. "What should I do now? Should I wait until after their nuptials?"

"No," Letitia blurted out so fast she almost made her head spin. "Greyson mentioned just this evening that he hoped you would be approaching him soon and that a double wedding would be perfect."

"Oh." He cleared his throat and smiled. "Well, then, I'd better tell him to expect a visit from me on Tuesday. I'd come before then, but I must escort my mother to her sister's house and won't arrive back in London until then. A double wedding. Aurora will be so thrilled."

"Did she tell you that?"

"I may have let it slip that I was going to ask her brother for permission to marry her. I wanted to be sure she wanted to marry me first."

"You and Aurora will be very happy together."

"Thank you." He stood. "Excuse me, but I must congratulate the happy couple."

As soon as Tuesday, there could be two happy couples planning a wedding.

After the bottle of champagne was empty, Warren and Hunter took their leave. Anastasia and Aurora left not long after, leaving Letitia and Greyson alone in the drawing room.

"Well, what a fitting end to the evening," Greyson said as he closed the drawing room door after his sisters left. When he reached the settee she sat on, he held out his hand. She immediately took it, and he pulled her to her feet and into his arms. "Warren asked for a meeting with me on Tuesday afternoon, and I can guess what it's about."

She wrapped her arms around his neck and pressed her body against his. "I'm sure you can."

Her not-so-subtle hint had him wrapping her in his arms and taking her mouth in a gentle kiss that quickly turned demanding and carnal. The man knew how to kiss, making her entire body quiver with need. His hands skimmed up her waist, his thumbs brushing the outside of her breasts, and she moaned into his mouth. Abruptly, he pulled back and kissed his way down her neck. One of his hands tugged down, first her little sleeves, then the front of her dress, freeing her breasts to the open air.

He leaned back, taking in her exposed flesh and pebbled nipples, then met her gaze with a lopsided grin. "You are beautiful. I can't wait for the day I make love to you. The masquerade ball is coming up. Will you be ready?"

His hot tongue laved one of her nipples, and he cupped her other breast with his warm, large hand. Her head dropped back, and she breathed, "Yes."

His teeth clamped down, and a jolt between her thighs made a moan escape her parted lips.

"You like that?"

"Hmmm," was all she could manage. Words weren't needed as he nipped her again, sending another lightning strike to her core.

He lavished attention on her breasts for several more moments before stepping back, his shaky hands running through his hair. "We must stop before I take you on the fine Aubusson rug."

The cool air settled on her wet nipples, and she shivered as she righted her clothing. She'd yet to meet his gaze, knowing her face was aflame with desire and embarrassment.

He picked up her shawl from the settee and wrapped it around her shoulders. "The carriage is ready to take you home. I think it's best if I remain behind."

She was disappointed he wasn't accompanying her, but she understood from the prominent bulge in his breeches. Something she couldn't wait to investigate when the time was right. That would be Monday night at Club Knight's masquerade ball.

With Greyson's help, she entered his carriage. "Thank you

for a wonderful night."

He leaned in and kissed her cheek. "I think that's my line. Good night. I'm going to dream of you. Forgive me, but I have family matters and business to attend to for the next two days. I will pick you up at half eleven on Monday night." He shut the door and knocked on the roof.

The carriage started, and Letitia whispered to herself, "I'm going to dream of you, too, Greyson, as you've stolen my heart and soul."

And when she climbed into bed not long after leaving Danbury Hall, snuggled beneath the coverlet, she did indeed dream of her brown-haired, green-eyed prince.

CHAPTER ELEVEN

As Greyson's eyes followed his carriage as it disappeared around a corner, taking Letitia home, his mind warred with itself. Too many things occupied it. He thought his head would burst, and he contemplated taking a bottle of whisky to his chambers and drinking it until he fell into oblivion. The problem with doing so was that he would feel like death in the morning, and he'd still have to accomplish all the things he needed to, except with one hell of a headache.

Instead, he ran up the stairs and down the hall to his chambers, where Dalton waited for him. "Just help me with my boots, Dalton, and then you may retire."

"Yes, my lord."

Dalton helped him with his boots, then left, closing the door quietly. Greyson undressed, put on a navy-blue banyan, and sat at his small writing desk in his room, scribbling several notes he needed to send the next morning. One was to the Duke of Tremont, or rather, Knight, requesting a private meeting to discuss his upcoming assignment in more detail. He also wanted to request several special considerations at the masquerade ball. He wanted everything to be perfect for Letitia that night. It was a big step in their courtship, and he wouldn't leave anything to chance.

He also penned a note to Hunter, reiterating what he had said tonight and welcoming him into the family, even though he was already considered family. As one of his two best friends, he couldn't be happier. The other note he wrote was addressed to Warren, stating that he was expected at Danbury Hall precisely at three on Tuesday afternoon and that he looked forward to discussing the marriage contract.

After folding and sealing all three correspondences, he left them on a tray on the desk for Dalton. Dalton had been with him since Greyson turned eighteen and sometimes knew what he wanted or needed even before he did. The man was very intuitive and precise in his duties, which reminded Greyson that it was time to give him a raise. Loyalty and honesty were traits Greyson insisted on, and Dalton embodied both and more.

Feeling tired, both physically and mentally, he removed his banyan and climbed beneath the covers. The night had chilled considerably, and Dalton had built a fire, giving the room a warm glow. The crackling of the logs helped lull him to sleep, and he dreamed of Letitia running through a wildflower field at Danbury Estate, laughing and removing her clothing as she ran.

Greyson noticed several things when he awoke: The blaze in the hearth had burned down to embers. Rays of sunshine were peeking through the gaps in the curtains, letting him know it was a bright day. He heard movement in his dressing room, which had two entrances, one to his chambers and one to Dalton's sleeping quarters, alerting him that Dalton was up and would be coming in momentarily.

As if he had conjured him up, Dalton opened the dressing room door and marched to the curtains, opening them. "Good morning, your lordship. I trust you slept well."

"Yes. Thank you, Dalton."

"There's hot water in the basin and fresh linens. Anything else?"

"See that the letters on the desk are delivered immediately. Have a tray brought to my father's study in half an hour. I'll be leaving at ten, so please have my horse brought around then."

"Yes, my lord."

Greyson threw back the covers and hurried into his dressing room to perform his morning ablutions. He dipped a small linen cloth in the basin of hot water, lathered it with soap, washed his body, and dried off with a larger linen cloth. Dressed in his riding clothes, he tugged on his boots and made his way down the stairs into the study.

His breakfast tray arrived. He ate the eggs and toast, then looked over Aurora's marriage contract, which his father had written up, while drinking his coffee. It was identical to Anatasia's, and he couldn't imagine Warren having any issue with it. His chest tightened. He had mixed emotions about marrying off his twin sisters. Life as they knew it would forever be changed. They would never live together at Danbury Hall again as a family. Oh, he knew it was the progression of one's life. Or hopefully it was. Marry, move away, and have children.

He wanted it for himself and certainly for his sisters. Change was necessary and expected in the sequence of one's life, but it was still sad to know that life, as he'd always known it, would disappear soon. But then his chest eased when he thought of Letitia and the life he hoped to create with her. Not once in his twenty-eight years had he met a woman he wanted in his life forever until her.

Ever since the first night he met her, he'd fought to remain calm, to not overwhelm her. He didn't want to frighten her with his desires and the need to claim her. Whenever he was privileged to be in her company, every nerve ending in his body tingled with awareness, making him wonder if that was what happened to Hunter with Anastasia. It was ridiculous to think he was the only one who felt this way when finding the person they loved. And yes, he loved Letitia to distraction. He only hoped it wouldn't be his downfall. It was high time he stopped making excuses for why he couldn't commit to her. If she would have him, that was.

A knock on the study door pulled him from his musings. "Forgive me, my lord," Henderson said. "Your horse is waiting."

Greyson sighed with relief once he sat on his favorite horse, Whisky. Whenever he was on horseback, no matter what was bothering him or occupying his mind, he relaxed. The scent of horse, leather, and freedom called to him. At least what he perceived as freedom, or as much freedom as one could have in the city of London. Already, the streets of Mayfair were crowded with carriages, hackneys, and horses. He entered the fray and rode with a smile on his face to Club Knight.

When he arrived, all was silent, as was the norm for a nighttime establishment. He dismounted and handed his reins to a stableboy who worked for Knight. Then he made his way around to the backdoor and did the secret knock. Samuel Cutter opened the door. "He's waiting for you downstairs." Greyson made his way down to their secret room and found Knight sitting in a chair with his feet up on another.

"Sit, Greyson. What did you want to discuss at this ungodly hour? You do realize I haven't slept yet, don't you?"

"Forgive me. I should've realized."

"Yes, you should've. But since you're here, let's get on with it."

"I have several requests regarding a room on the third floor for Tuesday's masquerade ball."

"Yes. What is it you want?"

For some reason, Knight had him feeling as if he were back at Eton, being questioned by the headmaster. He cleared his throat and rattled off several things he wanted prepared for the room.

"No problem. Consider it done. That better not be the only thing you wanted to talk to me about, because you could've sent a note with the instructions," Knight grumbled.

"Of course not," Greyson hurried to say. "I was thinking of Wednesday and the assignments."

"I have been as well. I'm calling a meeting for Tuesday at one. I feel as though we aren't as well prepared as we should be."

"I agree."

"Good. Get out of here and let me get some sleep. I have a

wife waiting for me at home."

"You are a fortunate man, Your Grace."

Knight nodded. "Don't I know it."

When he left Club Knight, he had a long list of people to see and things to do he'd been putting off. It was why he told Letitia he wouldn't see her until he picked her up for the masquerade ball. If he didn't buckle down on estate business and his family finances, he would get further and further behind.

CHAPTER TWELVE

O N MONDAY AFTERNOON, Letitia decided at the last minute to visit Blackstone Manor for afternoon tea with Emmeline and Lilly. She found herself in her carriage, stuck in slow traffic, as her driver made their way to Blackstone Manor.

She had desperately needed to get out of the house because the day before had been the longest of her life. After spending Saturday riding in the park with him and that night having dinner at Danbury Hall, her entire being missed Greyson. How could she be so attached to him that she felt his absence every second of the day? She shook her head and sighed deeply, disliking the feeling of wanting to be by his side at all times. She'd never felt that way with Rutherford, and it was quite unsettling, to say the least.

She also needed to get her mind off tonight because at the stroke of midnight, the masquerade ball at Club Knight began. Since waking up this morning, her stomach had been a jumbled mess of nervous anticipation. One moment, she was excited to spend time with Greyson, free to show affection without the risk of disapproval. Then she'd panic, thinking about sleeping with him. Would she please him? She and Rutherford had enjoyed their time in the marriage bed. But she worried she wouldn't please Greyson. She'd heard things, sexual things, discussed in drawing rooms. Things she'd never experienced with Rutherford.

Shocking things that left her curious. But it all made her insides ache with fear that Greyson would find her lacking in the bedroom.

It felt as though it had taken an hour to arrive at Blackstone Manor, and she was so very happy when the carriage stopped and her footman opened her door and helped her exit.

So now she sat in Blackstone Manor's drawing room, sipping tea and listening to Emmeline and Lilly discuss Lilly's pregnancy. She forced her worries aside and gave her attention to her friends. "Do you have morning sickness anymore?" Letitia asked.

Lilly smiled and placed her hand on her stomach. "Thankfully, not since my third month ended. I feel less tired, and my appetite has returned, which is good because Edmund was beside himself with worry about my health and the baby's during the first three months."

"I remember how worried Rutherford was. He was like a mother hen, hovering over me constantly, asking how I felt, whether I had eaten, and whether I had rested enough. It was sweet, but it began to annoy me the longer he hovered."

Lilly giggled. "That sounds just like Edmund."

"Since they can only watch us carry the child, it must be hard to understand, so they hover and drive us crazy with worry and questions," Letitia said.

"Well, I for one can't wait for Andrew to loom over me with worry," Emmeline said, placing one hand delicately on her stomach. "Can you ladies keep a secret?"

Lilly and Letitia exchanged a look, and Letitia's heart soared as she knew what Emmeline was going to say. "Yes," both Lilly and Letitia said together.

"Andrew knows, but I want to keep it private for as long as possible. I'm with child."

"This is wonderful news," Lilly said, covering Emmeline's hand with her own as they sat side by side on the settee. "Andrew must be over the moon with joy. And you . . . I'm beyond happy for you."

"Thank you. Andrew has already started hovering. I never knew he was such a worrier, but honestly, it's so sweet of him."

"Congratulations to you both," Letitia said, dreaming of one day giving Greyson a child and hoping they would marry soon. She knew, without him saying so, that he cared for her, even loved her. But would he propose and marry her? She tried not to let herself get her hopes up, but it was hard not to. She loved him so much that her heart called out to him when they were together. It was something she couldn't ignore, and she didn't believe it would ever go away.

"Thank you. It's still early, and I'm trying not to worry too much. I miscarried while I was married to my first husband. It was long ago, but I haven't forgotten how devastating and heartbreaking it was."

"I'm so sorry you went through that, but worrying won't do you or the baby any good," Letitia said. "But I understand worrying about your unborn child. I did the same while pregnant with Simon."

"Does the constant worry ever go away?" Lilly asked, looking expectantly.

"I wish I could say it does, but it doesn't. Not even after the baby's born or when they are two years old. I worry about Simon all the time. I suppose it's a mother's prerogative and curse to worry about their offspring. But it's worth it when you hold your little one close. There's nothing like the love you feel for your child, or the unconditional love a child returns."

"Ahhh," Lilly wiped a tear from her cheek. "I can't wait to hold my little one."

"Nor I," Emmeline added. "Enough of us. We heard that Hunter proposed to Anastasia."

"Yes. They are so happy, and I believe Warren is going to propose soon. A double wedding is in the near future."

"Greyson must be thrilled," Lilly said. "Two fine gentlemen for his sisters."

"Yes, he is," Letitia answered.

"Tell us all about you and Greyson," Emmeline said. "And don't leave anything out."

"I . . . I don't know where to begin. He is everything I ever wanted. He makes me laugh and melt."

"Have you . . .?"

"Lilly, I can't believe you said that," Emmeline chastised.

"Well, she's been married before, and it's quite acceptable for a widow to take a lover."

Letitia quickly covered her mouth to hide her shock, then began to laugh. Nervous laughter, since she planned to take Greyson as her lover that very night. When her laughter subsided, she took several deep breaths and said, "No. But I hope to soon. The man says he's waiting for the perfect time."

"So romantic," Lilly said. "He looks at you as if he's starving and you're his first meal in months. He also looks like he knows how to kiss."

Letitia found herself laughing again. "Oh, he can kiss."

"Who can kiss?" Blackstone asked as he entered the drawing room, making all three ladies blush and look at one another. Letitia wanted to crawl beneath the chair and hide.

"None of your business, husband," Emmeline said. "What brings you here?"

"Cook said she made biscuits. I'll grab a handful and leave you ladies to your visit."

When he left, all three of them giggled. "Oh my God," Letitia said. "I can't believe he heard me. I'm sure he knew who I meant."

"Yes, no doubt he did," Emmeline agreed. "He's probably sitting in his study, chuckling."

"Do you think he'll say anything to Greyson?" Letitia asked suddenly, in a panic.

"No. He wouldn't dare repeat anything he overheard in this drawing room," Emmeline said.

"Phew." Letitia's panic eased. She so wanted to tell them about the masquerade at Club Knight, but she knew she couldn't reveal anything about the secret club, even if she wanted their advice. She would have to rely on her own intuition. Not long after, she took her leave, thankful she had visited and learned about Emmeline's joyful condition. Too bad her nerves were still strung tight about tonight. She closed her eyes during the carriage ride home and forced her body and mind to relax. She would be with Greyson tonight. There was nothing to be anxious about.

When she returned home, she visited with Simon in the nursery for a spell, then went to her chambers to take a nap. She asked Jane to wake her at eight so she could eat dinner and prepare for the masquerade. She had asked Jane to create a costume and mask for her, and she was excited to see what Jane had made. Knowing Jane, it would be fabulous.

As much as Letitia wanted to nap, her mind wouldn't let her. As soon as she started to doze off, something else would pop into her mind. She finally gave up, rolled onto her back, and let her mind wander as it wanted. It wasn't just Greyson weighing heavily on her mind. Every little thing she'd neglected lately came to mind—things such as new clothing for Simon, who was growing so fast, and a new bed.

She took this time to worry about Lilly and Emmeline, and even Clarice. She missed Clarice terribly and couldn't wait for her to return from her honeymoon. She tried to keep her mind off Greyson and the masquerade, but she failed miserably. By the time Jane came in to wake her up, she sighed with relief. Having dinner and dressing up for the evening would keep her from jumping out of her skin.

Jane brought a tray of beef, carrots, and potatoes for her dinner, and Letitia forced herself to eat. Well, she ate the meat, mashed potatoes, and a roll. For some reason, the carrots were not to her liking tonight, even though the cook prepared them as she preferred. The beef, potatoes, and roll soothed her stomach. The carrots had the opposite effect.

When it came time to dress, Jane went into the dressing room and came out carrying a pile of white cloth. "What am I going to be?" Letitia asked.

"A shepherdess. Your simple, ankle-length dress will be tied at the waist with a gold rope, and it will have a fitted hood that will cover your hair, which you will wear down. And of course, you will carry a staff."

"I think I need to be dressed to visualize it, but it sounds exciting." Once she was dressed and looking in the mirror, she sighed with relief. The white shift fell to her ankles, revealing the tops of her brown boots. The sleeves were long and flowing. A gold braided rope encircled her waist, and the ends fell almost to the length of the dress. Her hair hung loose but was tucked into the fitted hood. Her half mask was white and adorned with thin gold braid. Overall, the costume was simple and plain, yet it made Letitia feel beautiful. Sometimes, simplicity was more alluring.

"As always, I knew I could count on you, Jane. It is perfect."

"Thank you, my lady. Your hair looks like spun gold beneath the hood. The costume suits you well."

"Thank you again, Jane. What would I do without you? You may retire for the night. Please don't wake me in the morning. I will call for you when I'm up."

"Yes, my lady."

After Jane left, Letitia took one last glance in the looking glass and couldn't help but smile. She picked up her staff, a tree branch someone had cut to her height and whittled off the bark, making it smooth as butter. It was exactly half eleven when she stepped foot in the entry hall and found Mr. Henry standing at the door, facing her.

"A carriage just pulled up, my lady." He handed her a dark brown cloak, which she didn't don, as she wanted Greyson to see her costume first. Mr. Henry opened the door, and she found herself face-to-face with Greyson, dressed as what she presumed was an American frontiersman, complete with a raccoon-tailed hat and a black half mask. He wore buckskin breeches and brown boots. A cream shirt, open at the throat, showed a smattering of brown hair, and he wore a brown buckskin vest with fringe. Her insides tingled. He looked wild and untamed, much like the American frontier. Or so she'd heard.

"You're staring, my dear."

Greyson's amused voice tore her thoughts away from the American frontier and back to the gentleman in front of her.

"Forgive me," she said, heat painting her cheeks. "I was thinking you look ready to join a wagon train, wrestle bears, and fight the elements as you stake your claim in the wilds of America." For one brief moment, she could see herself with him there.

He chuckled. "Then I'd say Dalton did his job with my costume." He looked her up and down, then grinned. "Where are your sheep? Have they run away, little shepherdess? Would you like my help finding them?"

His remark made her laugh. "Perhaps later. Right now, we have somewhere to be."

He held her hand as they descended the stone stairs. Greyson helped her into the carriage and joined her on the seat.

"My dear Letitia, you look positively alluring as hell, dressed all in white."

"I'm not supposed to be alluring. I'm supposed to be attracting my flock of sheep," she teased.

"I'll be one of your sheep. Just don't bring me to slaughter."

"Never."

"That's a relief," he chuckled. "You must be chilly. Let me help you with your cloak." Greyson took the cloak from her hands and draped it over her shoulders. She fastened the toggle at her throat and pulled the hood up.

"Better?" he asked.

"Yes, thank you."

The rest of the ride was silent. Greyson held her hand in his, and she wondered what he was thinking. She thought about tonight and being alone with him in one of the private upstairs rooms. Had he reserved one for them? Would he take her upstairs as soon as they arrived? Oh, my, her stomach did a silent tumble. She was nervous but excited about the prospect of making love with Greyson. No doubt he could teach her how to please him. And she could explain what she liked. Would she satisfy him? Again, her stomach tumbled.

"Is something amiss?" Greyson asked, his voice laced with concern.

"Just a little nervous."

"Don't be. As with our last visit to Club Knight, I will not leave your side unless you wish me to."

"Thank you." She squeezed his hand.

"Good. We have arrived. Oh, I forgot." He pulled a card from his jacket pocket and handed it to her. "This is your membership card. Guard it with your life." She took it from his hand. It looked identical to his. "Tonight, we pull up to the front door. No one will recognize us with our masks on."

She hoped he was correct in his assessment. He exited the carriage first, then leaned back in with his hand out, which she took and exited. They went to the back of the line to wait their turn to enter the club. She recognized the gentleman at the door from her previous visit. Tonight, he scrutinized the guests' cards and faces more closely because everyone was wearing masks. At times, she heard him ask questions, no doubt trying to recognize them by their voices.

When Greyson handed over his card, he merely glanced at it before handing it back. With trembling hands, Letitia handed hers to the doorman, held her breath as he studied it, and then said, "Welcome to the Club."

When he handed it back to her, she immediately slipped it into her white drawstring pouch that matched her costume. "Thank you."

The door opened, and they entered. Greyson helped her with her cloak, then handed it to a footman just inside the door. As they walked hand in hand up the stairs toward the ballroom, Letitia said, "That was terrifying."

"He was just doing his job."

"I know. But still terrifying." They entered the ballroom, and she took a moment to look around the dimly lit room full of costumed people. Some of the men and women were scantily dressed, and she tried not to gawk or gasp. An orchestra played a waltz, but the couples were not dancing it properly. They held each other shockingly close and swayed to the rhythm, their bodies nearly attached.

"What do you think?" Greyson asked, his voice loud enough to be heard over the music but not so loud that those around them could hear.

"I'm still taking it in."

"Me too. You forget I just became a member, and this is my first time attending a masquerade here."

"I've never attended one anywhere. Are the ones at the Pantheon and Vauxhall Gardens like this one?"

"No and yes. Masquerade balls usually attract some of society's seedier residents. Costumes can be just as bawdy. Some people let their inhibitions down, but once the masks are removed, *ton* standards are restored, at least for the members of the *ton*."

"Oh."

"Is that a good *oh* or a bad *oh*?"

"Just an *oh*. Not good or bad. More of an observation." She inhaled, her eyes fixed on a couple on the dance floor. "He's cupping her b-b-buttocks."

She could tell Greyson found her amusing, though he tried to hide it. "Yes, I believe he is. Like I told you, this is a place where people can engage in activities frowned upon in polite society."

She swallowed her nervous laugh. "Frowned upon? Come now, Greyson, she would be ruined, and the gentleman called out at dawn by a family member."

"There is that. Good thing nothing like that happens here."

"Should they not go upstairs?" she suggested.

"Part of the excitement is the prelude. Some people enjoy being on display."

"But . . ."

"No judging. We are members in attendance, so who are we to condemn another's actions? Come, let's dance."

Letitia allowed Greyson to lead her to the center of the dance floor, where couples surrounded them. He took her into his arms and said, "Follow my lead." He side-stepped, one, two, three, but they mainly moved in place. The crush left nowhere to go. "Relax."

She closed her eyes, her arms around his neck, his around her waist, their bodies brushing with each movement. With her eyes closed, she moved to the melody's rhythm, easing her tense muscles. She leaned into him until they touched more intimately. The swaying of their bodies, moving as one, the warmth of the room, and the intimacy of their mingled breaths transported her to another place, another time, where only the two of them existed.

One song turned into another, the melody similar, so they continued as they were. Greyson stroked his hands up her back, sending awareness throughout her body. Every nerve ending took notice. Heat pooled low in her belly and spread outward. It took effort not to rub her center against his thigh to find release. She was no better than the other couple. What was happening to her? Whatever it was, she would enjoy it while she could. Tomorrow, everything would go back to normal. But they had tonight. Greyson, his hands on either side of her hips, pulled her close to him, and she felt the hard bulge in his breeches press against her stomach. A moan escaped her lips. "Forgive me."

"Forgive me. I'm the one who rubbed against you. But I wanted you to know what it does to me to hold you close. I want you, Letitia. I want to make love to you until neither of us can move, until our bodies and muscles are pleasantly sore. I want to taste your lips, and I don't mean your mouth."

She moaned, and her head fell back as she remembered what she had overheard in a drawing room. So it was true?

"I believe now is the perfect time," he murmured in her ear.

Even though he spoke cryptically, she knew exactly what he

meant. "Yes," she exhaled.

He took her hand in his and led her out of the ballroom and up the stairs to the third floor. The entire time she walked, she didn't think her feet touched the ground. She glided on anticipation, excitement, and desire. Several people were milling about the dimly lit corridor, but she didn't make eye contact or say anything to them as Greyson led her to the second-to-last room on the left. He produced a key from his pocket, unlocked the door, and opened it, waving her in ahead of him.

She stepped over the threshold and gasped as Greyson shut and locked the door, then pocketed the key.

"Is something wrong?" he asked as he removed his mask.

She removed her mask to see the room more clearly. "Not at all. The room is beautiful."

"I'm glad you like it. I requested it especially for you."

"Me?" she blurted. Her eyes followed the trail of red rose petals from the door to the bed, where the white sheets and the turned-down counterpane were sprinkled with them. On one bedside table sat a tray of grapes and strawberries. On the opposite side of the bed stood a bottle of champagne and two crystal flutes. A low fire in the hearth cast a romantic glow throughout the small bedroom. "You thought of everything. It is beyond romantic."

He moved behind her and wrapped his arms around her waist. He lowered the hood of her costume, swept her hair aside, and pressed his warm, soft lips to her neck. "You bring out the romantic in me," he murmured.

A sigh escaped her lips, and her body liquefied. One of Greyson's hands slid up over her stomach until he cupped one of her breasts, his thumb swirling around her nipple. It hardened instantly under his touch.

"Your breasts are firm and made for my hands. The fit is perfect. May I remove your shepherdess dress? I do love you in it, though."

"Yes," she breathed, her body tingling with anticipation.

His large, capable hands untied the rope around her waist, teasingly slow, letting it fall to the floor. Then, with both hands, he reached for the hem of her dress. Again, he went tantalizingly slowly, pulling it up inch by inch, the fabric teasing her oversensitive skin, until it went over her head and fell carelessly to the floor. Cool air kissed her naked body, and she was shocked he'd removed her chemise as well.

"You said my dress." She shivered, not just from the cold.

"We both know your chemise needed to go." His voice sounded deep and strained, as if he were trying to control his eagerness and emotions.

Letitia still didn't move, her back facing his front. "Perhaps, Greyson, you should remove your clothing. It's only fair for you to be naked since I am."

He chuckled deeply. "Say no more."

She didn't dare look as the rustling of clothing came from behind her. She wanted to wait until all his clothes were removed so she could see him in all his naked glory. "Are you void of all clothing?"

"Yes," he groaned.

"Good," she whispered as she turned and found him about three feet away, perfect for her to look her fill. She tried not to think of him doing the same to her, even though she knew he was. Instead, she let her gaze drift slowly down his body. His shoulders were wide and his arms muscular. Not that this was new to her. She'd known this even with his clothes on. His chest was hard, sprinkled with light-brown hair. His stomach was flat, leading to a narrow waist. She skipped to his impressive thighs and calves. Then her eyes fell on his manhood, hard, large, and reaching out to her.

Greyson coughed. "Do you like what you see?"

She sputtered and crossed her arms beneath her breasts, then thought better of it when they looked more pronounced. "You are a fine specimen of the male species," she teased. "But you knew that already."

One side of his mouth quirked upward. "Thank you. Are you going to ask whether I like what I see?"

Heat scorched her cheeks. "No, I can see you do."

"Well, I'm going to tell you anyway. You are perfect, as I knew you would be. The blonde hair between your thighs intrigues me. I can't wait to taste you there." He inhaled. "I can already scent your arousal."

She inhaled and shook her head, hoping what he said was a lie. "You can't."

He reached for her, scooped her into his arms, and set her on the bed, scattering rose petals everywhere. "You're right. I can't, but I will when my head's buried between your thighs." He covered her with his body and took her mouth in a kiss that seared her entire being. Her tongue danced, retreated, then danced again with his. His teeth nipped her bottom lip as their desires flared out of control.

"Christ," Greyson said, breaking the kiss and burying his head in her neck as he gasped for air. "I need you. So badly. I may not be at my best. Forgive me, but I promise I'll make up for it next time." His hand moved down her body until he reached her core. Her hips rose to meet his hand. "Good. You are wet. Forgive me, but I need to be inside you. Just give me a moment." He produced a French letter from beneath a pillow and put it on, surprising her with his thoughtfulness in protecting her.

When he covered her body with his, she wrapped her legs around his hips and moaned as his hard cock pressed against her entrance. "I want you inside me just as badly."

He reached between their bodies, took his manhood in his hand, and guided it into her welcoming sheath. When her body accommodated his length and size and he was seated deep inside her, he looked at her in wonder. She felt like the most cherished and loved woman alive and smiled at him.

"Did I hurt you?" he asked.

"No. You feel amazing inside me. Why would you say that?"

He chuckled, and she felt his cock twitching inside her. "Because I'm better endowed than most."

"You may be, but you fit me perfectly."

Her words had him groaning. He leaned down and took her lips in another punishing kiss as he moved in and out of her. He tore his lips from hers, buried his head in her hair, and pounded into her until she tingled all over. She soared into the sky and exploded. Greyson buried himself deep, froze, and groaned loudly.

He rolled off her, removed the French letter, and set it on the bedside table. Then he took her into his arms and pulled up the covers. "Rest. I plan to have you again soon. And this time it won't be quick."

With his arms around her and his warm body pressed against her back, Letitia closed her eyes and fell asleep.

CHAPTER THIRTEEN

GREYSON LAY IN bed, holding Letitia in his arms as he listened to her sleep. He knew the moment she drifted off. Her breathing evened out, her body sank into the bed and against him, and she made the sweetest, softest noises. He thought about holding her in his arms for so long, and he couldn't believe it was happening. He'd been on the edge of release the moment they undressed, and he memorized every inch of her body. When she looked intently at his cock, it hardened to stone, and he knew he wouldn't last. He didn't think he'd disappointed her in bed, but there was so much he wanted to experience with her. He wasn't taking her home until they did.

After about half an hour, Letitia stirred in his arms and rolled over to face him, her cheeks flushed and a sweet smile on her face. "I fell asleep."

"You did. Are you refreshed?" he said, waggling his eyebrows up and down, hoping she took the hint.

Smiling, she rolled onto her back, raised her arms over her head, and stretched, sighing. "I'm very refreshed indeed. Enough so that I believe you made a promise to me?"

"You little minx," he said with a laugh as he swiped the covers off them both, leaving her flushed, naked body exposed in all its lush glory. She giggled as he came down on top of her and kissed her gently. This time, he wanted to take things slowly. Her soft, full lips tasted like the sweet wine she'd drunk earlier. His tongue explored the inside of her mouth, as if he were exploring a magical cave where one went to find one's heart's desire. It wasn't long before he took the kiss to the next level and devoured her mouth, forgetting his plan to take it slowly. Her tongue joined his, and they danced and twirled around, fueling the fire raging out of control inside him.

He pulled his lips from hers and kissed and licked his way down her neck until his mouth found the hardened peak of one nipple. His tongue swirled around and around, then sucked the nipple deep into his mouth. Not only did she moan, but she tried to get closer. Giving her nipple one last lick, he moved down her stomach. Nudging her legs apart, he stared at her exposed womanhood and inhaled. "Remember our conversation earlier, when I teased you about scenting your arousal?" He inhaled again. "I can now, and it's the most powerful and attractive scent I've ever had the pleasure of smelling."

Letitia groaned in what he believed was embarrassment. That groan turned into a moan as he parted her folds, licking one side, then the other, before sucking her nub into his mouth, causing her hips to rise off the bed. He wouldn't embarrass her again, but she tasted exquisite. Earthy and magical. Like the nectar of an ancient goddess. When he inserted a finger inside her, her hips rose again. He withdrew his finger, moved her legs over his shoulders, and slid it back in while teasing her nub with his mouth. He knew she was close. Her legs were vibrating, her insides tightening around his finger. When she came, he drank up her juices and was so thankful she trusted him enough to let him do that. When her orgasm subsided, he withdrew his finger, licked her nether lips one last time, climbed up her body, and entered her in one push.

"Greyson! Oh my, I think I'm going to die," she gasped.

"Not at all, my dear. I'll never let you die. Not while you're in my arms." He moved in and out of her wet sheath, which felt like a secret, magical place created for him alone. She fit him like a custom-made glove. It wasn't long before her insides were clamping around his cock, and they exploded together as one, his warm seed spilling inside her. It was then he realized he'd forgotten something.

When he rolled off her, he hugged her close and said, "I'm sorry. I forgot to protect you this time."

"It never dawned on me until I felt the wetness from your seed. We'll have to be more careful in the future."

His heart seized. "You will let me know if and when your courses come?" He would never admit it to her, but the idea of a quick wedding because she carried his child didn't terrify him as it once had. However, he didn't want to take her choice away from her, just in case she wasn't ready to marry him and have another child. He would ignore the ache in his chest at that thought.

"Can I ask you something?" He was all too glad to have his thoughts interrupted.

"Anything."

"What you did . . ." She paused and cleared her throat, her hands sliding up and down his arms as they held her around her waist. Her soft fingertips gave him the shivers. ". . . down there. Is that something everyone does?"

It never dawned on him that she might never have experienced that with Rutherford. From talks at his clubs, he knew of gentlemen who disliked tasting their wives or mistresses. He was not one of them, but Rutherford obviously was. "Many couples explore each other with their mouths, but I have heard some men prefer not to do that. Just as many women prefer not to taste a man's penis."

He could hear her mind working. She'd begin to speak, stop, then begin again, only to stop. "Feel free to tell me anything," he told her. "Remember, no secrets between us."

"Rutherford never did that," she said, shivering. Greyson tugged the covers up to keep them warm. "But if I'm being honest, I'm glad you were the first to taste me and give me pleasure that way."

Greyson's body trembled at her words. "I'm honored you have chosen me."

"Do you mind if I fall asleep? But promise you will wake me up in an hour."

He snuggled against her back and kissed her neck. "I promise."

He hoped he could keep his promise, but he was having a hard time keeping his eyes open. In fact, he was so content with Letitia in his arms that he did, indeed, fall asleep.

"Greyson," the voice of the woman in his dreams came to him again. He loved it when her soft, melodious voice whispered to him. "Greyson, wake up." Her voice changed. It was louder and more demanding. "Please, Greyson. We fell asleep. I need to get home before the sun rises."

His eyes popped open, and he sat up, instantly realizing where they were. Club Knight on the third floor. "I'm sorry. I fell asleep. I promised to wake you in an hour. Forgive me."

"Nothing to forgive. I fell asleep too." She pointed to her costume on the floor. "Can you bring me my clothes? I'll be ready to go in a moment."

He rose from the bed, picked up Letitia's shepherdess costume and her chemise, and handed them to her as she sat on the bed, the coverlet pulled up to her chin. He chuckled to himself, as it was a little late for modesty. He had seen, touched, and kissed every part of her body, and he couldn't wait to do so again. He put on his breeches, pulled his shirt over his head, then the vest, and plopped the raccoon hat on his head, but skipped the mask. He sank onto the bed and tugged on his boots while trying not to glance at Letitia, wanting to give her privacy while she dressed.

"I'm ready," she said as she came and stood beside him, resting her hand on his shoulder. She was fully clothed, complete with her mask and hood.

"Perfect." He stood, moved to the door, pulled the key from his pocket, and unlocked it. He transferred the key to the outside keyhole and left it there. He didn't want Knight complaining that he'd lost the key. "Come," he said, holding out his hand. Letitia placed her small, soft hand in his, and they made their way down to the entry. By the sound of voices carrying from the ballroom and the halls, there were still patrons of Club Knight there.

The doorman opened the door, and to Greyson's great relief, he saw his unmarked carriage parked just off to the side of the front entrance. He helped Letitia inside, then sat down beside her and knocked on the roof. Instantly, the carriage wheels turned. Wrapping his arm around her shoulders, he held her close for the ride to Rutherford Manor. Silence filled the air, and he wondered what she was thinking. Was she reliving their lovemaking in a pleasant way, or regretting giving herself to him?

A knot formed in his stomach. Don't be a fool, he chastised himself. It was the most intense and satisfying lovemaking he'd ever experienced, and he had to believe it was for her as well. There was no sense in doubting himself or her feelings for him. Joining Club Knight and accompanying him there was for his benefit. She had done this for him. To be with him. To understand him better. The knot in his stomach loosened a bit, and he forced his insecurities aside. Holding her now was what mattered most. The softness of her body against his. The scent of her floral perfume tickling his nose. She mattered to him. It was a strange and unusual experience to care for another person not related to him. Yes, he had cared for some of the women he'd had brief encounters with, but nothing compared to his feelings for Letitia. And he couldn't call them relationships because they never lasted longer than a month.

If he added up all the days he and Letitia had together, they would fall shy of a month, but that didn't matter. Time was irrelevant when the heart was involved. You couldn't put a time frame on love or on when it would take over your heart. For him, he fell for her the first night he looked across a crowded ballroom and locked eyes with her beautiful blue ones. In that second, he knew he had to get to know her and that he was looking into the future. A future with a blue-eyed goddess.

"Greyson," she nudged him with her body. "Are you awake? We're outside my home."

He removed his arm from around her shoulders and opened the door. "Forgive me. I must have dozed off," he lied. "Before we get out, I want to remind you that I leave town on Wednesday and won't see you before I leave."

"I know."

He stepped out of the carriage, then assisted her, keeping his hand in hers as they walked up the stairs to find the door opened by Mr. Henry.

"You didn't need to wait up," Letitia said as she stepped into the entry.

"I couldn't sleep, my lady."

"Thank you for a lovely night," she directed at Greyson.

Greyson bowed. "You are most welcome, and thank you." His feet didn't move until the door closed, and he realized he still stood on her stoop. He made haste to his carriage, practically jumping inside, and knocked on the roof before the door was shut tight. He estimated he had the morning to sleep away before he needed to be back at Club Knight for a Black Knight meeting at one. When his carriage came to a stop outside Danbury Hall, he made quick work of entering the home, running up the stairs and hurrying to his chambers, where he stripped off his clothes. He forgot to take off his boots and hopped over to the bed, his breeches down to his knees, and fell onto his back to catch his breath. Exerting oneself this late in the night or early in the morning, however you looked at it, was a bad idea.

He pushed himself up to a sitting position and tugged off his boots in three tries. His breeches fell off easily now, and he climbed beneath the covers and instantly fell into a deep sleep.

After Greyson dropped Letitia off at home, she prepared for

bed, climbed beneath the counterpane, and fell asleep a few minutes later.

When she awoke in the morning after a dreamless sleep, she rolled onto her side and faced two windows. The sun was higher in the sky than it usually was when she woke. Then she remembered telling Jane not to wake her. According to the clock on the mantel, it was eleven. Letitia stretched her sore muscles and was surprised by the tenderness between her thighs. But she shouldn't be, after being with Greyson. Her lips curved into a dreamy smile, and she almost giggled. She, Marchioness Rutherford, had made love with Viscount Greyson, and it was amazing—more than she could ever have envisioned. And oh, the things he did to her!

When he entered her, she felt as though they were made for one another. Their bodies meshed and became one. When Rutherford had bedded her, she'd enjoyed it, yet she'd always felt unconnected to him. They remained separate, though joined. She had found pleasure with her husband, but nothing compared to what transcended between her and Greyson. They tumbled off the precipice as one, soared through the universe, and returned as one, stronger and more in tune with each other than before. As she fell asleep in his arms, she felt treasured. And when he called her *my love*, she almost melted at his feet.

Realizing she needed to get up and start her day, even though she wanted to stay in bed and dream about Greyson, she threw off the covers, padded behind the screen to attend to her morning ritual, and rang the bell for Jane as she passed it. Then she entered her dressing room, washed up and wrapped herself in a robe, left the room to find Jane opening the curtains.

"Good morning, my lady," Jane said. "Would you care to dress before breakfast? I ordered a tray brought up to the family drawing room."

"Yes, a simple day dress will be fine. I'm not planning on going out."

"Yes, my lady." Jane entered the dressing room and returned

holding a green dress.

After Jane helped her into her clothes, brushed and styled her hair into a simple braid, she dismissed her. "Thank you, Jane. That will be all."

"Yes, my lady."

Letitia left her chambers right after Jane. But unlike Jane, who went down the stairs, she went down the hall to the family drawing room. A fire was blazing, taking the chill out of the relatively small, cozy sitting room. Her breakfast tray had already arrived. She sat on her favorite dark-pink-and-cream-flowered settee and poured tea into a cream china cup with a saucer with the initial *R* in gold. She sweetened it with sugar and added a splash of milk. Leaning against the back of the settee, she closed her eyes and sipped her warm tea. Just the temperature she liked. With her eyes still closed, she envisioned being naked in bed with Greyson again—something she wished to happen very soon.

CHAPTER FOURTEEN

G REYSON LAY ON his back, awake long before Dalton entered the room through the dressing room door and threw open the curtains, letting in the sunshine. He swung his arm up and covered his eyes, which didn't enjoy the sudden brightness of the room.

"Good morning, my lord," Dalton said as he went back into the dressing room and returned carrying a breakfast tray. The strong aroma of coffee made him smile as he inhaled his favorite morning scent. He placed the tray by his favorite overstuffed chair, facing the hearth, where the embers had long since died.

No need for a fire this morning, with the sun's rays filtering in through the windows. Tossing off his covers, he swung his legs over the edge of the bed and sat up, clearing his throat. "Please have Whisky brought around at half twelve."

"Yes, my lord."

Greyson stood, picked up his buckskin breeches from last night, and stepped into them. He moved to his favorite comfortable chair and sank into it, picked up his coffee with a dash of sugar, took a sip, and relaxed back with a moan. "That tastes good."

"I'm glad. Would you like me to lay out your riding clothes?"

"Please."

"There is hot water and clean linens for washing. Is there

anything else I can do for you, my lord?"

"One thing, Dalton. Send a note to Heartstone's Hothouse and have two dozen red roses delivered to Lady Rutherford."

"Right away, my lord."

When the door closed behind Dalton, Greyson savored his coffee, picturing Letitia's face as she found her pleasure. The soft moans escaping her lips, the wonder in her soft blue eyes. The vibration of her body as her legs wrapped around his hips. Magical. They'd experienced magic together.

His hand pressed against the bulge in his breeches, and he decided a change of subject was in order if he was to prepare for his upcoming meeting. Once he finished his coffee, he picked up his breakfast plate of poached eggs on toast and sausage. He devoured the food. He returned the empty plate to the tray, stood, raised his arms over his head, and stretched his tight muscles to prepare for a long day with many more to come, given his assignment to Bristol. He prayed all would go well and that no one would be hurt. He often wondered if Prinny had any idea how hard it was to keep the peace. He pitted the Black Knights against his seasoned Dragoons, yeomanry, or infantry soldiers. Not to mention the local militias, who inevitably showed up trying to keep their towns safe. Greyson didn't understand why the Prince Regent didn't tell all of them to stand down and let the Black Knights take control. He supposed it must be because the Black Knights didn't exist, and he wanted to keep it that way.

And he hated leaving town now that he was courting Letitia most seriously. He felt as if he were deserting her again. Knowing there was nothing he could do about it, he washed up and dressed in his riding clothes. He tied his own cravat in a simple knot and tugged on his boots. He would be lost without Dalton, but he preferred to dress himself when he could.

Making his way down to the entry hall, he greeted his butler. "Good afternoon, Henderson."

"Good afternoon, my lord. Whisky is waiting for you."

"Lord Warren is due at three today. If I'm late, have him wait in the drawing room."

"Yes, my lord."

Greyson enjoyed the ride on Whisky to Club Knight, but what he and his horse really needed was wide-open space to stretch their legs. That would have to wait. He wasn't taking Whisky to Bristol. He was taking Thorne. Thorne had better stamina for the long trek to Bristol. Hopefully, they would cover fifty miles a day, with stops every ten miles or so for feed, water, and rest for the horse. Thorne was the better horse for this.

He arrived at Club Knight with several other Black Knights and handed his reins to one of several young stableboys, who would take Whisky to the mews. The four men made their way to the back door, where Greyson knocked the secret knock. The door opened, and they filed in one by one, then down the cellar stairs into the secret room, where, as usual, eight chairs sat in a circle. Four were vacant, but not for long.

"Thank you for coming," Knight said, handing out brandy glasses. As far back as he could remember, they had opened every meeting with a glass of brandy. Knight was a superstitious fellow. Most sailors were. He had also learned that from Knight.

"Does everyone know their jobs for tomorrow?"

Seven yeses ricocheted through the small room.

"I'm still awaiting intelligence from our spies on the ground in Derbyshire, Nottingham, and Bristol. With any luck, it will all be for nothing, just rumors of more unrest. However, the closer we get to November, when the leaders of the Pentrich Rebellion are due to be executed, the more unrest we may see."

The Black Knights dispersed to prepare for their assignments. Greyson and Cooke were to meet at Club Knight an hour after dawn the following morning.

Greyson made it back home with ten minutes to spare before Warren was due to arrive. He sat at the desk in his father's study, sipping brandy to settle his nerves, not about the upcoming conversation and negotiations with Warren, but about Letitia. They hadn't had a chance for a proper goodbye when he'd dropped her off, not with Mr. Henry staring warily at him from his perch inside the entry. He hoped the flowers made up for the hasty way he'd left that morning. Perhaps he should send a note as well.

With a trembling hand, he raised the glass to his mouth and drained every last drop. He wanted another but didn't think it wise, since he was already feeling the effects of the two glasses he'd had at the Black Knights' meeting.

Leaning his elbows on the desk, he reflected that he should start thinking of the desk as his. His father would likely never sit at it again. He rested his head in his hands and exhaled, trying to purge his worries about Letitia and his father before Warren arrived.

A footman entered the study and announced, "Lord Warren to see you, my lord."

"Thank you. Please close the door on your way out."

"Yes, my lord."

"Warren," Greyson motioned to a chair. "Have a seat. Since we both know why you are here, let's get on with it." He opened the middle drawer, pulled out Aurora's marriage contract, and slid it across the smooth surface of the mahogany desk.

"Thank you for seeing me," Warren said as he picked up the sheet of paper. Greyson watched as he meticulously read every detail. He would be disappointed if the man didn't. This was a binding contract that would affect the rest of the man's life and his sister's as well.

"May I use your pen to change a few things?"

"Yes, of course." Greyson set the inkwell and quill within reach of Warren, watching his every move. When Warren was done, he pushed the contract back to him.

"Please look over the changes and let me know if you are agreeable," Warren said, looking a little flushed.

Greyson glanced down at the contract and noticed a few changes. So Warren's wealth wasn't as large as he had thought. Still, he had plenty to care for Aurora and their children from the income drawn from his estates. "On behalf of my father, I accept the changes and will have a new contract drawn up tomorrow for you to sign."

"No need to have it redrawn since I know your father is ill and he has already signed this one. I initialed all the changes, so it should be legal and binding." Warren pulled the contract toward him, dipped the quill in the inkwell, and signed his name.

"Wonderful," Greyson said. "All you need to do is propose to Aurora."

He cleared his throat and tugged at his cravat. "We have discussed marriage, and I plan to propose after this Friday's indoor garden party hosted by the Earl and Countess of Barstow."

"Perfect. Aurora does love a garden party theme." He frowned. Had he heard back from his cousin yet? Who would chaperone his sisters at the garden party if she were unavailable? Just another thing to worry about. How he hated leaving his duties and letting the people he cared about most down. But he loved his work with the Black Knights as well. Managing all his responsibilities and obligations was causing him great strain.

Warren stood and bowed. "Thank you again for seeing me, Lord Greyson."

"Aurora will make you a fine wife. She is kind and gentle, with a big heart. I know you will be a good, kind, and faithful husband in return."

The man looked ready to lose his lunch. "Y-y-yes," he stammered. "I will."

"Good day to you then."

"Good day."

Greyson chuckled to himself as Warren left. He hadn't meant to make him uncomfortable when he called him "good, kind, and faithful husband." The earl needed to relax. However, he meant every word. He hadn't said that to Hunter, but Hunter knew him, and he knew Hunter, so those words didn't need to be spoken. Hunter knew how he felt about marriage and what was expected of anyone entering the sanctity of it with his sisters. It was no less than what he expected from his own marriage. His hand found its way to his chest and rubbed at the ache radiating from his heart. He so wished his wife were Letitia.

Even though he planned to propose, he wanted to wait. His sisters deserved their time as they prepared for their wedding day, and he didn't want to take it away from them. If the banns were posted this Sunday, they could have their double wedding in three weeks. Anastasia expressed wanting the nuptials to happen quickly. Would that be what Aurora wanted as well?

He leaned back in his chair and exhaled loudly. He was so exhausted he could have fallen asleep right there. Instead, he left the study, climbed the stairs, and knocked on the door to his parents' chambers. "Come in," his mother's voice answered.

Slowly, he opened the door and stepped into the room. To his great surprise, he found both his mother and father seated in overstuffed chairs, facing a blaze in the hearth. His father's feet rested on a footstool, and a heavy blanket was draped across his lap. He still looked thin, fragile, and pale as a sheet. His mother, draped in a shawl, looked less tired, with color in her cheeks. Seeing them like that, he felt his emotions explode. He wiped the tears from his eyes and felt his chest ease. He nodded his head to the nurse as she tidied the bed.

"Doesn't your father look well?" his mother said.

"Yes. It's good to see you out of that bed, Father."

"It feels good, too. It took two footmen to carry me over here, but it was worth it."

"You've lost weight. I hardly think it was a strain on the footman carrying you," Greyson said.

His father laughed, but it came out as a snort. "I am rather thin. Tell me, son, what have your sisters been up to?"

"Hunter proposed to Anastasia, and Lord Warren is proposing to Aurora in a few days."

"Proposing? Proposing what? They are only fourteen. They are too young for marriage. And Lord Warren is as old as I am. Perhaps when she comes of age, she can marry his son."

Greyson and his mother shared a sad look. He might look better today, but his mind wasn't. His mother, once the belle of the debutantes with many suitors vying for her hand, looked ten years older than her forty-seven years. His father looked in his seventies, not fifty-five, with thinning gray hair and creases from weight loss. Greyson pulled a small chair from across the room, put it beside his father, and sat down. He sat for a spell just enjoying the silent company of his parents, as he did often, knowing time with them was limited. He closed his eyes and when he opened them again, he swore he'd dozed off. He stood and said, "Can I help do anything before I leave?"

His father didn't say anything, but his mother said, "We're fine, Greyson."

He bowed and left, shaking his head. He had no idea why he'd bowed to his parents. Only that he wanted to show his respect, and bowing seemed the only way. He made his way down the hall and past the staircase to the hall where his chambers and his sisters were. His eyes fixed on the door to his rooms, willing his body to move faster and faster. He was desperate for some time alone, where he could let his feelings come to the surface. Where he could relax from being Lord Greyson, head of his sick father's household and chaperone to his twin sisters. His shoulders were as tired as the rest of his body.

Finally, he was inside his chambers, behind a closed door. He tugged off his riding jacket, waistcoat, and his cravat as though they offended him, then left them lying on the floor. He sat in a chair near the fireplace, tugged off his boots, and sent them flying against the wall with a thud. Bending at the waist, free from the constraints of most of his clothing, he tried to take small breaths as his chest tightened, making it hard to get in the air he needed. Closing his eyes, he willed his body to relax rather than fight as he tried to draw air into his lungs.

He'd learned long ago that panicking when he couldn't breathe only made everything worse. He repeated the words, "I'm fine. I can breathe. My chest is tight, but I can breathe."

Thankfully, these episodes didn't happen often. He kept them secret. Even his family didn't know. If he could, he would go to his grave without anyone finding out.

"Ahhh," he inhaled deeply and exhaled, feeling his chest rise and fall as his lungs filled with air. He leaned back in the chair, his eyes still closed, focusing on his even breathing. His chest was no longer constricted, and his muscles relaxed. His lungs thanked him for the air passing through them. The sounds of the room, the wood crackling in the hearth, and the clock ticking on the wall began to fade as Greyson fell into a deep sleep.

THE DAY DRAGGED on for Letitia. After taking her breakfast in the family drawing room, she spent several hours with Simon until it was his naptime. She found herself back in the drawing room, taking afternoon tea alone. She had skipped luncheon because she'd taken breakfast so late.

The beautiful, fragrant red roses Greyson had delivered did brighten her mood for a spell. However, the thought of not seeing him for possibly a fortnight or longer pushed her bright mood aside, making room for self-pity. That was what she was feeling now. Brooding wasn't good. She couldn't rely on Greyson to be with her at all times. She needed to be happy and enjoy her life without him. That way, when they *were* together, her happiness and enjoyment would spill over into their time together.

During her marriage to Rutherford, she'd spent many hours each day alone. During her year of mourning, she had Simon and Clarice, yet she still spent much time alone. What had she done to fill her time? Whatever it was, she needed to do it now. She couldn't sit and agonize over him as she was. Indeed, she remembered what she'd done. She had done needlepoint and embroidery for which she had a cedar chest full of completed works. Perhaps she should take up watercolors. No. She was a terrible painter. Play the pianoforte? After the other night when Aurora and Warren played, and she sat with Greyson, she feared in this state of mind it would only remind her of him, taking the enjoyment she used to get from playing out of her.

She leaned back against the settee and sighed. If she truly put her mind to it, she would come up with something. She had to. Needed to.

She must have dozed off because when she opened her eyes, the sun was dipping low. Tonight she would have a supper tray sent to her room, take a nice hot bath, and perhaps read. Perfect. That was what she would do. And that's what she did. But now she sat in bed, propped up on pillows, a new gothic novel in her hands. It was a good book, but she couldn't concentrate. She couldn't get Greyson out of her mind. How come no one told her that being in love, truly in love, was all-consuming and painful?

After a while, she gave up trying to make sense of the words on the page. She closed the book, set it on the table beside her bed, snuffed out the candle, and lowered the pillows until she lay on her back. Staring up at the ceiling, she couldn't see it in the dark. It was a long time before her mind and body relaxed enough to let her fall asleep.

CHAPTER FIFTEEN

DAWN CAME FAST. When Dalton entered the room and declared it was time to rise, he wanted to pout like a young lad and tell him, no, he was staying in bed.

Dalton had packed his bag the night before. Since he was traveling on horseback, he could only bring what he needed most. He drank from a steaming cup of coffee and shoveled forkfuls of eggs from a plate Dalton held out while hurrying down the stairs. "Everyone thinks I'm traveling to Danbury Estate. If you need me, I left the inn's information in my middle desk drawer. Knight is remaining behind, and you can reach out to him if, God forbid, you have an emergency."

"Yes, my lord."

Another forkful of eggs, and by then they were in the entry hall. Greyson handed Henderson his empty cup. Oh, he almost forgot. "Henderson, please tell the housekeeper to prepare a room for my cousin, Lady Colbourn. She will arrive sometime today to chaperone my sisters." Thankfully, he had received a reply from his cousin just before retiring last evening.

"Yes, my lord."

Henderson opened the door. Greyson descended the outside granite stairs and mounted Thorne. They made good traveling companions. He flicked the reins, and off they went to Club Knight, where Cooke waited for him. "Are we ready?" he asked when he arrived, pulling on the reins to make Thorne stop.

"Yes," Cooke replied from atop his mount.

They rode at a fast pace, stopping every ten miles or so to tend to the horses and let them rest. Their first evening stop was a coaching inn called Houndstooth Hall, where they would spend the night. From the name, Greyson presumed the proprietors were Scottish.

Since it was the dinner hour, the taproom was filled with weary travelers. Knight was most proficient and had sent letters ahead requesting rooms for their travels. Greyson approached the middle-aged man behind the bar. "Are you the proprietor?"

The man paused while pouring an ale. "Aye. How may I help you?"

"I have two rooms booked under my name, Mr. James Barton."

The man excused himself, entered a back room, and returned with a middle-aged, plump woman who looked frazzled as she wiped her hands on her soiled apron and looked at Greyson with tired, dark eyes. The proprietor asked, "Will you be wanting a bit of scran before you go upstairs?"

"Yes."

"Gentry room, 'tis there." He pointed to a doorway across the room. "The missus will bring you scran."

"Thank you," Greyson said. He spoke briefly with Cooke, and they entered the private taproom, carrying their leather saddlebags. A well-dressed couple with two small children sat at a round table before the small fireplace, which looked newly lit. They settled at the only other table in the small room, placing their saddlebags beneath it.

"We made good time today," Cooke said just as the proprietor's wife, balancing a tray on her hip, approached. She set two tankards of ale, two bowls of stew with spoons, and two pieces of crusty bread on the wobbly table.

"Thank you, ma'am," Cooke said.

"Thank you," Greyson said as she hurried off. He stared at

what smelled and looked like rabbit stew. His stomach growled, reminding him that since his hurried breakfast, he'd only eaten dried beef and an apple while riding, and he was famished. He picked up the spoon and dug in. It wasn't until he'd soaked up the last of the broth with his bread and finished it that he said anything to Cooke. "That was good." He picked up his ale and drained the tankard.

Cooke did the same after finishing eating. "Yes. It shut my stomach up. It wouldn't stop growling the last mile we traveled."

Greyson chuckled as he wiped his mouth with his hand. "I hope the missus comes back with our room keys. I don't know about you, but my body's sore from riding all day, and dawn will be here before we know it."

She appeared several minutes later and said, "Follow me."

Greyson and Cooke picked up their saddlebags and followed the lady up the narrow wooden staircase, which was surprisingly solid, to the second floor and the first doors on the right and left. They always requested rooms closest to the stairs in case they had to get out in a hurry. Not something he anticipated tonight.

The owner's wife unlocked and opened Cooke's door on the left, then his on the right. "There is water and linens to wash. Clean bedding and logs for the hearth. All paid in advance."

"Thank you," Greyson said, and she went back down the stairs. "She seems well-spoken and English. I wonder how she ended up here."

Cooke snorted. "I'm too exhausted to care. See you at dawn."

Greyson entered his room, shut and locked the door. First, he started the fire in the hearth to take the chill out of the room. He washed up with cold water, a tiny clump of rough soap, and a small, clean cloth. He stripped off his clothes and fell into bed. His muscles ached, and he couldn't wait to sleep, which came immediately.

The next day of travel was rough, with wind-driven rain soaking them to the skin. The horses struggled on the muddy roads. When the Great Grouse Inn came into sight, Greyson wanted to weep with joy. The first thing he did when he entered his room was to set a fire in the hearth, strip off his muddy, wet clothing, and lay them near the hearth, hoping they would dry overnight. Dressed in dry, clean clothes, he met Cooke downstairs in the small parlor for lords and gentry.

Tonight's dinner was venison stew with a roll and ale. They both had seconds of the stew and ale. Greyson enjoyed the blaze from the stone hearth as it warmed his chilly bones. "Today was brutal. I gave the stableboy extra coin to clean and brush down our horses and to provide additional feed and apples for a treat."

"Good thinking," Cooke said, holding his hands out toward the fire. "My mind was frozen along with my body."

Since they were the only ones in the private parlor, Greyson shut the door and said, "We have roughly twenty miles to go tomorrow before we arrive at the Pheasant Lane Inn in Bristol. I have several names of mine owners and overmen who work for them. Hopefully, they are agreeable to meeting and discussing whether there's any contention among their workers that could prompt a rebellion. And if there's talk of unrest, perhaps we can help them be heard peacefully." He paused and took a drink of his ale. "Sometimes I wonder why Prinny formed the Black Knights."

"I think we all do at times. The idea of the Black Knights is brilliant in theory. I believe Prinny loves the secrecy surrounding us. But wouldn't it be easier and more productive to have his Dragoons do what we're doing? Instead of having them work against us."

"Agreed. Something we should address with Knight upon our return." Greyson drained the last of his ale and stood. "Time to retire. I'll see you at dawn."

"Dawn," Cooke mumbled.

Before Greyson climbed into bed, he poked the logs in the hearth, checked his still-damp clothes, and undressed. Then he fell into bed and into a dead man's slumber.

Dawn came quickly, and they reached the Pheasant Lane Inn by ten in the morning Greyson already dreaded the return trip.

Except he couldn't wait to return and see Letitia. He'd thought about her almost nonstop during the quiet ride.

The proprietor expected them and escorted them to their rooms. The first thing Greyson did was strip down and wash up with soap and water as best he could to get the stench of the road and Thorne out of his hair and off his skin. He buffed his skin dry with a large linen cloth and dressed in the only other pair of clean clothes he brought, dark-gray riding clothes. He left his dirty clothing along with several coins on a wooden chair for the maid who cleaned the rooms to launder.

Knight, forever the planner, must have sent letters to the three owners who controlled all the mines in Bristol and to their overmen. Six notes awaited him at the inn. All six men agreed to meet tonight at eight in the private salon at the inn.

Greyson was relieved. He thought he and Cooke would be riding all over Bristol today, traveling from mine to mine, hunting down the six men. Now they could have a fine luncheon.

Eight came quickly. Greyson had ordered ale and refreshments for the men and expected them at any time. They trickled in two by two until everyone sat at a long banquet table in the center of the room. Greyson had given extra coin to the inn owner to have the room to themselves.

"Welcome. I'm James Barton, and my associate is Stuart Brown. We've come because we're interested in purchasing mines in Somerset and have a few questions. I hope you, good gentlemen, will indulge us with our many questions as we research the profitability of owning such mines."

The meeting lasted nearly two hours. Yes, the miners and owners were frustrated with the prices they received for their coal, but neither he nor Cooke sensed any planned rebellion forming. They would spend another day or so investigating before Greyson felt confident enough to return to London and report their findings to Knight. They needed to be absolutely certain that no rebellion was brewing in Bristol.

CHAPTER SIXTEEN

LETITIA COULDN'T BELIEVE it was already Friday. She had expected the past three days to drag on with Greyson gone. She spent most of them with Simon in the nursery and outside in the garden. They even took a carriage ride with his governess.

She almost wanted to stay home today, but she had the Barstow Garden Party to attend and looked forward to seeing Anastasia and Aurora. She had received notes from both Emmeline and Lilly stating they were fine but not up to attending. Indeed, they were probably tired from being with child. Letitia remembered well how tired she had been carrying Simon.

She was dressed in a pretty pale-yellow dress with a matching pelisse, wide-brimmed bonnet, and parasol. The hat and parasol were originally meant to protect her from the sun. Now they would protect her from the rain.

Barstow Estates lay on the outskirts of London and bordered the River Thames. It was unfortunate that the weather was so foul. Letitia knew everyone would make the best of it, though. When she left her townhouse, a footman held an umbrella over her head so she didn't need to open her parasol or figure out how to enter the carriage while maneuvering it.

When they arrived at the impressive estate, carriages lined the driveway, waiting for their passengers to disembark. It was a slower-than-normal process because of the weather, but eventually it was Letitia's turn. Her footman opened the door and, once again, held an umbrella over her. She pulled up her skirts and picked her way around the puddles to keep her half boots from getting wet. Normally, she would wear slippers or shoes, but not on a rainy day. She'd be stuck in soaking-wet shoes all day if she had.

When she entered the estate, she handed her hat, parasol, and pelisse to the butler. She greeted her host and hostess on the upstairs landing outside the ballroom, which Letitia could see was decorated like the outdoors. How exciting and festive.

"Lady Barstow," Letitia curtsied. "I'm pleased to be among your guests today."

"I hope you enjoy yourself, Lady Rutherford."

"I'm sure I will." She curtsied again. "Lord Barstow, I am pleased to see you again."

"And I you."

Before she entered the ballroom, she took a few deep breaths. Receiving lines terrified her. She was thankful they hadn't mentioned Graham. He and Lord Barstow went back to their Eton days. Their eldest daughter was in her second season, and they were, most likely, hosting this party to give her a boost. Their daughter, Lady Samantha, was charming once you got to know her, but her shyness made it difficult to do so. She wished her well and much success in finding a husband.

Having woolgathered, her nerves had settled enough for her to enter the crush already filling the ballroom. Standing off to the side, she glanced around the room, seeking out Anastasia and Aurora, or even Hunter or Lord Warren. After two loops around the room, she finally found the four of them sitting on a quilt on the floor, a large picnic basket between them. Her heart dropped. They didn't need her joining their little private party. Instead, she wandered around the room, looking for someone, anyone she recognized. Her heart rose at the sight of Lady Samantha sitting with a young lady she didn't know. Making her way to them, she hoped they wouldn't mind if she joined their picnic.

"Lady Samantha," Letitia said with a smile. "May I join you and your friend?"

"Yes, please," Lady Samantha said, relief evident on her face.

She sat on the soft quilt, her legs bent and off to one side. After she tucked in her skirts, convinced no ankle or, God forbid, a calf showed, she sighed and looked to the other occupant of the blanket. "Good afternoon, I'm Lady Rutherford, but please call me Letitia."

The stranger frowned, giving her the impression that she wasn't a friendly person.

"I'm Lady Rose Templeton." She raised her head just enough to stick her nose up and look down at her, confirming her unfriendly first impression. "My father is the Duke of Templeton."

Now Letitia understood the relief on Samantha's face. "How fortunate for you." She rearranged herself to face Samantha. "How are you? I haven't seen you since the Westport ball at the start of the Season."

"I am well. I twisted my ankle at a soirée and had to miss several weeks of socializing, but I'm all healed."

"Thank goodness. How painful it must have been."

"It was." She frowned. "Mother thought I was feigning, but I wasn't, honestly."

Letitia reached forward and touched her hand. "I know you weren't. Why would anyone feign such an injury? Not with all the exhilarating functions to attend."

"That's what I told Mother." She lowered her voice. "May I ask you a personal question I've always wondered about?"

"You may ask. I may answer or not." Oh dear, when someone wanted to ask a personal question, it was never a good sign from her experience.

"I understand you were married to Lord Rutherford, and he was my father's closest friend. Why did we never meet? Why did you never accompany him when he visited? I never believed him when he said you were sickly, especially when his cousin accompanied him. He didn't treat her as one would a cousin."

Letitia wanted to turn and look at Rose to see if she'd heard Samantha, but she chose not to. It wouldn't change the facts. Tears burned in her eyes, and she refused to shed them. Rutherford told people she was sickly? How could he? And to flaunt his mistress in public, passing her off as his cousin? His deception knew no bounds.

"The truth is," Letitia whispered, "I don't know."

Now it was Samantha's turn to comfort her by touching her hand. "I'm sorry. I heard from my mother that Viscount Greyson is courting you. Is it true?"

Heat kissed her cheeks. "Yes."

"Mother had hoped for a match between him and me last Season, but he wasn't interested." She exhaled. "I'm happy for you. You deserve to be happy."

Letitia leaned forward and murmured, "Is there a young gentleman who's caught your eye?"

By the blush staining her cheeks, she had her answer. Just not the who.

Samantha leaned forward, and they were very close. "There is. He sends me letters because, like me, he is shy. He is actually here today. I don't think Mother knows about the letters, but I could be wrong. It could be why he received an invitation for today."

"Do I know him?" Letitia asked.

"I don't think so," she said, shaking her head.

"If you trust me, whisper his name in my ear."

And she whispered his name. "Lord Bradley."

"Ahh." Letitia had never been formally introduced, but she recognized his name from *Debrett's* and remembered he was worth a good deal of money, owned several estates, and had a townhouse in Mayfair. She was shocked; she remembered all that. "Have you spoken in person?"

"Once, when we were introduced. After I twisted my ankle, he wrote me long letters. He writes beautiful poetry. He's sitting a few blankets over by himself. He has red hair and is wearing a blue jacket."

She found him. He was hard to miss. "He's sitting alone. Why don't we join him?" Letitia suggested. Samantha's cheeks were no longer pink, but stark white. "It was just an idea," she quickly added.

It was then that Letitia noticed Lady Rose was no longer sitting with them. She glanced around for her, which was hard while sitting down, since many guests were standing around. She didn't see Lady Rose, but she did see Lord Bradley, strolling very slowly toward them. His complexion was pale with freckles. If memory served her from *Debrett's*, he was twenty-five. However, he looked like a sixteen-year-old lad. She felt sorry for him. It must be hard to be taken seriously when one looked so young and was shy. "Don't look now, but he is almost upon us."

"Who?" Samantha asked, looking ready to cast up her accounts.

"Breathe. This is what you want. He is who you want."

"Excuse me," Lord Bradley said in a deep voice. Letitia was shocked that it came from him.

Samantha turned her head and looked up at him. "Lord Bradley."

He bowed stiffly. "Lady Samantha, would you care to take a stroll around the room?" He held out his hands.

Perhaps he wasn't as shy as Samantha believed.

Without even turning around to say goodbye to her, Samantha said, "Yes." She took both his hands as he helped her rise to her feet. She turned back as she walked arm in arm with Lord Bradley, looked right at her, and smiled.

A few moments later, she heard, "I didn't believe Aurora when she said you were here. And you're sitting alone." Anastasia's voice came from above.

"Please help me."

Anastasia reached down. Letitia joined hands with hers and was tugged up to stand on legs that had turned numb from her awkward position on the quilt.

"Can you walk with me?" she asked. "My legs are asleep."

"Where? This place is a crush."

"We'll weave around the blankets, hoping not to step on anyone's fingers or toes," Letitia giggled.

"Are you well?" Anastasia asked, frowning. "Have you had too much wine?"

"Goodness me, I've had nothing. Is there any wine?"

"Perhaps Aurora and I should take you home. You don't seem yourself."

"Forgive me," Letitia said. "I'm in a strange mood today." Seeing the Earl and Countess of Barstow was disconcerting. Then her conversation with Samantha about Rutherford added another layer. She'd say her mood was odd. "I want you and Aurora to stay and enjoy the indoor picnic, but I'm going to take my leave. I'm no longer in the mood for socializing."

"What happened?" Anastasia asked, looking concerned.

"Perhaps another time. Go back to Hunter and give my best to him, Aurora, and Warren."

"Fine," she huffed. "But we'll miss you."

"I'll see you soon."

"Do you miss my brother?"

As if she didn't have enough emotional unrest to handle, Anastasia had to bring up Greyson. Tears threatened, and she blinked them away. "Yes. Now I must go." She couldn't hear what Anastasia was saying because she needed to get out of there fast and still needed to thank the hosts. Fortunately, they were by the entrance to the ballroom, so she stopped briefly to pay her respects. Down the stairs she went. She retrieved her things from the butler and requested her coach, for which the butler sent a footman out into the rain.

She felt bad for the footman. He always had to go out in bad weather. And now he had to find her driver.

It was a long five minutes before the footman returned, with rain dripping from his clothing. "Your carriage outside, my lady."

"Thank you."

The butler opened the door, and her footman was there with an umbrella ready. Such efficiency. She hurried down the stairs, her footman keeping pace. He opened the door and helped her inside without a single raindrop landing on her head. Inside, as the carriage wheels rolled, she finally let the tears fall. She hated feeling sorry for herself, but after hearing Samantha say she was sickly and that Rutherford had brought his cousin—or rather his mistress—in her place, how could she not? With the rain and the roads, she had perhaps an hour's drive before she arrived home. An hour to cry and feel sorry for herself. After that, it was chin up and no more self-pity.

Half of the tears she shed were for herself and what Rutherford had done to her, and the other half were for Greyson and how much she missed him. He'd been gone three days. He'd said he'd be gone, most likely, a fortnight. Suddenly chilled, she reached for the blanket beside her, covered her lap, and closed her eyes. Perhaps a nap would make her feel better.

The carriage stopped, and the door opening startled her awake. She stared at the footman's gloved hand.

"My lady. We have returned home."

"Thank you." She placed her hand in his and stepped out of the carriage. The first thing she noticed was that the rain had stopped. She entered the townhouse and handed Mr. Henry her hat and parasol. "When did it stop raining?"

"About an hour ago, my lady," he replied.

"I'm going to my chambers. Please have Cook send up a tea tray."

"Yes, my lady."

The nap she took in the carriage had left her sleepy and foggy, and she looked forward to relaxing for the rest of the day. Jane was waiting for her in her chambers. "I want my night rail and robe. I don't plan to leave my chambers again today."

"Yes, my lady." Jane disappeared into the dressing room and returned a moment later with her night clothes. Letitia stood still as Jane removed her picnic outfit and dressed her in her night-clothes.

"Cook is bringing up a tea tray. Will you set it on the table beside the chaise longue? I'll undo my hair."

"Yes, my lady."

Letitia sat at her dressing table and pulled out all the pins. She ran her hands through her tresses, searching for any missed pins. She found two. Picking up her brush, she ran it through her hair to remove any tangles, then went to her chaise longue and rested on it.

"Would you like a blanket and a pillow, my lady?" Jane asked.

"Yes, Jane. That would be nice."

Jane placed a pillow behind her back, tucked her in with a soft blanket, then hurried to answer the knock at the door. She returned with a tea tray and put it down on the table next to the chaise longue. "Thank you, Jane. You may go."

"Yes, my lady."

Once Jane left, Letitia decided she was too tired to do anything but snuggle down and sleep. And sleep she did. In fact, she spent the next two days in bed with an upset stomach and cramps, a reminder that her courses were due.

CHAPTER SEVENTEEN

GREYSON AND COOKE stayed another full day after the meeting with the mine owners to be certain all was well. They visited several pubs and eavesdropped on conversations among the locals and miners. Nothing seemed out of the ordinary. Just the usual complaining, with nothing about any planned gatherings or rebellions.

Feeling confident they could return to London, they left at dawn the next morning. After two and a half days of travel, a road-weary Greyson returned to Danbury Hall eight days after he had left. He almost went straight to Club Knight, but decided a note to Knight with a quick summary of what they had found would suffice until tomorrow. Right now, he needed a bath, a good meal, and sleep, in that order.

He left an equally road-weary Thorne by the roadside, then ascended the stairs and entered through the door as Henderson opened it. "Welcome home, my lord."

"Thank you, Henderson. Please have someone take care of Thorne. He needs extra feed and a thorough brushing."

"Yes, my lord. Will there be anything else?"

"Have a footman bring my saddlebags to my chambers." He dumped the bags at Henderson's feet, too tired to lug them up the stairs. "I need a bath."

His butler made a face. Obviously, he agreed. "Coming right

up, my lord."

Stinking and not fit for company, family or not, he sneaked up to his chambers, hoping not to run into any of his family members until he'd cleaned up.

Dalton greeted him when he entered his chambers. "Welcome home, my lord."

"Thank you, Dalton. It's good to be home."

"Your bath should be ready soon. In the meantime, let's get you out of those clothes," Dalton said, wrinkling his nose.

"Yes."

While he was undressing, four footmen entered carrying a large metal tub which they placed in front of the hearth. They promptly left and returned carrying buckets of hot water which they dumped into the tub. After they left, Greyson sank into the hot water and sighed. "You may leave, Dalton. Come back in half an hour."

"Yes, my lord."

He didn't move for a good ten minutes as the heat of the water soothed his road-worn body, one muscle at a time. He sat up and washed his body and hair, dunking his head several times to rinse the soap. It wasn't until the water cooled that he finally stepped out of the tub and dried off, throwing on a blue banyan Dalton had laid out on a wooden chair. He raised his arms and stretched from side to side, reveling in the feeling of being human again. He may be all of twenty-eight, but riding horseback for two and a half straight days, then doing it again several days later, was brutal on one's body.

When Dalton returned, he dressed in casual clothes and went down the stairs into the drawing room, where he could hear voices from the hall. Before he could speak, his cousin, Charity, said, "Greyson, you have returned!"

"Brother," Anastasia and Aurora said together. "Welcome home."

"Thank you. It's good to be home." He sat beside Charity on one of the two settees; the twins were seated together on the other one.

"How did you get to Danbury Estate and back so quickly?" Charity asked.

He hadn't expected to be questioned about his timing. Nobody ever had before. Leave it to Charity, his ever-inquisitive cousin. "Two days' ride back and forth. Four days seeing to things. Our estate manager does a great job overseeing everything. I even visited all the tenant farmers."

"Did you perhaps," Anastasia fluttered her lashes, "hurry home because you missed Lady Rutherford?"

Aurora jumped up. "Warren proposed."

He stood and hugged her. "Congratulations. I'm so happy for you." He looked over Aurora's head at his other sister. "For both of you. Does this mean a double wedding is in the near future?"

Aurora sat back down. "Yes, as soon as the banns are posted. You never requested that they be posted at St. George's Hanover Square, so we have to wait another week. Although Anastasia's were read."

"Forgive me. It wasn't that I forgot—I left before Warren proposed. What if he hadn't, and the banns were read on Sunday? Another sennight gives you two more time to prepare."

He couldn't make out Anastasia's mumbling, but he could guess what she thought about that. Needing a change of subject, he asked, "Charity, can you stay for a visit, or do you have to return home?"

"Oh, no. I can stay for a few more days. Colbourn is away doing whatever it is he does."

"Good. Let's invite Lady Rutherford, Hunter, and Warren for a celebratory dinner tomorrow night. Charity, can you take care of the menu with the cook?"

"Yes. It will be my pleasure."

"Sisters, will you send invitations to your intendeds? I will invite Letitia."

"We will do it right now," Aurora said. "Come, Anastasia."

The twins hurried from the room, leaving Greyson with

Charity. He should have thought his plan through more carefully. It wasn't that he didn't enjoy spending time with her, it was just that his cousin was the most intuitive person he'd ever met, and she no doubt picked up on his emotions, both about his recent assignment and about Letitia.

"So," Charity said, her voice smooth and deceiving, "tell me about Lady Rutherford. I didn't get a chance to meet her at the Barstow picnic; she left before I had the opportunity. Although I must say, she seems lovely and is quite beautiful."

"She is. Lovely and beautiful, that is."

"I remember Lord Rutherford. By all appearances, he was an affable and loyal gentleman. That is, until you learned he would leave his sickly young wife at home and escort his fake cousin, whom everyone knew was his mistress and the mother of his bastards, to social events in her place."

"Sickly?" Had he heard Charity correctly? Letitia wasn't sickly. "I had no idea he used such an excuse. Letitia never came right out and said Rutherford had a mistress, but I knew he lied and hid things from her. Not to mention the fact that I heard all the rumors. That does explain why she came right out and asked if I had a mistress."

Charity gasped, then giggled. "I already love her."

"As do I," he thought, unable to believe he'd just told his cousin he loved Letitia. He did, but he'd yet to tell Letitia. How strange it seemed to have confided in his cousin that he loved Letitia before he'd even told her. "You will love her even more when you actually get to spend time with her tomorrow night."

"I'm looking forward to it."

"If that's settled, I'm going to spend the rest of the day and the night sleeping. It was a grueling trip."

Charity hmphed, "One day I will get to the bottom of your disappearances."

"I wish you good luck." As he left the room, he schooled himself for saying what sounded like a dare. Never dare Charity. She'd make it her mission to find the answers. He hurried up the stairs, briefly checked on his parents, who were both resting. He spoke briefly with their nurse, then entered his chambers, stripped off his clothes, dove beneath the covers, and fell asleep with visions of Letitia dancing in his arms.

⟫⟫⟫✦⟪⟪⟪

AFTER SPENDING THE past two days in bed, Letitia woke on the third day much improved. Jane entered the room, her eyes widening when she found her standing at the window, looking out at the partly cloudy sky.

"My lady," Jane exclaimed, "it's so good to see you up and feeling well."

Turning around, Letitia smiled. "I do feel better, and I'm famished."

"That's more good news. I'll be right back." She left the room, leaving the door open, and came back in with her breakfast tray. "I left it out in the hall in case you weren't hungry."

"Thank you. Put it near the chaise longue."

"Oh, my lady, I almost forgot." She set the tray down and handed her a note. "This just arrived for you."

One glance at the wax seal sent her heart skipping. Greyson. It was from Greyson. Did that mean . . . ? She broke the seal and unfolded the missive.

My Dearest Letitia,

I have returned from Danbury Estate and would like to invite you to dinner tomorrow night at eight. A celebration is in order for both of my sisters' engagements. Unless I hear otherwise, my carriage will pick you up at a quarter to eight.

Greyson

Now she felt even better, knowing that Greyson had returned to London. Oh dear, what to wear? "Jane, I'm attending a small dinner party at Danbury Hall tomorrow night. What shall I wear?

I also need two engagement gifts. We need to go to Bond Street."

"Yes, my lady. But first, you must eat to have the strength to shop. Then we must dress and fix your hair."

"Yes, of course."

Two hours later, the Rutherford carriage pulled up in front of Madam Serena's. Her footman opened the door and assisted her and Jane in alighting. Letitia insisted that Jane come along to help her pick out engagement gifts for her friends. But first, she hoped her modiste had a new creation she could impress Greyson with tomorrow night.

The bells on the door rang as they entered the shop. At this early hour, there were hardly any people inside, which was to her advantage.

Madam Serena stepped through the curtain separating the front of the shop from the fitting and stock room. "Good morning to you, Lady Rutherford," she said cheerily. "May I help you find something?"

"Actually, I'm attending a dinner party tomorrow night and was hoping you might have an evening dress."

"Ah, you know me too well. I always have a few beautiful things prepared for just such an emergency." She swung the curtain back. "Come with me. Your maid can wait out here."

"I won't be long, Jane."

"Yes, my lady."

Before Letitia had a chance to glance around the fitting room, Madam Serena brought over a forest-green silk dress trimmed with gold lace and ribbon that looked stunning. Letitia could imagine how it would look on her.

"I just finished this last night. It may need a few minor alterations, but I can have it delivered in plenty of time for tomorrow night. That is, if you like it?"

"Like it? I love it."

"Then let's get you undressed and into my latest creation."

"It is perfect," Letitia said as she turned from side to side, admiring the dress. At first glance, one might think it was a simple silk creation with a wide square neckline, and short sleeves. But when the light hit the dress, the gold thread woven into the green silk made it sparkle and shine.

As it turned out, it only needed a little tuck here and there and a hem. Not only did she take the stunning dress, but she also bought the matching cloak. She joined Jane in the storefront. "I found the perfect evening dress."

"Wonderful, my lady. Shall we look for those engagement gifts?"

"Yes. I have the perfect shop in mind. I've never been there, but I hear it has a wide variety of goods." Her carriage was parked right outside the dress shop. "Soho Bazaar," she told the driver.

Two hours later, they arrived back at Rutherford Manor. Letitia was too excited about the gifts she had bought to have them delivered, so she took them home in the carriage. She purchased a lovely mother-of-pearl sewing box with needles and thread for Aurora, whom she knew loved all sorts of threadwork. For Anastasia, she bought a mahogany lap desk and wildflower stationery. For Hunter and Warren, she picked out heavy crystal brandy decanters with four matching glasses.

Now all she had to do was stay busy until tomorrow night, which she managed to do.

CHAPTER EIGHTEEN

O
N THE DAY of the dinner party, Greyson and Cooke met at Club Knight and informed Knight of what they had learned. He had yet to hear from anyone else about their assignments.

For the rest of the day, he stayed busy with estate business and visited with his parents. His father was more lucid than on some days, which eased his sore heart. Then he looked at his mother, pale, thin, weary, and sad, and his heart ached again. There was no denying they were both dying. Would they get to see their daughters married?

Dalton helped him dress for dinner in his black evening wear. As he descended the stairs, voices resonated from the drawing room. He'd come down late on purpose, hoping Letitia would already be present. He listened outside the open doors without looking in, and sure enough, he heard her melodious voice, and awareness spread throughout his body. Ever since they'd made love, he'd dreamed of doing it again. Was tonight the night? His body was hoping.

He entered the room and went straight to her. He had eyes only for her. Everyone else in the room disappeared. Her deep-green loveliness stole the very air from his lungs. Her hair was a curled masterpiece, and her eyes held more green than blue. When he stood before her, their eyes met, and he felt her essence deep within his soul. He took her hand, bowed over it, and brushed his lips across her gloved fingers. "Letitia," he said when he stood tall, her hand still in his. "You steal my breath with your beauty."

He could tell he'd shocked her. Clearly, he hadn't complimented her enough. Something he needed to remedy. A soft blush colored her cheeks, and she smiled. "Thank you. You look handsome in your evening wear."

"I see you have met my cousin, Charity."

They were deep in conversation when he entered the room and now stood side by side. "Yes, I didn't know she was visiting. But I'm so glad she is. I believe we will be good friends. She was telling me about you as a young boy and what a hellion you were."

He cleared his throat and glared at Charity. "Please say no more. I'd rather keep those years behind me."

Both Letitia and Charity laughed.

Thankfully, he was saved by the bell signaling dinner. They filed into the dining room and took their seats. He noticed place cards at each setting. Anastasia, Hunter, Aurora, and Warren sat on one side, while Letitia, Charity, and he sat opposite. He was in between the ladies, which had him sighing in relief. He didn't have to worry about Charity talking to Letitia nonstop through dinner with more embarrassing tales of him.

The conversation around the table touched on nothing serious, which was good, considering it was a happy occasion. Before he knew it, they were retreating into the drawing room. He poured sherry for the ladies and brandy for the gentlemen. Before anyone could claim either settee, he held out his hand to Letitia. "Come. Let's sit."

She took his hand, and they crossed the room to sit on the settee. "We haven't had time to talk." He rubbed his thumb across the top of her soft, bare hand. He loved it when dinner ended, and usually nobody put their gloves back on.

"How was your time at Danbury Estate?"

"Fine. I was worried over nothing. The manager has everything under control and is doing an excellent job."

"I'm glad to hear that. Perhaps you won't have to leave London for a while."

"Perhaps." He couldn't really say one way or the other. What he did know was that he needed a different excuse if he was sent on another assignment soon.

Charity clinked her sherry glass to get everyone's attention. "I think I speak for Greyson, Letitia, and myself," she nodded at both of them, "when I say how happy we are about the engagement of two wonderful couples, Anastasia and Hunter, and Aurora and Warren. May you have happy, fruitful, and loving lives." She placed her empty sherry glass on the sideboard. "I'm going to retire and give you happy couples time to yourselves."

"Shall I take you home?" Letitia's eyes widened, and Greyson quickly added, "I hoped we could spend some time alone."

Her lips curved into a teasing smile. "You did, did you? I think that can be arranged. Except who is going to chaperone?"

Greyson jumped up and hurried out of the room, frantically looking for Charity. He ran down the stairs. His pounding heart subsided when he found her in the entry hall, speaking to Henderson. "Charity, I need you back in the drawing room."

She didn't appear shocked by his statement as she slipped her arm through his. "Are you going somewhere?"

"I'm escorting Letitia home."

"And when will you return?"

"My dear, Charity." He winked. "That is none of your business. But I would be forever grateful if you would stay in the drawing room with my sisters until Hunter and Warren leave."

After saying their goodbyes, they left in the Danbury family carriage with a matching set of four. Greyson wished he'd never gone away, because there was a distance between them tonight he didn't care for. Like now, as they rode in silence, it was not the comfortable silence they sometimes shared. He hoped to break it. "Did you do anything interesting while I was gone?"

"Yes. I spent most of my time with Simon. We went riding in

Hyde Park and spent time outdoors in Rutherford Manor's gardens. Simon loves chasing bugs and bees."

He loved hearing the happiness in her voice when she talked about her son. But his heart also dropped. For the first time in his life, he couldn't wait to get married and have children of his own with Letitia. Could he wait a month before proposing? Would his sisters mind if he didn't wait? He didn't know if he could. He wanted the woman beside him to have his name, his heart, and his soul. She already had the latter two.

The carriage stopped. He opened the door, climbed out, and leaned in with his hand out. "My lady."

She giggled as she slipped her hand into his. "You're certainly being charming this evening."

"I'm trying." And he was. He'd never really courted anyone before, so he could only hope he was doing it right.

"We should get inside. It's cold, and the nosy neighbors are probably watching us from their windows."

"Really?"

"Perhaps. Although I have good neighbors, I wouldn't want to test their desire to spread gossip."

"Then by all means, let us get inside." He tugged on her hand, and they hurried up the stairs and into the entry hall, since Mr. Henry had the door open by the time they reached the top step.

Greyson handed his greatcoat and gloves to Mr. Henry, then assisted Letitia in removing her cloak.

"That will be all for the night, Mr. Henry."

"Yes, my lady."

Greyson had a moment of weakness because he was afraid to look at Mr. Henry and see the disapproval on his face. Except he was only looking out for his mistress, and he appreciated that. He just didn't want the steady butler to protect her from him.

When they were alone in the entry hall, Letitia whispered, "Did you tell your driver to leave? People will definitely gossip if your carriage stays outside my townhouse all night."

He hadn't wanted to be presumptuous, but he had told his driver to leave. It wasn't that far to his family home. "I did, knowing I could walk home if I needed to." She slipped her arm through his and led the way up two flights of stairs and down a corridor, where she opened the door to her chambers. "We could've gone to Club Knight."

After they entered, she closed and locked the door. "I know, and I thought about it. I told my maid I was not to be disturbed. She takes her job very seriously."

"I'm glad. Come here." He wrapped an arm around her waist, pulling her against him. "I've missed you."

"Me too."

His mouth claimed hers. He tried to be gentle, but it wasn't always in his nature. Instead, he kissed her as if he could never get enough of her, as if she might vanish any second and he had to make his mark while he could. She understood his desires and kissed him back just as desperately. His entire body tensed with need. His cock was hard. He pushed his hips against her stomach so she knew what she did to him. Only she could make him this needy, this hard, this desperate for release.

"As much as I love this dress, it has to go," he said, turning her around so her back faced him. His fingers shook as he untied her laces, tantalizingly slowly. He could feel her body trembling beneath his fingers when he slipped the dress down over her hips until it pooled at her feet.

"I'll do the rest," she said as she stepped forward, turned, and locked sultry eyes with his. He broke the contact and followed her fingers as they caressed up her stomach to her breasts, where she untied her chemise. His chest tightened. He couldn't breathe. The top fell but got hung up on her hips, which she shimmied until it landed on the floor with the rest of her clothes. Standing naked before him was the most beautiful, alluring goddess that ever existed.

His hands moved quickly and with precision. Moments later, sans his coat, waistcoat, and shirt, he moved to the bed and sat down to remove his shoes and hose.

"Let me," the goddess said.

She bent at the waist and removed first one shoe, then the other, and his eyes never left her full breasts as they bounced with her movement. Then she slid her hands beneath his breeches and rolled down the hose on each leg, tossing them aside.

"Stand."

He obeyed. Her delicate fingers brushed against the front placket of his breeches, causing him to inhale. He held his breath until she unbuttoned him and slid his breeches over his hips and down to his ankles. He now stood in his small clothes, which did nothing to hide his erection. She used her hand to tug the front down, freeing him. Her eyes widened, and she smiled. Then she cupped him, forcing a groan from his lips. He wouldn't last long with her hands on him. He reached down and stilled her. "Later."

He lifted her, spun around, and they fell onto the bed exactly where he wanted her. He shed his undergarments. "I'll be right back." He found his jacket and took a French letter from the pocket. He wanted a child with Letitia, but he preferred that they be married first. He covered his penis and tied the ribbon tight.

He rejoined her on the bed and kissed her with all the love and devotion he wanted her to feel from him. When her legs wrapped around his hips, he entered her, sending sparks throughout his body. Every time he pulled out and pushed back in, more sparks ignited inside his veins. Soon he was pounding in and out, and she met his rhythm with her own. Her insides clamped down on him, milking his seed. They both panted and went over the edge together.

He rolled onto his back. Removed the French letter. Then turned onto his side, pulling her close. "Thank you."

"You don't have to thank me every time we make love."

"I do. I want you to know how much I appreciate you." He inhaled, then said the words he'd never spoken to anyone but his immediate family. "I love you."

Silence. She took a deep breath and, as she exhaled, said, "I love you, too." He was shocked to find himself hard again so quickly, and he showed her how much he loved her.

She lay in his arms asleep and he followed her soon after.

Greyson was dreaming he was in bed with Letitia, but an annoying knock kept bothering him and wouldn't stop. He popped his eyes open and realized he'd fallen asleep and that someone was actually knocking on the door.

It opened, and he covered them both just as Letitia awoke and said, "Who is it?"

"Jane. I'm sorry, my lady, but I have a message for Viscount Greyson."

"Leave it on the floor inside the door."

"Yes, my lady."

Luckily, they'd left some candles lit. Greyson climbed out of bed and walked naked to the note on the floor addressed to him. He snapped the seal of Tremont and scanned the contents. "I'm being called away," he said as he hastily dressed.

"Called away?" she mumbled sleepily. "It's the middle of the night."

"Yes."

"Is it your father?" she asked, sitting up.

He hated lying to her, but she gave him the perfect excuse. "Yes, he has taken a turn for the worse, and I must return home."

"Yes. Of course. Give me a moment to find my dressing robe, and I'll see you to the door."

"You stay here." He moved to her side of the bed. "I'm sorry our night was cut short. I'll make it up to you. I promise." He kissed her cheek. "Goodnight, my love." Of all the nights to be called away, it had to be tonight. From experience, if Knight had hunted him down, something significant had to have happened. The sooner he left, the sooner he'd understand the situation.

He moved hastily and silently out of Letitia's house. No surprise, he saw Mr. Henry out of the corner of his eye, lurking just off the entry hall. He should be offended, but he was thankful and knew Letitia would be safe with him to guard her.

Down the street stood an unmarked black carriage. Greyson hurried toward it, opened the door, and climbed in to find Knight waiting for him. "What happened?" he whispered.

"When the stones were thrown at Prinny's carriage back in January, it was bad, but this time someone shot at him as he exited his coach around one this morning. The bullet grazed a footman's arm. Both were fortunate."

"Thank God no one was killed," Greyson spat.

The carriage came to a stop. "Come, the Prince is waiting."

They approached the entrance to Carlton House and were met by four guards, who let them pass. At the main door, two more guards stood watch and, upon recognizing them, let them pass. Inside, another two guards met them and escorted them to Prinny's private residence, where he sat at his desk in his study, looking weary.

"Your Royal Highness," both Knight and Greyson said, bowing.

"Please take a seat."

Once Knight and Greyson sat in leather chairs facing the desk, Prinny said, "What a night. Will this madness ever end? It's been going on too long. One of these days or nights, I'm going to get hurt."

"Was he caught?" Knight asked.

"Oh, yes. He's in the Tower as we speak. You can both question him when you leave."

"Good," Knight added.

The Prince Regent let out a heavy sigh. "I'm frightened for my family. What if someone goes after them next?"

"We will do everything in our power to make sure it doesn't happen," Knight said.

"Princess Charlotte is at Claremont House in Surrey and due to have my grandchild soon."

"Send some of your Dragoons to Surrey," Knight recommended.

"I already made the arrangements. They leave at first light."

"Good." Knight touched his mask, which hid his burned face, a gesture Greyson knew he made when frustrated. "Where are your Dragoons?"

"Some are out scouring the streets, questioning anyone they see. Others are here, protecting those in residence. I'm quite convinced this person didn't act alone. He's a poor farmer and should've wielded a pitchfork or some such tool, not a pistol beyond his means."

"We will find out what we can," Greyson said. "Forgive me, Your Highness, if this is the wrong time, but there's something I've wanted to ask you."

"Go on."

"With the Home Office, the Bow Street Runners, and your Dragoons, I don't understand why you created the Black Knights."

"Because I don't trust anyone! There could be spies anywhere. Your job is to keep me safe and alive, weed out any spies, and keep my subjects from marching on London with any weapon they can find to protest government laws. And most importantly, keep England from having a bloody revolution."

"We will try," Knight said.

"You'd better do more than try, Knight," Prinny bellowed. "I expect you and your men to succeed in curbing all this unrest."

"Pardon me, Your Highness," Knight said. "But we are only eight Black Knights, five of whom are out on assignment."

"Yes. Eight men you handpicked with my approval. Now is not the time to expand the Knights. I will, however, for the time being, turn over to your command six of my most skilled and trusted Dragoons."

"Thank you, Your Highness. Please tell them to bring their weapons, but leave their uniforms behind. The Black Knights need to blend in. As regal as their uniforms are, they have no place on Black Knight assignments."

"Understood. I expect an update by ten."

After being dismissed, Knight's carriage took them to the

Tower, where they were met by a guard who escorted them to the farmer's cell. The guard unlocked the gate and handed Greyson a lantern, then they entered the small chamber, where a middle-aged man sat huddled on the cold, dirty floor, shivering.

"What is your name?" Knight demanded.

"Timothy Burke."

"Who gave you the pistol and told you to shoot the Prince Regent?"

The prisoner looked up, his eyes glowing white in the lantern light. "It be mine."

Greyson knew Knight could be ruthless, but for some reason he wasn't tonight. "I don't believe you. As a farmer, it would take a year's profit to buy such a fine pistol."

"I won't tell you nothing," he spat.

"If you don't, you'll hang."

"I'll hang anyway."

"Let me tell you something," Knight said. "The Prince Regent is trying to keep his subjects safe. He is trying to stop these rebellions before they begin. Not because he fears for his own safety, but because he fears for his subjects'. He doesn't want bloodshed. He is trying to prevent it. We," he said, pointing from Greyson to himself, "are trying to help those marching toward London to see that nothing but arrests and bloodshed will come of it. That is the last thing the Regent wants. His heart breaks when his subjects die for the greed of others who instigate these rebellions. Those who create these uprisings don't march alongside you. They are snakes that slither and hide."

"I'm still not talking."

"Fine. But know that my people will continue to prevent farmers like you from ending up in jail or, worse, hanged. And know that we will do anything in our power to make your troubles heard."

Knight banged on the iron bars to get the guard's attention. He unlocked the gate and let them out. Back inside his carriage, Knight said, "I fear more marches are ahead. But what bothers me is that he had a pistol, and he was alone. Large crowds can get unruly, but one man can move stealthily and undetected. Prinny was lucky tonight. He's expecting me back to report to him in the morning. I'll tell him of my fears and advise him to increase his Dragoons' security. Meanwhile, I'll drop you off and go home myself. We both could use some sleep."

"You're right." The rest of the ride was silent, and Greyson found himself nodding off to the sound of the horses' hooves.

"Greyson, wake up." Knight's voice startled him.

"Sorry."

The carriage stopped in front of Danbury Hall. "Thank you for the ride."

"Anytime. Meeting tomorrow at noon. Let's hope more Black Knights have returned."

"Yes." Greyson let himself out and hurried into his family's home as the sky began to lighten with the approach of dawn. Exhausted, he slowly made his way to his chambers. He fell back on his bed, clothes and all, and slipped into a deep slumber.

CHAPTER NINETEEN

A FTER GREYSON LEFT, Letitia climbed out of bed, slipped into her dressing room, and put on a night rail. Back in bed, she couldn't sleep despite being exhausted. She kept thinking about Greyson's father. Had he died, making Greyson the Earl of Danbury? She couldn't imagine calling him Danbury instead of Greyson. If her prayers were answered, his father would remain alive.

Lying on her side, she'd wanted to celebrate when Greyson told her he loved her. But now, given the circumstances surrounding his father's health, she couldn't. It didn't seem proper. After a while, her eyes closed. The last thing she remembered before sleep came was hoping to receive a note from him the next morning with favorable news.

The sun peeked through the curtains the next morning as she awoke. The day looked promising weather-wise, but her thoughts were somber, wondering whether Greyson's father had died. If she didn't receive a note from him soon, she would write one asking about his father's health. Otherwise, she would worry all day. If the worst happened, would he welcome a visit from her? Would he prefer to mourn alone with his family? "Stop," she said to herself. Stop wondering what he will or will not want. It was foolish, since nothing could be done now.

How difficult it must be for a title to pass from father to son, knowing someone had died for it. All the felicitations to the recipient of the new title, while the recipient mourned the loss of a loved one or family member, felt contradictory. She certainly didn't envy Greyson and his future title of earl.

"Good morning, my lady," Jane said as she entered, carrying her breakfast tray and placing it on the table beside her chaise longue. Recently, it had become normal for her to break her fast in her chambers instead of the morning room.

"Good morning, Jane." She climbed out of bed, put on her robe, and sat on the chaise longue, fixing a cup of tea. As she sipped, she heard Jane tidying her chambers and wondered whether she should mention last night. She trusted Jane and all her servants. However, she'd never had a man in her bed before. Not since Rutherford. "Jane. About last night."

"You needn't worry, my lady. I will never speak of it. Only Mr. Henry and I know the viscount was here, and you can trust him."

"I know. Thank you."

"I will return shortly to help you prepare for your day."

"Thank you." Letitia said, setting her empty teacup and saucer on the tray. Then she picked up a cold piece of toast with raspberry jam and nibbled it, trying to catch the crumbs as they fell. After another piece of toast, she brushed the dry crumbs from her lap, stood, and made her way to the large window facing the street, pushing the curtains aside. She should go for a walk to clear her head, but she didn't have the energy. Instead, feeling restless and unwilling to wait another moment to hear from Greyson, she sat at her dressing table, which doubled as a writing desk, and penned a note to Greyson inquiring about his father's health. When she finished, she rang for a footman and handed him the note. "Please have this delivered immediately."

"Yes, my lady," he said, bowing and hurrying off.

She spent an hour with Simon, then did some embroidery until luncheon was served in the family drawing room.

A footman entered the room and bowed. "Excuse me, my

lady. A note has just arrived for you." He stepped forward and handed over the correspondence. Recognizing Greyson's seal, she snapped the wax with trembling hands, unfolded it, scanning the words as they were revealed. His father was still alive and improving. She was happy for Greyson and his family, yet still felt unsettled and bored. She left the drawing room for her chambers and had Jane help her change into a lovely cream day dress with a matching pelisse, hat, and gloves. She decided to go to Blackstone Manor for afternoon tea.

Ready for her outing, Letitia made her way down the stairs and into the entry hall, where she found Mr. Henry standing ready to open the door.

"The carriage is ready, your ladyship."

"Thank you, Mr. Henry, but how did you know?"

"Miss Jane. I told the driver to go to Blackstone Manor."

"Thank you."

He opened the door, and she descended the stone stairs and entered the carriage as a footman held the door open. Once inside, he closed the door and knocked on the roof. Her capable driver guided the carriage and horses smoothly and carefully into the street. Blackstone Manor was only a few streets from Rutherford Manor, so it wasn't long before she was greeted by the Blackstone butler and escorted into the drawing room by a footman.

"The Marchioness of Rutherford," announced the footman.

"Letitia," Emmeline said with a smile. "What a pleasant surprise. Please sit with us."

"Forgive me for coming without sending word."

"Nonsense. You are always welcome. No note or invitation is necessary."

Since Lilly sat in a chair, Letitia joined Emmeline on the settee.

"Please forgive me for saying this," Lilly said. "But you seem out of sorts. Are you unwell? Has anything happened?"

Emmeline poured her tea and handed her the cup and saucer.

"Thank you. I'm perfectly well. I've been worried about Greyson's father all day since I heard he had taken a turn for the worse last night."

"Oh, how frightening," Emmeline said. "Is he any better?"

"Yes, I received a note from Greyson saying he has improved, but I feel it's only a matter of time. He's been unwell for quite some time."

"Yes, we know," Lilly said. "It must be difficult for Greyson to wake each morning and wonder whether it will be the last day he spends with his father."

"Indeed," Letitia said. "I think about that as well."

A footman entered the drawing room and announced, "Lady Aurora and Lady Anastasia."

Letitia turned her head to see the twins following the footman into the room. They were both smiling, easing Letitia's worry. They wouldn't be smiling if their father's health had declined further, or worse.

"Anastasia, Aurora," Emmeline said with a warm smile. "What a lovely surprise. Please sit and join us for tea and biscuits."

"Thank you, Your Grace," Aurora said as both sisters curtsied. Aurora took the chair beside the settee, and Anastasia took the one opposite the settee, next to Lilly.

Emmeline poured them tea, then said, "Congratulations on your engagement to Hunter, Anastasia."

"Thank you. Warren proposed to Aurora after the Barstow picnic. We're going to have a double wedding."

"How wonderful," Lilly said. "Congratulations to both of you."

"Thank you," the twins said together.

"Letitia just told us your father was quite ill last night," Lilly remarked. "How is he doing today?"

The sisters looked at one another and frowned, making Letitia's stomach tighten. "I don't know where you heard this, but Father has rallied over the past several days. He's better than he has been in months," Aurora replied.

Letitia found it hard to breathe, and the pain in her stomach intensified. Still, she managed to say, "Forgive me. I must have misunderstood Greyson."

Her eyes fell to the cup of tea she held. Her cheeks burned, her hands trembled, and her head throbbed. Greyson had lied to her. He *lied* to her. The one thing she couldn't tolerate in a gentleman was lying. It wasn't so much the lie, because everyone told a fib now and then. It was what it triggered inside her. The memories of Rutherford's lies and how she couldn't live through something similar again.

She reached beside her, set her tea down, and stood. "Forgive me, ladies, but I must return home."

It would be hard to miss the look Lilly and Emmeline shared. Emmeline rose. "I'll see you out."

Letitia bid the remaining ladies good day and followed Emmeline out of the drawing room. As they neared the entry hall, Emmeline said, "What was that about? I don't believe you misunderstood Greyson. Why did he tell you that about his father?"

Letitia couldn't hide her frustration and hurt, and she rubbed her forehead. "I don't know. I didn't misunderstand. I know exactly what he said. It was an obvious excuse to get away from me last night."

Emmeline took her hands in hers. "Don't do anything rash. I know Rutherford lied to you for years, and how much it hurt when you found out he had a longtime mistress and sired several illegitimate children with her. But Greyson is not Rutherford. Ask him about it. Give him a chance to explain before you decide to end the courtship. You both care deeply for one another. It's obvious to anyone fortunate enough to be in the same room with you both."

"Thank you, Emmeline. You're a good friend." She pulled her hands away. "I promise I'll give him a chance to explain, but I can't promise anything regarding our courtship." She covered her heart with one hand. "I don't think my heart can survive being lied to by another man I love."

Emmeline hugged her and whispered, "Be kind to yourself. Go home, soak in a hot bath, and take a nap. Those two things will help you see things clearly. If not, at least you will feel soothed and rested. If you need me, send word, and I will come. Blackstone and I have nothing on our calendar for tonight."

"Thank you," Letitia said, hugging Emmeline back. "You are a good friend." She swallowed the lump forming in her throat and fought back the tears gathering in her eyes. She wouldn't embarrass herself by crying in front of the duchess. She would cry in the privacy of her chambers after she took Emeline's advice and took a relaxing bath. She also had no social engagement for tonight, which was good, because all she wanted to do was have a good cry and sleep away her broken heart.

THE MORNING AFTER Letitia found out that Greyson had lied about his father, she sat up in bed, her breakfast tray across her lap, yawning. Sleep had eluded her for most of the previous night, and she had the beginnings of a dull headache to match her poor mood. The lie Greyson had told her was nothing compared to the lies Rutherford told during their marriage.

How foolish and naïve she'd been when she entered their marriage at eighteen. All his trips to his clubs and dinners out with friends were spent with his mistress and their children. His natural-born children. He lived another life with another woman. She'd often wondered whether their marriage meant anything. She understood at the beginning of their marriage that he'd married her to produce a legitimate heir. But as the years went by and they suited one another, she'd thought they had shared much more than that.

She learned after his death from their solicitor that he had set up a trust for his other family and that they were well cared for. She was at least glad he had looked to the future and planned for his death. She often thought about reaching out, since she knew the woman's name. But her embarrassment and pride stopped her.

Even though she knew why Rutherford had lied to her, she didn't know the extent of those lies. Nor how they affected her. How insecure they made her. How she believed she wasn't enough of a wife to satisfy her husband. She knew she wasn't enough for Rutherford, but she also believed it would be the same if and when she married again. She tried to make herself understand that Rutherford had been in love with his mistress for ten years before they'd even met. Though Rutherford had cared for Letitia, he never loved her as he loved his mistress. And nothing she had done or not done would ever have changed the facts of his life before her. But it still hurt. Her heart still ached at the truth.

On the night her husband died, something happened to her besides the trauma of witnessing him fall to his death. It triggered a connection between lying, death, and guilt. She knew it wasn't rational, but she couldn't help what her mind believed. Greyson's lie to her made her fear his death and triggered the debilitating guilt she felt after Rutherford's death. If he hadn't lied, if she hadn't gotten angry and argued with him, he would still be alive. In her mind, the sequence of events started with the lie and ended with death. Upon discovering Greyson's lie, it sparked these fears in her. Indeed, she was upset he lied and he would have to explain his reasoning at some point, but until then she would struggle with her irrational fears.

She sipped her hot chocolate and picked at her eggs and toast. Nothing tasted good. It was bland and flavorless. While Jane was busy in the dressing room, preparing her clothes for the day, she set the breakfast tray aside. Tossed the covers off her body and left the warm bed, shivering as she put her dressing robe on. Making her way over to the fireplace, which had been set, she stood in front of the warm blaze and sighed deeply.

What was she going to do about Greyson? So many scenarios had run through her mind during her sleepless night. Some were so ridiculous she almost laughed at the memory. Most left her heartbroken, tears soaking her pillow. Should she ignore his lie and pretend all was well between them? Even if she did, his sisters would no doubt mention their conversation in Emmeline's drawing room. Then he would know she knew he had lied to her.

What a dilemma. Deep down, where her heart was hiding, she wanted to forgive him. She believed he had a good reason for the lie and could still hope that it wouldn't happen again. Emmeline had given her wise advice, and perhaps she would consider using it.

"My lady," Jane said, stepping out of the dressing room with her arms full. "Are you ready to dress?"

"Yes, Jane. I'm going to call upon Lady Anastasia and Lady Aurora this morning." After Letitia was dressed in a pale-blue day dress and pelisse, Jane styled her hair in a neat chignon low on her neck so her yellow bonnet would fit perfectly.

"Please go tell Mr. Henry to have the carriage brought around."

"Yes, my lady."

She made her way to the drawing room, looking out the front windows while awaiting the arrival of the carriage. Lost in thoughts of Greyson, when Mr. Henry announced that the carriage had arrived, she was startled. She hadn't seen it pull up.

"I'll be right there, Mr. Henry." Taking a deep breath, she raised one hand, and her gloved fingertips grazed her bonnet. Nothing was out of place, so she couldn't put off her excursion to Danbury Hall any longer. Exiting the drawing room, she paused as Mr. Henry bowed and opened the door. She descended the several steps and entered the coach as a footman held the door open. Once he closed the door, he knocked on the roof, and her driver, Mr. Burke, set the horses and wheels in motion at a steady pace.

Her insides quivered, and she leaned back against the squabs, wrapping her arms around her stomach. She had second thoughts about visiting Danbury Hall. Yesterday, it hadn't felt right, but today she felt she needed to. She didn't have much to discuss with Anastasia and Aurora, since she'd seen them yesterday, but of course this visit was a ruse to see Greyson and gauge his reaction to her coming to his home. Oh dear, she covered her mouth and fought the urge to gag. "Stop this, Letitia. You are making yourself sick with worry." If only she would listen to herself.

When the carriage came to a halt, she almost yelled at the driver to go home. Instead, a footman from Danbury Hall opened the door and offered her his hand. She took it, hoping he didn't notice how it shook. "Thank you," she said as she stepped onto the pavement, then made her way up the stairs and through the door the butler already held open. She handed over her calling card. "I'm here to see Lady Anastasia and Lady Aurora."

The butler bowed. "Yes, Lady Rutherford. Come with me."

She followed him up one flight of stairs to a set of double doors, partly ajar. He opened them wide and announced, "Lady Rutherford." It was the same drawing room she'd been in when she'd come for the celebratory engagement dinner. It seemed like a lifetime ago.

Both Anastasia and Aurora rose from their seats on one of the two blue velvet settees and closed the distance between them. "Letitia," Anastasia said, taking her hands. "What a lovely surprise. Come sit down and have tea with us."

"Yes, do," Aurora said as the three of them sat down. Letitia settled into the vacant settee.

"We are thrilled by your visit, but did we not see you yesterday?" Aurora said, pouring her a cup of tea. "Milk and sugar?"

"Yes, please. I saw you both yesterday, but I thought I would stop by today."

"We're glad you did," Anastasia said with a smile and an inquisitive look. "But if you are calling on us hoping to see our brother, you will be sorely disappointed. We were told he left early this morning."

She ignored the silent tumble her stomach took at the knowledge that he was not home. "It would've been nice to see him, but that is not why I came," she lied, which she despised.

"Both Anastasia and I wanted to say thank you for the engagement presents. They were perfect. Also, Warren and Hunter were both thrilled with their brandy decanter and matching glasses."

"I'm glad to hear it," Letitia replied. "Where is Charity?"

"She has a headache and is resting," Anastasia answered.

"I'm sorry to hear this. Give her my regards."

They made small talk for the remainder of her visit, discussing wedding plans. Thirty minutes later, she bid them farewell and left Danbury Hall with a heavy heart and a more jumbled-up mind. Until she came face-to-face with Greyson and talked things through, she would be a mess of contradictory emotions.

Instead of going home, she had the driver take her to Bond Street and to her modiste, Madame Serena. She had been there several days earlier and had picked out the green-and-gold evening dress, but she was in the mood for something else. She entered the crowded shop and looked over bolts of fabric while she waited for Madame Serena to come out of the back room. Perhaps she should've made an appointment. She was just about to leave when she heard, "Lady Rutherford, how nice to see you again. How may I help you?"

"I would like to order a ball gown."

"Come," she said, holding back the curtain separating the storefront from the back.

"Thank you."

"Do you have a color in mind?"

"I do. Do you have any blue fabric?"

"Yes." She went to a shelf full of bolts of cloth in every color and fabric, and pulled out a beautiful sky-blue taffeta. "This just arrived yesterday."

"It's perfect." After reviewing several style plates, she combined several to create the perfect ball gown and matching cloak. Then they went over trimmings and embellishments until Madame Serena had everything set aside.

"I will send a note when it's ready for your fitting sometime next week," Madame Serena said. "It's going to be the most beautiful gown I've created yet."

Letitia found herself laughing and feeling more like herself. "You say that every time someone orders a new gown."

"Yes. And I mean it every time," Madame Serena laughed.

Letitia left the modiste with a lighter heart and walked down Bond Street, window-shopping and enjoying the bright, sunny day. Since it was mid-October, it would be too cold to enjoy window-shopping much longer, especially if it snowed. She stopped outside a clock shop and listened to the sounds coming from inside. The proprietor, who designed the clocks, was a true master. She knew his clocks graced many royal homes. Several of his clocks also resided in Rutherford Manor. One masterpiece sat on Rutherford's mantel in his study, a gift from her for their first anniversary. Her deceased husband had been a lover of clocks and timepieces. She hoped Simon would someday enjoy his father's love of clocks and his collection.

"What brings you here, Lady Rutherford?"

At the sound of Greyson's voice, her heart skipped a beat and her insides warmed. Then she remembered she was upset with him. More than upset. Heartbroken and disillusioned. "I just came from the modiste and decided to window-shop and get some fresh air and sunshine. You?"

He stood a little too close for propriety's sake, but she didn't move. "I was riding in my carriage, minding my own business, when, out of the corner of my eye, I spied the most beautiful, enchanting lady I've ever seen, and I knew I had to make her acquaintance."

"Who was she?"

His deep chuckle made her skin tingle. Damn her traitorous body. She needed to keep reminding herself that she was upset with him. "As if you don't know. Would you like to accompany me to Gunter's for lemon ices?"

Lemon ices sounded heavenly. "Forgive me, but I must return home now to spend time with my son."

His posture straightened, and he frowned. She saw it in his reflection in the large glass window. "Perhaps another time, then."

"Yes. Perhaps another time." She did need to talk to him about his lie, but here on the street or at Gunter's with an audience wasn't the right time. Thankfully, her carriage was right there. She pivoted and climbed in with her footman's help. Against her better judgment, she glanced out the window at Greyson standing in front of the clock shop, his eyes on her. She shivered and tried not to feel guilty about hurting his feelings. It was right there in his expression. It hurt her as much as it did him for her to turn down his offer to go to Gunter's. Her entire being, against her wishes, wanted to be with him at all times.

CHAPTER TWENTY

Greyson was having a hell of a morning until he spotted Letitia standing in front of the clock shop, staring into the window. The tightness in his muscles eased, and his mind, preoccupied with Black Knight business, relaxed. If he was being honest, every time she was nearby, his disorderly world straightened. The sky grew bluer. The clouds fluffier and whiter. The birds chirped more melodiously. He could go on, but he didn't need to convince himself. After what they shared at Club Knight and the other night in her chambers, he knew how connected they were, how right they were together. Letitia needed convincing. Or perhaps she didn't feel what he did? No. He didn't believe that for a moment. He understood she wanted to spend time with her son instead of going to Gunter's with him. Yet he had the strangest feeling she wanted to avoid him.

Feeling disconcerted, he walked up and down Bond Street on both sides until he came upon a hothouse. He went inside and ordered two dozen red roses to be sent to Letitia that afternoon. He hoped she would understand their significance. Red rose petals had spread across the bed and the floor the night they made love, the night of the masquerade ball. He hoped that night meant as much to her as it had to him. He wrote on the card that would accompany the flowers:

My Dearest Letitia,

Roses for the lady who holds my heart in the palm of her delicate hand.

Greyson

When he returned to Danbury Hall, a letter awaited him. He frowned at the handwriting he recognized as Knight's, along with the seal belonging to the Duke of Tremont. He wondered how Knight managed to be a husband to his new wife while running Club Knight, leading the Black Knights, and, of course, being the Duke of Tremont. And how did the duchess feel about it? It gave Greyson hope when it came to Letitia and making her his wife. If she'd have him. He realized he was stalling about reading Knight's note. Nothing good ever came of receiving a note from him.

And once he'd read it, he knew he was right. Knight had heard a rumor that a group of protesters was planning to march to Carlton House that night in protest of the upcoming executions of the Pentrich Rebellion leaders.

It was one of the reasons Prinny created the Black Knights, to defuse situations by stopping the protestors at the outset before any bloodshed occurred. Greyson knew Knight paid significant sums to spies spread throughout England, reporting on any rebellions rising up. But somehow, Knight hadn't gotten word of this one before the people formed. Once the good people of England gathered in protest, carrying whatever crude weapons they could find, the Black Knights would find keeping the peace difficult. Prinny wanted peace in England, but the task was difficult.

Before he went up to his chambers to change, he said to Henderson, "Please send a footman to the mews and have Whisky brought around. I'm going out, and I don't know when I'll return."

"Yes, my lord."

He hurried to his chambers to change into riding clothes. He tucked a loaded pistol into each jacket pocket and hoped like hell he wouldn't need them. But anything could happen, and it was best to be prepared. His assignment was to keep the peace and protect the royal family. Not always an easy thing to do.

Dalton helped him with his boots, frowning the entire time. His driver Reed, the groom Stevenson, Henderson, and Dalton knew of his secret work with the Black Knights. He needed their help on occasion, especially Reed and Stevenson. But tonight, he was taking his horse, not the unmarked carriage.

When he was ready to go, Dalton said, "Be safe, my lord."

"Always," he replied, then exited, descended the stairs, went out the door, and mounted Whisky. It was nearing four in the afternoon, and the streets were crowded with horses and carriages as the *ton* made their way to various parks throughout London. Hyde Park was the most frequently visited, and unfortunately, he needed to pass right by the entrance, which was why he was on horseback. He could weave his way around the slow carriages and riders.

Finally, he arrived at Club Knight, dismounted, tossed his reins to the stableboy, and hurried to the back door. After knocking the secret knock, Cooke let him inside. "Good, you're the last to arrive."

"Everyone is here?" Greyson couldn't believe all the Black Knights had returned to London from their assignments.

"Yes."

They made their way down to the lower level. The closer they got to the room, the louder the voices grew. Inside the room, Cooke shut and bolted the door, and Greyson took his usual seat in the circle.

Knight stood and began pacing the room, looking anything but happy. "Drink your brandy and I'll make this quick. The protesters are five miles west of London. If we hurry, we may intercept them and persuade them to return home. If the Dragoons, the yeomanry, or infantry regiments reach them first, there will be bloodshed and arrests. We need to prevent this."

"Where are the Dragoons who were joining us temporarily?" Greyson asked.

"I sent them to Carlton House."

"Good."

"Any questions before we saddle up?" Knight asked, stopping his pacing and looking each member in the eye. When no one spoke up, he said, "Good."

They filed out of the room, up the stairs, and out the door to the front of Club Knight, where each of their horses was waiting. Greyson mounted Whisky.

"Ride with me, Greyson," Knight said. "The rest of you pair off. We need to blend in and avoid drawing attention. You saw the map. We'll meet at the grove of trees I pointed out, two miles from here."

There was no need for words as the men rode off in pairs in different directions, looking like two gentlemen taking a late afternoon ride. Greyson and Knight were the last to leave, taking the busy London streets in plain sight, straight through fashionable Mayfair. The entire time they rode, Knight was silent, and Greyson wondered what the duke was thinking. Did he worry about his wife if he never returned? Something Greyson had never worried about until he met and fell in love with Letitia. Well, he did occasionally worry about his family, but he knew his cousin, Jacob Morton, would step in and care for them.

Thirty minutes later, they met the rest of the Black Knights in the grove of trees outside London proper. "Greyson, you'll ride in front with me," Knight said. "Cooke and Sweeney, take up the rear. When we approach the marchers, let me do the talking."

Greyson once again rode alongside Knight. "Do you think they will listen to reason?"

Knight looked over at him. With his mask covering his deformed face, it was hard to read his thoughts. "If their leader is a reasonable man, possibly. No doubt they know the consequences of marching to Carlton House. Even if Prinny told the Dragoons, the yeomanry, and soldiers to keep it peaceful, anything can

for his life, pulled the weapon out and ran, leaving him on the ground, breathing through the agonizing pain radiating down his leg. Blood quickly soaked his tan riding breeches.

Retired Captain Sweeney reached him first. "Christ! What the hell?" he yelled as he removed his cravat and used it as a tourniquet to stop the bleeding. Greyson gritted his teeth to keep himself from screaming. The pain was so intense that the world swirled around and around, then faded away.

The next thing he remembered was waking up in a strange room, on a strange bed, with a physician working on his thigh, which burned and stung at the same time it was tingly and numb.

"Wh-what are you doing?" he said in a raw voice.

"Easy, Viscount. I'm the duke's physician, and I'm trying to save your leg. I've cleaned your wounds. Had to pick out dirt, grass and rust first. Now I'm packing the puncture wounds. You were lucky the pitchfork didn't go deep enough to hit bone."

Had he said *trying to save your leg*? He tried to lift his head to see his leg, to no avail.

"Be still."

"I want to see my leg."

"You can later. Right now, I need you to stay still and keep off it. You're under bed rest for the foreseeable future. And let us hope infection doesn't set in."

"Where am I?"

"Tremont Manor. I've done all I can for now." He removed a brown bottle from his valise and using a dropper put some into a cup. The doctor helped Greyson raise his head. "Drink this. It will curb the pain and help you sleep. What you need is sleep and rest to heal and fight infection if it happens upon you."

Greyson drank the entire contents of the cup, knowing the doctor put laudanum in it to help him with his pain.

"Rest. Do not, under any circumstances, get up from this bed." The physician placed the spoon and laudanum on the bedside table. "I'm sending a nurse to keep watch over you. She will have instructions."

"Thank you, I think."

"Don't thank me until we know if your leg can be saved."

Once again, those words. Sweat broke out on his brow, and he couldn't move his arms or anything as he drifted into an unnatural slumber in which he dreamed of being bitten in the leg by a huge, vicious dog.

CHAPTER TWENTY-ONE

FOR THE PAST three days, Letitia had spent more time than usual in the nursery with Simon, trying to take her mind off Greyson, whom she hadn't heard from. The last time she saw him was the day in front of the clock shop, when he asked her to go for ice at Gunter's. Oh, how she wished she'd gone.

Sitting in the family drawing room, taking tea alone, she wished now that he'd call upon her. Resting on the settee, sipping her warm tea, did nothing to ease her worry over him. After making love several times, she loved him more than ever. She believed those nights were a pivotal turning point in their relationship. She wiped away her tears, angry at herself for shedding them, and wondered if she knew him as well as she thought.

"My lady," Mr. Henry entered the room. "This just arrived for you."

She held out her hand, and Mr. Henry handed her the note. "Thank you. That will be all."

He bowed. "Yes, my lady." He then left.

Letitia quickly unfolded the paper and read it.

Dear Lady Rutherford,

We want to let you know that our brother has been gone for three days. It dawned on us this morning that you may be wondering why you haven't heard from him. No doubt he is away on some secret viscount business and will call on you upon his return.

Your friends,

Ladies Anastasia and Aurora

Letitia reread the letter, thinking it odd that they had sent it. Oh, she was very glad they had, as it explained where Greyson was—or wasn't. At least his absence didn't seem to have anything to do with her. He wasn't staying away because he didn't want to see her. He was away because he just was. He had mentioned his little disappearances, and she had thought nothing of them. But for some reason, she had a niggling feeling that something was wrong.

There could be many reasons her intuition was worrisome. However, there was nothing she could do about it. The good thing was that if his sisters hadn't heard from him, then all was well. Or was it?

For the next thirty minutes, she alternated between pacing the room and staring out the window, debating with herself about Greyson. She still hadn't found any answers or solutions to their courtship, such as it was, when Mr. Henry returned. "Another note for you, my lady."

"Please put it on the table."

"Yes, my lady."

She took one last look out the window at the late-afternoon sun, turned and walked to the table beside the settee, picked up the note, and frowned. The wax seal was that of the Duke of Tremont. She cracked the seal, unfolded the paper, and read:

Lady Rutherford,

I'm writing to you because Viscount Greyson was injured and is asking for you. He is staying with me at Tremont Manor. I have also sent a note to his family. Please come as soon as you can.

Tremont

Injured? What did he mean by that? And why was he at Tremont Manor instead of his own home? *Please come as soon as you can.* Her stomach coiled into a painful knot. His last sentence sounded ominous. As if time were short.

She left the family drawing room, hurried to her own chambers, and when she burst through the door, she called out, "Jane. I need my cream pelisse. And can you put my hair up?"

She hadn't bothered with her hair today, except to brush it, since she hadn't planned to leave the house. Anxious to get to Tremont Manor, she wished she'd had Jane style her hair earlier in the day. She sat at her dressing table. "A simple knot will suffice. And please make it quick. Oh, dear, I forgot to have the carriage brought around."

"I'll return in a moment," Jane said, setting the hairbrush down on the dressing table and hurrying out the door. She returned a minute later. "The carriage is on its way."

"Thank you, Jane."

Jane's nimble fingers worked magic on her long, thick tresses, and she was presentable in no time. With her pelisse on, a matching hat and gloves, and her reticule gripped for dear life in her hands, she hurried down the stairs and into the entry hall. "I will be at Tremont Manor if you need me. I don't know when I'll return," she said to Mr. Henry.

"Yes, my lady," Mr. Henry said as he opened the door. "Should Burke wait for you?"

She hadn't considered that. "No. He should return home."

He followed her down the stairs and spoke with her driver while a footman helped her into the carriage. A moment later, they were caught in the flow of carriages. She stared out the window, feeling sick to her stomach ever since reading the duke's cryptic note. Would his sisters be there when she arrived? Was it that serious? Oh dear, she hugged herself, trembling. Couldn't Burke make the horses and carriage go any faster? What was taking them so long? She was about to scream in frustration when the carriage pulled up to a grand manor house.

A footman opened the door, lowered the steps, and held out his hand to assist her in exiting. "Thank you."

As she ascended the stairs, the door to the home opened, and the butler greeted her. "The duke and duchess are waiting for you in the drawing room. Please follow me."

They went up a set of stairs and down the hall to a large burgundy drawing room, where she found not only Knight and his duchess but also Hunter, Anastasia, and Aurora. The room was quiet. The overall atmosphere had her hand flying to her chest.

"Everyone, please sit down," said Tremont, or Knight, as she also knew him. Everyone sat on various chairs and the two settees facing one another, Letitia sat next to Aurora. Tremont remained standing; the expression on the side of his face she could see was somber, and his posture tense. "You may hear me say things in this room that you must promise never to repeat."

Anastasia sat opposite Letitia on the other settee with Hunter. They both looked worried. Aurora reached for her hand and held it tightly.

"First, I will tell you about the Black Knights." Everyone in the room fell silent as he explained about them, what they did, and who they reported to. Letita didn't think her heart could survive if it beat any faster. "We were trying to stop protestors from reaching Carlton House three nights ago when a skirmish broke out, and Greyson was stabbed in the thigh with a pitchfork."

Gasps broke out among everyone in the room. Aurora squeezed her hand tightly, but it didn't matter. All Letitia could think about was Greyson and seeing him. She needed to see him and know he was well and alive. Before she realized what she was doing, she tugged her hand from Aurora and stood. "I need to see him."

Greyson's sisters and Hunter stood saying the same thing.

"You can all see him. My physician has been caring for him, and a private nurse, highly recommended by Dr. Hanson, has been as well. I owe Dr. Hanson my life after sustaining injuries in the war. Please believe me when I say Greyson is receiving the best care available."

Letitia was having difficulty breathing. Her heart and pulse were racing, and she felt lightheaded. She reached behind her for the settee and sank down. "What are you not saying?" she whispered, praying the room would stop spinning.

"The pitchfork was dirty. Dr. Hanson did everything he could to prevent infection in the wound. This morning, Greyson woke up delirious with a fever. Dr. Hanson came and unpacked and drained the wounds, cleaned them, and packed them with a foul-smelling cream he swears by. As do I. It's what the good doctor used on my burns to help prevent infection and promote healing. Dr. Hanson is doing all he can to save Greyson's leg and his life." He paused to let everyone in the room comprehend the serious-ness of the situation. "He's been thrashing about and calling out in his sleep. Your name is often spoken, Letitia."

Tears trickled down her cheeks in a steady stream, and she didn't care. There wasn't a dry eye in the drawing room. Even Hunter wiped his eyes. She wasn't surprised to see Hunter here, since he was Greyson's best friend. But she was shocked Lady Charity wasn't.

As much as Letitia wanted to see Greyson at once, she felt obligated to grant his sisters the honor of visiting first. "Anastasia and Aurora, go to him."

Anastasia went into Hunter's open arms and cried as he held her close, murmuring to her. Aurora was by a window, her head down, her arms wrapped around her middle, and her shoulders shook with silent tears.

"He's been calling out for you," Aurora said from across the room. "Go to him."

Letitia swallowed back more tears, clogging her throat in hopes of speaking loudly enough to be heard, but nothing came out.

"If you're ready, Letitia. I'll take you to him," the duchess said.

Letitia tried hard to remember her name but came up empty. "Thank you, Your Grace."

"No need for formalities at a time such as this. Charlotte will do."

"Thank you, Charlotte." The duchess led her up a flight of stairs and down the corridor to the left. Another time, if Letitia ever found herself inside Tremont Manor again, she would allow herself to take in the beautiful interior, the sweeping grand staircase winding off in two directions. But today wasn't the day for admiring architecture.

"This is his room," Charlotte said, knocking, then opening the door a crack. "May we come in?"

A lady's voice answered, "Yes."

Charlotte opened the door wide and let Letitia enter first. "If you would like, I can stay with you."

"Thank you. I would appreciate it."

"Nurse Pendergrast, go to the kitchens and get something to eat. I'm sure you could use a break."

"Thank you, Your Grace." Nurse Pendergrast curtsied, checked on Greyson, then left the room, leaving the door slightly ajar.

Letitia took a deep breath and forced her feet to move forward until she stood beside the bed. There were so many things to notice that she didn't know where to look first. He was sleeping. She'd never seen him look so flushed, even after all his outdoor activities. The man loved to ride his horse. His usually clean, light brown hair was matted to his head and darker than usual. He had several days of facial hair growth. Every so often, his body twitched, his head moved from side to side, and he moaned.

He was wrapped in blankets so that she couldn't see the wound on his leg. The leg would be wrapped in a linen cloth to keep it clean. Part of her wanted to see the infected flesh for herself, but she would trust the doctor, as Tremont had told them to. Besides, what did she know about caring for wounds?

Nothing. His hand was visible, poking out from the side of the covers, and she curled her hands around it. The palm of his hand burned against hers, no doubt from his high fever.

She stood, holding his hand, ignoring the tears streaming down her cheeks. The large, strong, and vital Greyson seemed to have disappeared, replaced by a sickly man with none of the vibrancy Greyson had. Her thoughts turned dark. What would her world be like if he died? Could she survive another broken heart? She had loved Rutherford, but that love couldn't compare to the all-encompassing love she had for Greyson. Only two people filled her heart to near bursting—Simon and Greyson. Would the half that loved everything about him continue to beat if he no longer breathed? Could a person keep living if half their heart died? She would have to, for her son's sake.

What would happen to his parents? His sisters? Who would take over his father's title if he died? A sob escaped her, and she didn't care. Charlotte brought a small chair to the bedside. "Sit before you fall."

"Thank you," she sobbed as she sank into the small wooden chair, never breaking the bond between her hands and Greyson.

"I'll leave now and give you some privacy. Ring the bell if you need anything."

Letitia's eyes never left Greyson's sleeping form, but she knew from the sound of her soft footfalls that Charlotte had left the room. Letitia continued to hold his hand and watch every twitch and subtle movement his body and face made as he slept. His breathing appeared labored, which she knew was due to his fever. Time ticked on, and she listened to the clock on the wall. Eventually, the sound faded, and all she could hear was his breathing and the rustling of the sheets and blankets as he moved. Once or twice, he shifted his injured leg and moaned in his sleep. The pain was obviously great if it penetrated his slumber. Even in sleep, his body recognized the injury.

Several times, Letitia was startled to hear her name escape his dry lips. Whatever he was dreaming about bothered him greatly, as he moaned and kept repeating the words, "Forgive me." She had a feeling he was apologizing for something far more intense than the one lie she'd caught him telling. Could it be about his involvement in the Black Knights? Another lie by omission. She had heard the reasons he'd claimed for his disappearances from both his sisters and himself. More lies, but she understood now his need for them. He couldn't risk his life or the lives of the other Black Knights if their existence became widely known.

Because he was a member of the Black Knights, he now lay in bed with a dangerous infection and a wound that could very well end his life. His loyalty was admirable. She sobbed loudly again, bent forward at the waist, and rested her cheek on their joined hands. Her tears leaked onto their hands and the blanket. She would try her best not to think his lie would lead to his death.

"Don't cry," Greyson said in a hoarse voice.

She stopped breathing, waiting to hear whether he would speak again, confirming she hadn't imagined hearing his voice.

"Letitia, please don't cry," he whispered, allowing her lungs to take in much-needed air.

"Greyson," she gasped, lifting her head and wiping the tears from her eyes so she could see him clearly. When she looked into his dull, green eyes, full of remorse and plagued by pain and fever, she sniffed and smiled. Her heart sped up with hope. "You're awake."

His dry lips curled into a weak smile. "I am." He used his free hand to cup her cheek. "Thank you for coming."

She covered his hand with one of hers and leaned into his gentle, searing touch. "There's no place I'd rather be than by your side." Unabashed tears trickled from her eyes. "You've given everyone quite a fright."

He licked his cracked lips and inhaled. His chest shook with the effort. "Not my intention. The Black Knights are the peacekeepers. We try to avoid shedding any blood."

"So Knight has explained." She quickly added, "We have been sworn to secrecy."

"We?" he closed his eyes.

"Hunter and your sisters."

"Hmmm."

"The Black Knights have nothing to fear from us."

He inhaled and exhaled, and she heard a rattling in his chest. She frowned. Had the infection spread to his lungs? Oh, dear God, lung infections were bad. Very, very bad. Clarice's husband, the Duke of Stanton, nearly died when an infection from a gunshot wound spread to his lungs when he was a young man. It took him months to regain his strength.

She fought the panic that threatened to overtake her emotions. It wouldn't do any good for Greyson to see her frightened. It took everything to control her emotions and remain calm. At least on the outside. "Do you need anything?"

"A drink."

On the table next to the bed sat a glass of water and a bowl of what looked like broth. She picked up the bowl and spoon, then took a sip to confirm the contents. It was cold, but it would do. "I have broth for you. Can you lift your head?"

He raised his head just enough for her to give him several spoonfuls of chicken broth. He rested his head back on the pillows. "Thank you," he said, sighing and closing his eyes. "Forgive me for lying to you the night I hurried from your house. I had no choice."

"I know that now. Rest. I'm calling for the nurse," Letitia said, rising from the chair and going to pull the tassel on the wall. Several moments later, a maid entered the room and curtsied.

"How may I help you, my lady?"

"Could you please send for Nurse Pendergrast?"

"Yes, my lady."

The maid hurried from the room, and the nurse returned minutes later. By then, Letitia had returned to Greyson's bedside, sat in the chair, and held his hand as he'd fallen back to sleep.

The nurse approached the bed. "Did he wake up, my lady?"

"Yes, for a brief time. I gave him several spoonfuls of broth."

"Good. He needs to keep up his strength."

"I'm afraid for his lungs. I heard them rattling."

"Yes. It's not a good sign. Doctor Hanson is due to arrive soon. We are watching him closely and doing all we can."

"Thank you," Letitia said, standing. She placed her hand on Greyson's cheek, biting her bottom lip to keep from crying. "Thank you," she said again to the nurse as she took her leave. Her legs barely held her up as she made the trek out the door and into the hall, where she leaned against the wall. She wrapped her arms around herself, bowed her head, and gave in to her despair. How had Greyson, over the course of several days, come to be on death's door?

Soft voices and footsteps in the corridor had her raising her head and swiping away her tears. Hunter, Anastasia, and Aurora came into view. They would learn soon enough how sick Greyson was.

"How is he?" All three asked at once, their expressions hopeful.

She tried to school her features, but failed miserably as her face fell and tears continued to fall. How many tears could one cry? "It is bad. Go see him." They entered the room, and Letitia stayed where she was until she felt she could rejoin Knight and Charlotte in the drawing room. She joined them a few minutes later to find them sitting together on the settee, with a fresh serving of tea, sandwiches, and fruit and cheese on the table between the two sofas.

Knight stood as Letitia entered the room, looking hopeful. "How is he?"

"I don't know. But there's a rattle in his lungs that worries me," she said.

"Sit, Letitia, before you collapse," Knight said, wrapping an arm through hers and escorting her to sit beside Charlotte, where he previously sat.

"Thank you, Your Grace."

"Knight. I prefer Knight."

"Even by those who know nothing about your club or the Black Knights?"

"I don't socialize with many people who don't know about one or the other of those things," he said, his dark eyebrow raised. "For obvious reasons."

It was strange how the more times she came into contact with him, the less she focused on the mask hiding his burn scars, and the more she saw the whole gentleman. The mask was just a part of him, the only way she'd ever known him.

"I see." And she did. She could imagine the stares he would draw at a ball. Charlotte poured her tea and placed two tiny sandwiches on a plate for her.

"You should eat something, my dear," Charlotte said, looking concerned. "You are very pale."

"Thank you." Letitia picked up the cup of tea and sipped. If her stomach settled after she drank it, she would risk some food. "When is the doctor due back?"

Knight paced the room, sipping from a glass that looked like brandy. "Soon. I sent a footman to fetch him."

"I'm glad."

"Did he wake up when you were with him?" Charlotte asked, stood, went to the sideboard, and returned with a decanter of golden liquid, splashing a dash into both their teas. "I think we could use a little brandy to settle our nerves."

"Thank you," Letitia said, wholeheartedly agreeing. "He did wake up. He seemed lucid. Had some chicken broth, then fell back asleep. My imagination is running wild with concern." All her emotions were muddled, making it hard to sort things out. She didn't often panic over little things, like when her son caught a cold. However, given what Knight said about the rusty, dirty pitchfork, there was much to be concerned about for Greyson.

"Both Charlotte and I discussed our concerns about his lungs. I have to keep believing that Greyson is strong and a fighter, and that he will be out of that bed, walking around, and riding his horse in no time." He paused and looked right at her, his dark eyes filled with guilt and sorrow. "I can't allow myself to think otherwise."

She understood his dilemma. As the leader of the Black Knights, he felt responsible for his Knights. He took anything that befell them as a personal affront. He believed he was responsible for whatever happened to them. Just as he felt responsible for the men who served under him in the Navy. The man had a huge heart.

A footman entered the drawing room, spoke briefly with Knight, and then left. "Doctor Hanson has arrived and gone up to see Greyson."

A tiny bit of Letitia's insides eased at the doctor's return. Moments later, Hunter, Anastasia, and Aurora entered the room. Greyson's sisters looked a mess, with red, blotchy faces and swollen eyes from crying. She suspected it was very much what she must have looked like when she'd entered the drawing room and Knight hurried to her side to assist her in taking a seat. Hunter, pale and worried, had an arm around each of the twins, and the three of them squished onto the vacant settee opposite Charlotte and her. Knight hurried over with an empty glass, splashed some brandy into it, and handed it to Hunter.

"You look like you could use this."

"Thank you," Hunter said, downing it in one swallow.

In the meantime, Charlotte poured tea for the twins, adding a splash of brandy to each cup.

Anastasia and Aurora gladly picked up their teas and took deep sips.

Letitia could only imagine how they must be feeling. Their only brother was lying in bed, his leg wounded and very sick from an infection.

"The doctor's here," Hunter said as he helped himself to another pour of brandy, this time sipping it.

"Did he awaken while you were there?" Letitia asked.

"Yes," Aurora replied. "He's worried about Mother and Father and about us." She paused, finished her tea, and set the cup and saucer on the table. "I told him we're fine, and he should just get better so I can beat him in a horse race."

"Oh, what did he say about that?" Letitia asked.

"He laughed, then had a coughing fit and gasped for air." Aurora wiped a stray tear from her cheek. "I've never beaten him in a race, but I had to say something."

Anastasia took her sister's hand in her own. "It was the perfect thing to say."

"It was," Hunter agreed. "You know how he is about his horse. I'm surprised he hasn't joined Stanton in opening his thoroughbred farm. Stanton asked him. I believe it's only a matter of time before he's as thoroughbred-racing crazy as Stanton. I may have to join them as well."

Letitia knew Greyson loved horses and racing, but she didn't know that Stanton had asked him to partner in his thoroughbred farm. She believed he would excel, and if Hunter joined them as well, the three of them would produce some of the fastest thoroughbred horses ever. All it would take was for Greyson to recover and keep his leg. She worried about him if the doctor had to amputate. Sometimes, when an infection set in, they remove the infected appendage to save the patient's life. However, she believed the infection had already spread, and removing the leg now would not do any good.

If the doctor found he needed to remove his leg, would Greyson come to terms with it? It wouldn't matter to her whether he had two legs or one. All that mattered was that he was alive so she could love him for the rest of their lives, however long that may be.

CHAPTER TWENTY-TWO

GREYSON HAD BLINKED the sleep from his eyes and couldn't believe what he saw. Letitia sat beside his bed, her hands blanketing his. The warmth of her hands was almost more than his fevered body could bear, but he would die before he pulled his hand from between hers. Before he'd opened his eyes, he'd known she was there. Her floral scent and the sound of her breathing were familiar to him; he would recognize them anywhere. Even as the fever ravaged his body, he recognized her as an extension of himself.

They belonged together. They completed each other, body, mind, and soul. He prayed he had the strength to fight the pitchfork wound and the infection that no one needed to explain was running rampant through his body. He only needed to inhale, and the pain in his lungs stoked his greatest fear—the fear of dying on his family. Not being there to take care of them. Not being there to handle the burdens they would face if he were gone.

He trusted his cousin, but it wouldn't be the same. He didn't know or love them as he did. And when it came to Letitia, whom he loved to distraction, who would look after her? Her son, Simon, was many years away from being able to care for her. If Greyson died, he prayed she would fall in love again with a gentleman worthy of her—one who would cherish and love her as he did. Knight would step up and watch over her. With him and Charlotte, he could rest easy knowing she had friends who cared for her, along with Clarice, Emmeline, Lilly, and their husbands. She also had his sisters, Hunter, and Warren. She would be fine.

His chest ached. He wouldn't be fine. He'd be dead. No. No. No. Don't think that way. He needed to fight with everything he had. It was the only way to survive.

He forced his eyes open and said, "Don't cry." It seemed the perfect thing to say at the time.

He was so thankful she had come to him. No doubt Knight had sent word. And if Knight had sent word, he was very sick indeed. Forcing his fears aside, he enjoyed the time he spent with her. Even if he wished he had the strength to pull her into bed with him and make love to her. He had to believe the time would come when he could. He would not give up. He would not give in to his fears and worries. Even if he lost his leg, he would be alive and could still love Letitia if she'd have him, cripple and all. And she would. She had the biggest heart of anyone he knew. She loved him now, flaws and all. She would love him with one leg.

When she spoon-fed him chicken broth, tears welled in his eyes at the gentleness of her soul. Everything she felt for him was evident, and he would fight with everything he had to experience her gentle soul again and again until they were old, with gray hair and wrinkles. Until their grandchildren were old enough to marry and have children of their own. This was what he had to remind himself he was fighting for. Fighting for a future with Letitia. If he didn't fight and death took him, those children and grandchildren would never be born, and how tragic would that be?

When she finished feeding him, he tried to keep his eyes open—tried to speak and tell her how he felt, how he loved her enough to reach into the sky and give her a star. But his body had other ideas, and he drifted back into sleep, full of fitful dreams and an uncertain future.

He'd woken again briefly when Hunter and his sisters visited, then again when the doctor arrived.

"Are you awake, Viscount?" Doctor Hanson said as he lifted his eyelids, and he moaned, shocked that moving them could hurt.

"Perhaps."

"Good. Nurse Pendergrast and I are going to raise you just a little on a pillow so we can get you to take some nice warm broth."

He had to keep sucking in air to keep from screaming because the pain in his leg was so intense.

"I'm sorry," the doctor said. "But if you are to keep up your strength, you need nourishment."

"Open," the nurse said.

He obeyed, and the warm broth slid down his throat and eased his thirst. They repeated this many times until he croaked out, "Enough."

"You did well, Viscount. Now we're going to try something to help your lungs," the doctor said. "We're going to put a linen towel over your head while you breathe in the mist from the boiling water, which I've infused with a medicinal mixture. Whatever you do, don't move. I don't want the water spilling and burning you. Do you understand?"

Greyson tried for patience. Not easy when all he wanted to do was sleep. "Yes."

"Good. I'm putting the cloth over your head now, and Nurse Pendergrast will hold the bowl. Breathe in and out. Hopefully, this will help your lungs clear. This needs to be done often. That's good. Keep breathing it in. In case you're wondering about your leg, it hasn't improved, but it hasn't gotten worse. Before I leave, I'm going to repack it with a fresh poultice and clean bandages. One more thing. I don't know what His Grace has told you about me, but I use unconventional practices to help my patients."

The doctor saved Knight's life when every other physician had given up and left him to die. Not Doctor Hanson. The good doctor never gave up, and that was why Knight was still with them. He cleared some of the mucus from his throat and whispered, "Do whatever you need."

"I will, and I am."

The tightness and pain in his chest and lungs lessened from whatever he was breathing in. It had a minty smell.

"That's good for now," Nurse Pendergrast said as the towel and the bowl were removed. She did something at the bedside table, then held out a cup. "It's time for your laudanum. Please drink this." When he finished dinking, the doctor and nurse helped him lay back down.

"Nurse Pendergrast will be taking care of your breathing treatments," Doctor Hanson said, "Once the laudanum takes effect in a few minutes, I'll tend to your leg. I'll return in the morning."

Greyson winced in pain and opened his eyes in what he thought was the dead of night. Pain he had never known before radiated through his injured leg. His head and eyes hurt as if a red-hot poker were being pressed against his temples. Sleep was a much better option than being awake. Several candles glowed in the room. As he glanced around as best he could, he saw the nurse sleeping on a pallet in the corner and Knight slumped asleep in a chair beside his bed. He cleared his throat and whispered, "Knight."

"Hmm, what?" Knight mumbled, sitting up straight and opening his eyes. "Greyson."

"You look extremely uncomfortable sleeping in that chair."

He stood and stretched. "I was, but I wanted to talk to you about what happened, and the only way to do that was stay here until you woke up."

"I remember clearly what happened."

"I'm sure you do. I wanted you to know that the lad who stabbed you made it home safely."

"Good. I don't want him punished."

"I knew you wouldn't. I'm still trying to get Prinny to agree to let the leader from that day go free. Hanging him is not going to accomplish peace. I won't relent until he agrees. Meanwhile, don't worry about the Black Knights or make any decisions about whether you will come back until you are back up on your feet." He touched his shoulder. "Sleep and get better, my friend."

After Knight left, he closed his eyes hoping to shut out the pain and sleep.

FOR A WEEK, this routine continued. Letitia watched as Greyson's fever slowly subsided, his lungs, though still raspy, improved, and even his wound on his leg was less angry. When the doctor said, "He will keep his leg and live," she nearly collapsed to the floor and wept.

Knight and Charlotte were so kind as to offer her a guest room to stay in and sent for clothes, which Jane packed and sent with her driver. Letitia had sent a note to Mrs. Hartman about Simon. She would miss him terribly and would make up for her absence when she returned. She would plan a day doing all his favorite things. Anatasia, Aurora, and Hunter went home but spent hours each day with Greyson.

On the morning of the tenth day since his injury, she entered his room and found his valet, Dalton, shaving his face while Greyson sat up tall in the bed, looking freshly cleaned, his hair damp.

"I'll be back," she said, blushing.

"No," Greyson said. "Stay. Dalton is almost done."

She stood near the door and waited for Dalton to finish, pack up his things into a valise, and leave the room, smiling as he walked by her.

"Why was Dalton smiling?" she asked as she crossed the room and lowered her hip on the side of the bed where his good leg was.

"Perhaps because I'm going to recover and he needn't find a

position as a valet in another household."

She giggled. "I think it's something else. You were whispering."

"It's a man-to-man thing."

"I hear you're being moved to Danbury Hall today."

"Yes. I can't possibly continue to impose on Knight."

"He has been most kind and generous. I've packed my things and sent them along to Rutherford Manor." She frowned, and her heart plummeted. "I'm going to miss being with you. Even when you were a terrible patient."

"You can visit Danbury Hall every day. According to Doctor Hanson, I need to keep off my leg for another week. He made me these wooden crutches so I can get around until my leg is strong enough to support me and switch to a walking stick."

"I'll visit you every day." She paused to gather courage, as she had news to share with him. News she had no idea how he would take, though she was beyond happy. "Now that you're on the mend, I have something to say. Let me finish before you interrupt—no need to look concerned. I'm not breaking off our courtship. In fact, I'm hoping you will marry me."

He placed his hand on her cheek. "Do you have something to tell me?"

"My courses are a fortnight late, and I'm never late. I also recognize all the signs from when I was pregnant with Simon." She held her breath as she studied his features, praying he was as thrilled with this blessing as she was. His eyes widened, then softened. He grinned widely and caressed her cheek with the hand that rested there.

"Thank you," he said in wonder.

"You enjoy thanking me."

"I do, and I hope I never stop. You have made me so pleased with this news. His hand moved from her cheek to her stomach, where he rubbed her reverently. "Our babe. We need a special license."

"I believe we do." She leaned forward and kissed him with all the love in her heart. "Once you're settled at home, you can apply for the special license. I have one more thing to ask, are you going to continue with the Black Knights?"

He didn't answer right away. Eventually, he said, "That is something I can't answer now. You were there when Doctor Hanson said I may need a walking stick because my leg may never be right again and that riding on horseback may be too painful to bear. When the time comes, we will discuss it together. I would never want to cause you undue worry because of my involvement with the Black Knights."

"Thank you for including me."

"Of course.

"Meanwhile," she leaned forward once more, "I could use a few more kisses."

"I'm yours, always and forever."

"ARE YOU COMPLETELY sure you don't want your double wedding at St. George's Hanover Square?" Greyson asked Anastasia and Aurora while he sat in the drawing room on an overstuffed chair, his leg up on an ottoman, a week after returning from Tremont Manor.

Letitia stood beside him, her hand resting on his shoulder, waiting patiently for his sisters' answers. They had heard that Greyson had proposed, which was partly true. After she asked him to marry her, he asked her that night, and everyone was so happy that the twins mentioned a triple wedding. Neither of them thought they meant it, but eventually they did.

"We want our wedding here at Danbury Hall," Aurora said. "Nothing would be better than sharing our day with you and Letitia. Soon to be our sister."

Tears slid down her cheeks at the love coming from the twins. "What about Hunter and Warren?"

Anastasia giggled. "According to Hunter, the quicker we marry, the better."

Greyson coughed, then chuckled. "Sounds like him. What about Warren?"

Aurora beamed. "He said if it's what I want, it's what he wants."

"Then it's settled," Greyson said. "A triple wedding in two days since Warren also procured a special license. Their banns are one week shy on being read. Anastasia and Hunter met the three-week requirement."

"Oh my," Letitia gasped. "I have so much to do."

"Us, too."

"In two days, there will be three weddings. I'd better tell Cook," Greyson chuckled.

EPILOGUE

THE WEDDING DAY arrived. Letitia sat at her dressing table while Jane put the finishing touches on her hair. She wore the stunning blue taffeta ballgown Madame Serena had created for her. Her eyes, staring back at her from the looking glass, were bluer than blue. She wore sapphires in her ears and at her throat. Gifts from Greyson. If she didn't know better, she'd swear he had spies inside Rutherford Manor. Otherwise, how did he know she was wearing blue? Most likely he had guessed, knowing it was his favorite color, and had become hers, too.

"It's time," Jane said, wiping tears from her eyes. "I'm so happy for you, my lady, and for Master Simon."

"Thank you, Jane."

Letitia took a moment to breathe before standing and making her way down the stairs into the entry hall, where Simon stood, dressed most handsomely, beside his governess. "Mama," he said with a big grin.

"Good morning, my son." She held out her hand. "Are you ready for my wedding?"

"Yes."

Mr. Henry opened the door and bowed. "My lady."

"Thank you, Mr. Henry."

They descended the stairs and were met by Danbury's footmen and driver in full Danbury livery. They had traveled so often in Greyson's unmarked coach that she was unaccustomed to seeing his father's colors, and it brought tears to her eyes as she thought of Greyson's father, the Earl of Danbury. He would not be attending the wedding, which was unfortunate for Anastasia and Aurora. However, their mother would be attending.

Sitting in the carriage on one side, while Simon and his governess sat opposite, she was very thankful she wasn't experiencing any morning sickness this morning. She noticed Simon was unusually quiet today, and she hoped he would acclimate to having a father. Greyson would become his father today, and they would be moving to Danbury Hall. Letita's heart couldn't be any fuller.

When the carriage stopped outside Danbury Hall, her nerves calmed, and an extraordinary warmth overtook her. Her dream of marrying for true love was coming true. The carriage door opened, the stairs lowered, and she took the footman's hand as she stepped down. She giggled when the footman tried to help Simon, but Simon climbed out himself, followed by Mrs. Hartman.

Holding Simon's hand, they ascended the stairs. They stepped over the threshold into the entry hall, where her eyes fell on Anastasia, splendid in a cream silk gown. Aurora looked lovely in a pale-green taffeta gown with a lace overlay. They both beamed when they saw her.

"It's our wedding day," Aurora said, fighting back tears.

"I know," Letitia agreed. "Henderson, will you take Mrs. Hartman and Master Simon to the drawing room where our guests are waiting?"

"Yes, my lady."

"How much time do we have?" Letitia asked as she removed her cloak and handed it to a footman. She ran her hands down her skirts to smooth out any creases that had formed in the carriage.

"Not long," Anastasia answered. "Henderson informed us right before you arrived that all our guests and husbands-to-be are in the drawing room. That's why we felt safe meeting you in the entry."

"Well, then, let's not keep our gentlemen waiting." They decided to enter in the order they were engaged. When it was Letitia's turn to enter through the drawing room's double doors, she almost faltered in her steps. Greyson stood, looking splendid in his evening wear. But what stunned her and brought tears to her eyes was that he stood on his own, aided by a walking stick. Other than the man she loved, she didn't notice another person in the room.

Their eyes stayed connected the entire time she walked toward him. It all seemed like a dream. It felt as though she were floating on a cloud toward another cloud where Greyson waited for her. When she reached him, she joined her hand with his free one. "Greyson."

He cleared his throat and murmured, "You look beautiful."

Warmth kissed her cheeks. "Thank you."

They stood side by side, holding hands as they awaited their turn with the minister. Letitia barely heard the vows spoken by her soon-to-be sisters-in-law. Her entire being was centered on Greyson. How his large, warm hand felt in hers. Even though he leaned on a walking stick, he towered over her, making her feel safe and warm. His woodsy scent eased her straight to her soul. The sound of his clear, even breathing had her thanking God he was alive. She was so thankful to be able to spend her life loving this man. As far as she was concerned, no greater, kinder, or more loyal gentleman existed.

The minister came and stood before them. Greyson squeezed her hand. She spoke her vows softly. They were for Greyson alone. He recited his just as softly. He placed a delicate sapphire-and-diamond ring on her finger, matching the jewelry she was wearing.

The minister addressed their guests and announced all three couples were wed. Greyson and Letitia paid no attention. They snuck out the adjoining door that led into the dining room. Exited that room into the corridor and paused so Greyson could rest his leg. "Can you make it up the stairs?" she asked because she could see pain radiating in his green eyes, and she was concerned it would be too much.

"Nothing will keep me from bringing you to my . . . our . . . chambers," he said with a grin and a wink.

"Well, then," she exhaled. "Shall we?"

It was slow going up the stairs and down the long corridor, and finally, a deep sigh, as they entered his chambers. Greyson closed and locked the door behind them. She stood, tears of joy dripping down her cheeks. Hundreds of red rose petals covered the floor and the bed. She reached for his hand, raised it, and kissed it. "Thank you."

"I love you. I would do anything for you. I am yours always and forever, and I plan to spend my life cherishing you."

"Then let me help you undress so you can cherish your new wife by making love to her."

"Your wish is my greatest desire."

THE END

About the Author

Christine Donovan is an International Bestselling Author who writes romance that touches the heart, soothes the soul and feeds the mind. In addition to writing historical romance set in the Regency era, she also writes contemporary romance.

When she landed her first job at sixteen as a cashier at a supermarket, the first thing she did each week on payday was stop at the local bookstore and buy the latest historical romance. It was a dream of hers back then to become a romance author.

She lives on the Southeast Coast of Massachusetts with her husband. She has four grown sons, two granddaughters, two cats, and a black lab named Luna. In her spare time, she can be found at the beach, reading, painting, or gardening. She loves to tackle DIY projects.

Website: authorchristinedonovan.com
Newletter: www.authorchristinedonovan.com/newsletter
Amazon: amazon.com/Christine-Donovan/e/B00APR743Y
Facebook: authorchristinedonovan
Instagram: christinedonovan6